LET'S KILL
ALL THE
LAWYERS

LET'S KILL ALL THE LAWYERS

If You Prick Me, Do I Not Bleed?

TIM HOWARD

BROWN
DOG
BOOKS

Published under licence by Brown Dog Books and
The Self-Publishing Partnership Ltd, 10b Greenway Farm, Bath Rd,
Wick, nr. Bath BS30 5RL

www.selfpublishingpartnership.co.uk

ISBN printed book: 978-1-83952-330-4
ISBN e-book: 978-1-83952-331-1

Cover design by Kevin Rylands
Internal design by Andrew Easton

Printed and bound in the UK

This book is printed on FSC certified paper

For Kate

CHAPTER 1

The High Court Writ lay on his desk in front of him, like an unexploded grenade. He stared at it unseeingly, while a stream of pictures, thoughts and fears tumbled through his mind in a chaotic torrent. 'What the hell do I do now?' he thought.

'Are you all right, Nick?' Maeve said. She was a partner in the general practice. 'You look as though someone has just punched you.'

She had been walking by the open door of his room in the surgery, and had seen him sitting at his desk with his head in his hands. She was a wise and cheerful Irish doctor, and had been a partner in his Practice for five years less than him. She was a voice of sanity in the turbulent world of medical care, a constant source of common sense and wisdom.

'It feels as though someone just has' he said. 'The bastard; how could he do this to me, after all I did for him.'

'Done what?' she said. 'And how?'

'He's bloody well suing me in the High Court,' he answered. 'Blaming me because he became ill. How could he? The bastard.' And once more, 'after all I did for him.'

Maeve was on call for emergencies. It had been a quiet day,

and she had come into the surgery, like him, to catch up on the piles of paperwork that constitute so much of a doctor's everyday work.

She pulled up a chair next to him, the one in which the patients usually sat, and lowered herself into it. She looked at the anxious face in front of her. 'Try not to worry too much,' she said. 'It'll all come out in the wash. You know you're a good doctor. And don't let it spoil your holiday.' Then her phone rang, and she went off to deal with another problem.

But spoil the holiday it did. Completely. He felt the calmness and sense of wellbeing of it fall away like a cloak, and was aware of his heart thumping in his chest. 'A fight or flight reaction,' he thought, 'or more likely, just fright.'

*

It had been a good holiday – much better than he could have hoped for. For once, the fickle weather of the English summer had smiled on them, and the two weeks on the south coast of Cornwall had been the stuff of childhood memories. His wife had been slowly returning to her extrovert self, and seemed to have got over – as much as she ever would – the tragedy of their son, although the rift between them that his loss had caused would never heal. The cottage they had rented had been lovely, right on the water. The pasties had tasted good. And the stresses of everyday life as a busy GP had sloughed away like the old skin of a snake, and been replaced with a benign sense of calm wellbeing that was a new and curious sensation.

He had taken real pleasure in making his ancient sailing dinghy keep up with the smart competitive boats and energetic young men in the local sailing club, and to his surprise had actually won a prize in the regatta that was the culmination of the holiday. Only a third place in the mixed class, but a prize none the less. Even packing up the boat, getting its mast down and stowing it on its trailer, had gone according to plan, recalling previous holidays when his son had been there to help. Even the long slow drive back home to Sussex had been – and the word surprised him – happy.

As he always did, he had gone into the surgery on the Sunday evening before he started work again on Monday, to sort through the backlog of post, catch up on what the Practice had been up to during his absence, and to update himself on the patients whom he had left behind. The place he worked helped him get back into doctor mode. It was a beautiful Georgian building in the Sussex market town where he worked, hopelessly impractical in its function as a surgery, but friendly and charming in its place in the community. Doctors had practiced from it for generations.

However much he hoped to pass the responsibility for his patients to others in the Practice when he was away, there were always some whose problems he carried with him. The patients who were very ill, the patients who were dying, and most of all, the patients who had problems that he had failed to unravel or solve. All these sat in a sort of file marked 'pending' at the back of his mind, wherever he was. He had tried to break himself of this sense of responsibility over the years, but without success, and had got used to the sensation of subliminal concern about some patients, even when he was on the other side of the world. 'Curious' he had said to himself when he actually thought about it. 'Perhaps it's a genetic hang-over from the single-handed practices that his father and grandfather had run, when they were never off duty. Or perhaps just an over sensitive conscience. Or the paternalism of a slightly Victorian upbringing. Or something.' But it was a nuisance, although he had got used to it. He had learnt to live with it, and managed it by coming in before his holidays ended in order to keep on top of what had happened in his absence.

And that is how he found that, for the first time in his professional life, he was being sued for negligence. Every professional has a lurking anxiety about the possibility of this, the ultimate sanction. The fear that he, whoever he is and whatever profession he follows, will be exposed to the cold analysis of a Court of Law, and his judgement and his alleged failings laid bare before a critical public and a voracious Press. And the possibility of the ultimate failure, of being found negligent, of failing in his professional duties, with all its consequences for reputation and career.

So, as he drove home on that Sunday evening, back to his wife still basking in the glow of the holiday, he thought bitterly of the sheer unfairness of it all. That you could work your socks off for your patients for year after year, do your very best for them, and receive casual thanks or just acknowledgement. But make one mistake – just one error of judgement in the hundreds of decisions that you have to make each week - and you became subject to the full weight of the law and the opprobrium of the world.

With a conscious effort, he put that thought to the back of his mind, for in that direction lay anger and bitterness and disillusion. He must cling to the words of his Irish partner, he told himself, that he was a good doctor, and most, in fact nearly all his patients liked him and needed him. This was an episode to be got through, like an exam. Or so he told himself.

CHAPTER 2

I learnt the bare outlines of all this a few days later. The details, the thoughts and fears and emotions, only emerged piece by piece, over the next months and years, as he let them drop in unguarded moments.

I, too, had been on holiday, taking a break from my busy and successful legal practice in London. I had come back to my solicitor's office off Covent Garden tanned and rested, but less relaxed than the doctor had been. We had been to Barbados, my rich husband and I, and although we had done all the lovely things that successful people like us do on expensive holidays like that, the time to think had allowed me to realise that I had a problem. A cloud the size of a man's hand that had been hovering on my horizon for many many months had coalesced into a definite patch of cumulo-nimbus, and forced itself into my hitherto satisfactory life. And the cloud said that he wasn't as nice as I had thought; nothing like as nice.

My musings about this were interrupted by my secretary, a middle-aged and rather bitter lady. She came into my office without knocking. This always annoyed me, and she knew that it annoyed me, but it was just part of the undeclared war between women who have achieved a professional status and those who have not. Just a tiny crack in the glass ceiling which lies between the employer and the employee. An irritant. A fleabite.

'I think you might want to listen to this,' she said. Without waiting for my reply, she turned on the speaker on my desk and pressed a button. It repeated a message the ansaphone in the outer office had taken.

'Hello' the speaker said, in a metallic male voice. 'The Medical Defence people have given me your number to ring. I've just received a Writ.' And then, realising the uselessness of this message by itself, the caller gave his name and phone number, and went on 'the Writ expires in four days – I'm afraid I've been on holiday. I haven't a clue what to do about it. Can I come and see you please?' Then, as an afterthought, 'the patient who is complaining about me is one I thought that I had done my best for, my very best. I can't think why he's going after me.'

That was intriguing. My usual clients were rather depressing. Lots of doctors who were at the lower end of the competence scale, or who were rude, or who were lazy, or who had just made mistakes. Everyone makes mistakes. The 'good doctor having a bad day' defence was well recognised in my business. But this sounded different. A seemingly competent doctor who couldn't see why he was being sued. That sounded really interesting. Not something I should palm off onto a junior.

'Four days' I said to my secretary. 'We'd better get cracking. If there is a defence worth lodging, that is. What's the diary like?'

'Full,' she said, 'as always. Cancel or work late?'

'Cancel. You chose. Tomorrow, if possible. Anything not

directly concerned with a current case.'

'There's the Law Society intern interview at 3.00pm', she said. 'I'll get James to see him. He sounded a bit of a wimp on the phone anyway. James is good at dealing with wimps.'

'OK' I said. 'This sounds as though it might be an interesting challenge.'

*

I was agreeably surprised when the doctor was shown in just after three o'clock the next day. I have the bad habit of painting a picture in my mind's eye from what I hear on the phone. I had imagined a slightly red-faced and bucolic country doctor, dressed in tweed. Paternalistic. Probably quite a good shot, I thought, and maybe even a churchwarden. Definitely a pillar of the local community. Everyone's idea of a country doctor. Or, from his name, a Russian émigré, with a tired aquiline face.

The figure that came in was very different. Smallish, slim, thinning hair, but quick and alert, with a pair of penetrating blue eyes and a firm, rather humorous mouth. He was wearing a smart dark suit, and looked more like a business man, perhaps a senior manager. Nothing like the country doctor I had expected.

'Hello,' he said. 'I'm Nick. Nick Malenkov. '

'And I'm Antonia, Antonia Grey.'

His handshake was firm, but he was nervous. His palm was sweaty, and he crossed and uncrossed his legs as he sat on the other side of the desk from me. I watched him taking in the room, his clear eyes noting the pile of briefs with their pink ribbons on my desk, the framed law certificates on the wall, and the impressive legal tomes lining the bookshelves.

'Thank you for seeing me so quickly,' he said. A quiet voice, but firm.

'That's OK,' I replied. 'All part of the service. Tell me what the problem is.'

He took a deep breath, and his eyes focussed inwardly for a moment. Then he looked up, and I was struck by their intensity and the directness of the gaze.

"I came back from holiday on Sunday,' he paused, 'and found this waiting for me.'

'This' was a High Court Writ. I had seen hundreds of them, but they always produced a frisson of excitement in the professional bit of me. Rather like Sherlock Holmes, I thought: 'the games afoot.' This one could turn out to be nothing, but it could - might – be a significant event in my legal life, a real challenge.

He pushed it across the desk to me, and I glanced at the first page. The only thing that mattered at this point was the date. Writs are, put simply, accusations, and unless the person accused denies the accusation, the High Court accepts them as being true and awards damages accordingly. And the time allowed for the response is short – fourteen days. The dates on the first page indicated that we had three days left to deny it. But before committing myself to doing this, I needed to know whether it was worth denying, that the accusations could be reasonably defended. And to do that, I needed to know the story.

'Tell me what led up to this.' I asked.

Another big breath. He seemed a sensible individual, who thought before he spoke. I watched, interested.

'When I first saw it, I could only remember the outlines. The whole thing happened over 3 years ago. But I've thought about it long and hard since, and the sequence has come back to me fairly accurately, I think. The main memory I have of it all is one of frustration.'

'Go on. Start from the beginning.'

'He was young, humourless and a red head' he said. 'I hardly knew him before the main event kicked off. He had only been to see me a few times for minor problems. A mild go of bronchitis, an attack of athlete's foot, a cut on his arm, but nothing of any consequence. I found him difficult to make contact with; I feel that I may be able to help my patients better if I can form some sort of relationship with them. But he held me at arm's length, and so our exchanges were strictly professional.' He looked across at me and smiled, a friendly smile. I could see his patients liking him 'Not a big point, but possibly significant for what happened later.'

I nodded encouragingly. My tutor in the Law Department at Cambridge had held that if you kept quiet but looked encouraging, you would get the essence of the story far more quickly and accurately than if you asked leading questions.

'He made an urgent appointment to see me one Monday morning. Mondays are always busy as hell, but I squeezed him in as an extra, and was glad that I did. He complained of vague tummy ache and diarrhoea which had been going on for a couple of weeks, and a bit of weight loss. Nothing out of the ordinary, you might think. Probably a dodgy curry or something, but all my clinical hackles went up, and I examined him properly, and went by the book.'

'What do you mean by that?' No harm in testing him a bit, seeing how he might respond to cross-questioning. I would need to know that if it went to court.

He paused, and looked at his hands. I noticed that they were small and neat and that the nails were cut short. There was no wedding band on the fourth finger.

'To answer that, you need to understand the way General Practice thinks and works', he said. 'It is nothing like the structured process that goes on in hospitals. Its basic principle is about taking calculated risks'. He paused, and I could see he was about to embark on an explanation. I interrupted him - no need for that now. He was obviously capable of stringing coherent thoughts together.

'OK. Let's put that on one side for the time being. You can give me your take on it if we need it later on.'

I was only too well aware of the medical process of taking a history, examining a patient to look for pointers, forming a hypothesis about what the problem was, confirming it with tests, and so on. I also knew that in the real world of the 7 minutes consultation, this was simply not possible, and most doctors, especially GPs, simply had to fly by the seat of their pants.

'I was just seeing how you responded to being challenged a bit.'

He laughed, and I was surprised at how his face lit up. He

had one of those faces that wasn't good-looking in the ordinary sense, but was sort of ugly attractive. It was the kind of face which would draw people to it, I thought. Children would trust it.

'Sorry. You nearly got me onto one of my hobby-horses.'

'Do you have lots of those, then?'

'Herds of them. Don't get me started.' and he laughed again. 'It's a dreadful habit, having opinions.'

We smiled at each other. He was a nice man.

I picked up the phone and asked my secretary to rustle up some coffee for us. The coffee came in, and we went through the little ritual of pouring and drinking. A useful way of getting people to relax, I always thought; a way to get the real story out of them.

'I wonder if we ought to get back to your little problem?'

'Where were we?' he asked, putting his cup down. 'Oh yes. The red headed socialist.'

'Socialist?' I queried.

'Oh yes. He was a socialist all right,' he said. 'The whole nine yards. But that wasn't relevant then or now, of course. More importantly, there was something about his medical state when he came to see me that rang alarm bells.'

'Can you be more specific?'

'It's hard to say. You must have the same sort of feeling about whether someone is telling the truth or not, a sixth sense. In his case, it was a combination of things. His pulse was a little too fast. His skin was a little too translucent – even for red-head.' he smiled. 'And his abdomen felt odd – a little too diffusely tender, even for a very strong curry. So I did all the right things. I did his routine bloods – screened him for a whole range of physiological norms. Sent off urine and stool samples to the lab. Gave him symptomatic treatment for the diarrhoea. And told him to come back and see me in a week, or before if he was worried. And, unusually for me, made quite good notes. I'm sure of that.'

'So what happened next?'

'He beat me to it. He came in on Friday, much worse. As soon as I saw him I knew he was significantly ill now. You can tell, just by looking; you don't need fancy tests and full examinations. One look, and you know they are significantly ill and need to be in hospital.'

'What was it?'

'I was fairly sure I knew by then. Crohn's disease. Acute inflammation of a bit of bowel He confirmed it when I asked him about his stools – poo, to you and me. He described blood and slime. He was gaunt and pale, and the weight had fallen off him in just those few days. His bloods had just come back, and confirmed that he was very anaemic, with raised inflammatory markers – a sure sign that something significant was going on. So I admitted him to our local hospital.'

'Were you right?'

'I thought that was the most likely diagnosis, and suggested it in the letter I sent in with him. The snooty junior doctor I spoke to on the phone to arrange a bed asked if I had done a biopsy to confirm it, and was put out when I suggested that perhaps this was his job. Ignorant lad. It has always amazed me that all GPs have to do several years working in hospitals to learn their ropes, often in irrelevant specialities, but hospital doctors never have to do any part of their training of what it's like in the real world of the community. Sorry – that's another hobby horse.' And he smiled wryly again.

'Yes,' I said. 'It is.' This doctor seemed to have a perspective that I found interesting, to say the least. And his vivid blue eyes were unsettling.

He took another sip of his coffee, and went on with his story.

'And then I put him out of my mind. It was the holiday season, with other partners away, so the rest of us were covering for them, and I was busy as hell. Usually I try to visit my patients in hospital, but I didn't have time to visit him, and even if I had, he wasn't easy to talk to, so I might have used that as an excuse not to go.'

'And?'

'A whole month went by, and I had forgotten all about him. But then his girlfriend asked for a home visit him for him. I rang before going, as I do with all visits, to see if it was really necessary, and got an earful about doctors not caring and trying to avoid work, so I went to see him. He lived in a house on a new estate not far from the surgery, but I learnt later that he was renting it.'

'So?'

'He was bloody ill. Worse than when I sent him in. I don't shock easily, but I was shocked. The quite well built man of a month ago was a skeleton – he looked as though he had been in a concentration camp.

I asked him 'What on earth has happened to you?'

'Everything' he replied. 'Or nothing.' He was very angry. 'Bloody hospitals. Bloody doctors' he said. 'Useless. I don't expect you to remember.' A sneer.

I asked him to slow down and help me understand what had happened, and why he was so upset. It took quite a lot of tact and gentleness to calm him down. If he hadn't been so obviously ill, I might have been less patient with him. Eventually the story of the last month came out.

He had been admitted on a Friday afternoon – possibly the least good time to go into hospital as an emergency. The on-call teams that covered emergency admissions are more concerned with stemming the flood of emergency work than in solving the clinical problems. They were just holding the fort until the heavy guns – the specialist teams – came back on Monday. And it was in August, one of the two worst months to be admitted as an emergency.'

I raised my eyebrows. 'Explain please.'

But before he could do so, the phone on my desk rang.

CHAPTER 3

Interruptions are always irritating. I had clear standing instructions that I was not to be interrupted when I was with a new client. So this must be something important I glanced at the doctor in apology and picked up the phone. It was my husband. My secretary must have put him straight through.

'Sorry darling,' he said, 'But there's a crisis at school. Sophie's vomiting and they want her taken home. I'm in a case conference.'

Of course he was. He was a barrister, and his work always took precedence over mine. In his opinion, anyway. I was, after all, merely a solicitor.

'So am I.'

'Well, you'll have to leave it.' And the phone went dead.

I looked up, to find the blue eyes watching me.

'A problem?'

'Yes. Give me a moment. I'm so sorry.'

It took ten minutes to track down my best friend and to bribe her to go to Sophie's school and pick her up.

'Not again.' she said. 'You'll have to get your life a bit more organised, Antonia. And why the hell can't Richard sort it out?' The words 'pompous prat' weren't spoken, but I could feel her thinking them. She couldn't stand Richard. But she went, and I returned to my office, aware that I had pushed my luck a bit too far, and irritated by it. Bloody husband.

I popped into the Ladies before going back into my room. As I washed my hands after going to the loo, I looked into the mirror above the washbasin, and tried to see the me that my client saw. What I once thought of as a reasonably pretty face, was now starting to show the signs of age. The fine lines in the skin, the shadows under the eyes, and for the first time I saw there was a permanent crease between the eyebrows. The dark hair, cut in a bob, definitely had a few grey hairs in it. There wasn't much happiness in that face now, I thought, but it would just have to do. It was, after all, the only one I had. I touched up my pale lipstick, straightened my blouse and jacket, and went back to my room.

'OK?' Nick Malenkov turned back from the window, where he had been watching the crowds ebb and flow below him in Covent Garden

"Yes, thank you,' I said. 'Sorry about that. The problems of balancing personal and professional life. Sorted now. And….'

I found myself very nearly telling him about my husband and his infuriating self-importance. Not appropriate.

'And…?' he queried.

'And nothing', I said briskly. But I was aware again of the penetrating eyes. 'Go on with what happened.'

'Well,' Nick Malenkov said, 'he told me that the team that admitted him were very busy, and that they specialised in diabetes anyway. It is coincidence which team is on call at any given time. Medical care in hospital is dealt with by teams that deal with sub-specialties – diabetes, chest problems, hearts, and so on. But they all take part in emergency on-call in turn. So if you have a fit or a coronary, you may be dealt with at night by someone with a different skill-set. The on-call team performed quite reasonably though, it seemed. They did all the correct routine tests, they put up a drip and rehydrated him, and they gave him the standard treatment for Crohn's disease. Then they rushed off to deal with the next admission, and he was left alone in a side ward ('in case you're infectious'). And there he stayed for the weekend. Miserable. A bit frightened. Feeling lousy. And frustrated that he didn't know what was going on. On Monday, the hospital returned to normal working, and he was transferred to the care of the gastroenterology team, the specialists that dealt with bowel conditions. Which should have worked, except that the consultant in charge of the team had just gone on holiday himself, and the other specialist gastroenterologist was away in London, examining for the membership of his Royal College. And then he, too, was going on holiday. At that time no one questioned whether it was reasonable for the two leaders of a single department to be absent at the same time. Fortunately, things are different now.'

'That sounds like a recipe for a cock-up,' I said. 'What a ludicrous way to run a hospital. And what about August being dangerous?'

'That's easy. Junior doctors rotate through jobs in their training, most of them every six or twelve months. The usual change-over date is August, so if you are admitted on the 1st of

August, the first doctor you see may only have been qualified for a day or two, and will be very inexperienced.'

'Wow. I never thought of that.'

'We all have to start somewhere. You must have had a first case as well.'

He paused, and reached for his cup of coffee, which was getting cold.

'Another?' I asked.

'No thanks' he said. 'It makes me pee too much.' And he smiled, the creases at the corners of his eyes very apparent.

'So for the next month, he was managed by the so-called junior doctors, senior house officers who are starting their specialised training and the registrars who are getting near to finishing it. But haven't finished yet.

They were faced with that most difficult of decisions – how bad is bad? How long do you persevere with medical treatment that is working a bit before taking the plunge of admitting that he was escaping from control, and that the time had come to call in the surgeons. A surgical solution to Crohn's disease is pretty radical – the removal of large sections of bowel, leaving the patients with a colostomy for life. But if it is necessary, it has to be done. If the decision to do it is left too long, people die. Crohn's disease can kill you.'

'Wow' I said again. 'I had no idea.'

'Yes' he went on. 'And the medical treatment – giving the patient steroids – can rack up the risks of surgery greatly. Steroids for any serious illness can be lifesaving, but at a cost. So they dithered. They sat and watched as he got weaker and weaker, and poo-d out much of the protein that had made him a fit man. Sometimes he got a bit better, and the medical treatment seemed to be working, but after a few days, the bloody diarrhoea returned, and he got weaker and iller. And angrier. And no one was senior enough or experienced enough to have the courage to call for help.

'Bloody doctors', he said to me when I visited him in his home. 'All arrogant and self-opinionated. Talking with posh accents. Most of them went to public schools, I should think.'

'Gosh' I said. 'How awful.' I had been to a public school myself, and my wife always says that I 'talked posh'. He was quite unaware of the irony. I didn't feel that this was the moment to discuss medical school entry with him – which is predominantly state educated. I remember thinking that he was almost a parody of a class warrior.

After nearly four weeks, he had had enough, he said, and told the nurses that he was going home. 'This place isn't doing me any good', he told them, 'I'm getting weaker by the day, and no one seems to care or do anything. I'd be better off out of here. At least I'd be amongst friends.'

They tried to dissuade him, he said. Lots of staff explained at length the risks of not being properly monitored, of not having intravenous fluids when he needed them, of the hazards of his illness, but he had made up his mind. His girlfriend brought in some clothes, and they struggled down to the main hospital entrance, and caught one of the taxis that always sat waiting there. Illness is a good source of income for taxi owners. And managed to get home.

And then they rang me.'

Quite unconsciously, Nick Malenkov got up from his chair, and paced round the room. He was re-living an episode that must have left a deep impression. And he was finding it difficult to put it into dispassionate words. I reminded myself that this was a man whose professional ability was being challenged, who was having to defend himself.

He swung round to face me:

'I told him, quite clearly, that unless he got proper hospital treatment that he might die,' he said, looking at me with those disarming eyes. 'I spent an age talking to them both – the angry redhead and his droopy girlfriend. She had the kind of hair that hangs down both sides of her face in curtains, and she used it effectively as a screen to hide behind. Never said a thing. I made him very aware of the risks he was facing if he stayed at home. I said that I would try to find another doctor or another team to look after him, that we could admit him to another hospital, and that I would personally act as his spokesman to the doctors caring for him. 'Caring!' he sneered. 'They don't know the meaning of the word. It's all tick boxes and shifts now. Nye Bevan would turn in his grave.' I used all my hard-learnt skills at persuading and manipulating him into doing what I was pretty sure was the only way to save him from medical disaster. I used every argument I could think of, but he was adamant. 'I'm not going back in,' he said.

So after an hour, I asked them both a direct question: 'You asked me to come and see you, quite rightly, in all the circumstances. What do you want me to do?'

Of course, they couldn't give a sensible answer to that, so it merely led to another outburst of resentment. But at the end of it, he said that he would go to his parents in Newcastle.

'Where?' I asked.

'North of Newcastle,' he said. 'A place called Blyth. At least the folk up there will look after me, even if the NHS down here won't.' By sheer coincidence, I had visited Blyth as a student years before, and mentioned this to him. 'Not much of a place, is it?' he said. I had to agree; my memory is of back-to-back miner's terraced houses, almost archetypal slum dwellings.

So that is what he did. I remember being very worried about the risks of a long drive for someone in his condition, and told him so. I managed to get him to remember the name of his parents' GP, and wrote a detailed letter by hand then and there, for him to give to take to him. I expected them to read it on the journey. Most patients read doctor's letters. And I reminded myself to ring the GP there when I had a moment. I gave him some simple medicine to quieten his tummy during the trip, and then I left. The workload had been building up while I spent all this time with him, and I rushed through another half dozen or so visits before going back to face the afternoon surgery. Only when that was over, did I get round to ringing his GP in Newcastle. Sod's Law meant that his surgery was shut by then, but I left a long and detailed message. And went home, completely knackered, and not a little angry.'

'So,' I asked. 'Why the complaint?'

'I simply don't know,' he said. 'I can't think of anything I could or should have done differently. That's what so unsettling about this damned Writ. It doesn't say what he thinks I did wrong.'

I pulled the Writ towards me, and ran quickly through the Heads of Allegation. They were vague in the extreme. They just used a standard form of words – 'Failure to provide adequate care, leading to serious consequences for Mr ….' Nothing of any value there. I sat thinking for a moment, and then pulled myself together, and used my 'I am in control' voice.

'Right,' I said. 'This is what we'll do. First and foremost, we will respond to the Writ, denying any and all its allegations in their entirety. That is just a form of words, and you can leave that to me. As long as the High Court has it by tomorrow at close of play, there is no problem. That will send the lawyers acting for him a clear message that we are not a push-over, and that we will fight tooth and claw. Providing, ' and I looked directly at the clear blue eyes, 'providing that you really didn't make a mistake. And we'll only know that for sure when we've got the notes and the expert opinions.'

'This could be a fishing expedition', I went on, 'an attempt by an ambulance chaser to see if there is a chance that you might just give in and cough up some damages. We see lots of those, and sadly they are frequently successful. Especially in secondary care, as hospitals are in the curious position of not being allowed to insure against negligence, and have to rely on the Crown Indemnity system. And for lots of claims, it's cheaper to settle for a small sum and avoid the legal costs than it is to defend the claim, or even to see if the claim is defensible. It's one of the things that has stoked the fires of medical litigation.'

"Yes', he said. 'I was vaguely aware of that. It seems very unfair and wrong.'

'You must remember,' I went into my default lawyer mode, the one in which I warned the client of the pitfalls ahead, 'that there is a gulf between the three things that we are talking about – justice, fairness, and the law. Each is a separate concept, and is governed by its own rules and standards. You mustn't confuse them, as that will just hurt you. Don't look to get fairness from justice, or justice from the law. Accept the whole process that you are going through as an occupational hazard, like a pilot having a near miss, or a rugby player an injury. It isn't fair, but it goes with the territory.'

'Thanks. ' he said. 'That's helpful, really helpful. Let me know what you want me to do, and I'll do it. Otherwise, I'm in your hands.'

'Correct.' I said. I got up from behind my desk, indicating that the interview was over. 'Write down a comprehensive history of what you have told me – tell the story, if you like, and I'll do the technical legal bit. I'll get in touch if and when I need to. Get hold of the notes – that's important. They are the confirmation that what you have told me actually happened. And don't forget, it may just go away.'

So Nick Malenkov left, with another firm handshake, and another direct look from those clear blue eyes. And I went home to Sophie and her upset tummy.

CHAPTER 4

So I did the technical legal bit to formally deny the allegations, and waited to see what would happen. And waited. Nothing. Not a squeak out of the lawyers representing the redheaded socialist. Nick Malenkov sent me a comprehensive account of his recollection of the sequence of events, which confirmed the story he had given me when we met. We were still unsure of exactly what he was perceived to have done wrong. The opening shot in a Writ is often vague: in this case it said "by failing to readmit Mr Harrison to hospital, Dr Malenkov failed in his duty of care, thereby allowing the disease from which Mr Harrison was suffering to take hold. As a consequence, Mr Harrison suffered severe and ongoing physical suffering, with consequences for his wellbeing and lifestyle that will be life-long." So we were still uncertain what specifically he was being accused of failing to do, and the one thing we needed to refute things was Harrison's medical records. Without them, it was one person's word against another.

I explained all this to Nick on the phone. 'I'm chasing up the medical notes,' he told me, but that 'could take some time.' I recalled wryly that at any one time up to fifteen percent of all

NHS notes are missing, or at least not where they should be, so 'some time' might turn into 'a long time.' The notes were probably sitting in some warehouse somewhere, waiting to be delivered from one GP to another. I had almost put the case out of my mind as just another fishing expedition. I had other more pressing things to deal with, both professional and personal. Not least, my marriage.

There is a curious separation between liking someone, fancying them, and loving them, and combining all of those enough to want to live with them for a lifetime. I knew the hazards of mistaking one of these emotions for another, just as most of us do. Growing up as a girl, especially as a pretty girl, which in retrospect I was, has all the hazards that lead to such mistakes. And the other bear-trap, waiting to catch the unwary, is the realisation – or lack of it – that girls and boys develop and deploy their emotions and consequent behaviour very differently.

The boys at school, both attractive and unattractive, had a strangely ambivalent way of demonstrating that they liked you. They tended to kick at stones on the pavement outside school, stutter about things like football, and eventually ask, without looking you in the eye, whether you felt like having a coffee, or coming to the cinema. At Cambridge, things were different. The male confidence was more on show, bolstered by the realisation that getting to Cambridge already made them a winner in life's lottery. The arrogant young men were more cocky, the charming young men were more charming, and the unspoken invitations were more overt. Of course the most attractive were always beyond reach, already surrounded by a cluster of admiring high achievers of both sexes, and the rest of us could only look on and admire. The golden boys and girls basked in the sunshine of their beauty and success. And the people who were not so beautiful, the bashful, the spotty, those with regional accents and the gingers, relapsed further and further into their shy and defensive shells, and watched with envy.

I, of course, fell passionately in love with a golden boy. He was in his last year at Pembroke, a small but elitist College, and had been to a good public school. He already had a Blue, and was looking forward to getting the inevitable First in PPE, before taking up his rightful job in the City and making his fortune. He knew, with sublime certainty, that he would then get a safe Conservative seat, and rise rapidly up the greasy pole. He was beautiful, well-off, charming, and deeply, subliminally arrogant. I was overwhelmed and overjoyed when he chose me, little me, from a suburban background and with a grammar school education, to go to the May Ball in my first year. I borrowed a dress from one of the new friends I had made at Newnham – I thought I had scrubbed up quite nicely. He danced divinely, introduced me to his numerous and equally beautiful friends, gave me much too much to drink, and expected me to be made love to on demand in return. Which I did with amateur enthusiasm. It seemed the only courteous thing to do, and after all, everyone else was doing it. When, after a few delirious weeks, he dropped me like a stone for another and more attractive girl, my heart was broken, and the world seemed to be ending. I cried outside the door of his set of rooms one night, until he finally came out and sent me away with a few cutting remarks about bourgeois upbringing, and middle class morals. Then I hated him, even though I still worshipped him. I think that that experience was the start of the cynicism that has pervaded many of my relationships ever since. I seem to be inherently suspicious of everyone and everything. Perhaps this is what allows me to do my job so dispassionately and efficiently. I have developed a protective carapace which assumes that all human contact comes with an ulterior motive, and that only the self-protective survive.

So I went into marriage with my eyes wide open, and a degree of wariness. The man I married was, I thought, a good man, though. He came from a background a bit up the social scale from mine, and had the same sort of outlook on life. We were both driven to achieve, and we both loved the shining principles of the law we were starting to practice. I had just got my job in a well-known London firm of solicitors, and he had completed his pupillage with flying colours, and his call to the Bar had coincided with getting into a popular chambers. As the best man said at our expensive wedding in a beautiful Cotswold setting, 'if ever a couple were made for each other, it was these two'. And made for each other we were, to begin with.

But, as in all relationships, be they marriage or anything else, the initial gloss slowly wore off. Irritating traits and habits became apparent, and were either tolerated or bickered over. Ambitions were compared and contrasted, and motives were examined. But for the first few years, our marriage was no worse, and quite a lot better, than the vast majority of those of our friends and colleagues. We were happy, bed was wonderful, we were making good money, and having a good time if the work allowed. So what if he drank a little too much, and flirted a little too ostentatiously?

I think the first crack came with children. It would be a surprise to me, at least, if any marriage survived children without major fissures and difficulties. The profound, almost overwhelming, change in the focus of a woman's life when she has produced a baby is something that no man can fully comprehend, and he definitely cannot experience it. This extraordinary devotion to a noisy, demanding, entirely dependent scrap of humanity is such a big and unexpected feeling that a man can only watch and wonder. And quite soon, my man started to resent it. He had been the centre of my life until then, the focus of all my attention. Now someone had taken his place, and although he had been a willing partner in producing his competitor, he found being edged out a deeply disrupting change to come to terms with. We struggled through the first year of Sophie's life, me tired and depressed and frustrated, he inefficient at home, busy at work, and increasingly distant.

I went back to my solicitor's office eight months after giving birth, and the pressure of work was added to the tiredness and worry and angst of being a young mother. That he expected me to be entirely responsible for the fetching and carrying, the day nursery pick-ups, as well as the broken nights ('I'm in Court tomorrow'). This all contrived to reinforce my subliminal view that there is no man who can really be trusted.

It was a shock when I became pregnant again – although my parents expressed quiet pleasure, and his overprotective mother rushed down from the Cotswolds to congratulate him, and took us out to lunch near Lincoln's Inn.

'Anyone would think that I had nothing to do with it,' I grumbled later, but he laughed.

'You know Mum,' he said. 'She knows that the sun shine's out of my bum.'

'Sometimes' I said 'I think you do as well.'

He looked at me, smoothing back his well-cut hair, and hung up the jacket of his expensive suit. We were just going to bed, and I was feeling queasy and tired.

'Pull yourself together, darling,' he said. 'She's got every right to be pleased.' But there was a distance between us, and I felt a frisson of anxiety.

*

I struggled through the second pregnancy, but at least I knew what to expect. Richard was not particularly interested in how I felt; his mind was on his first application to become a Silk, and the doors that that would open. However, he bought off my protests by making me go privately to have the baby.

'Nothing but the very best for you, sweetheart,' he said, and packed me off to Wimpole Street as a way of paying for not being there for me. That didn't work either. I instinctively disliked the rather overweight and florid obstetrician I was sent to see. He had moist hands, and called me 'little lady'. I would much rather have been cared for by the cheerful Jamaican midwife who had seen me through Sophie's birth.

'He's the very best,' Richard said. 'Several minor Royals have been to see him, and lots of well-off ladies from the Middle East.'

'Hardly an objective recommendation,' I huffed. 'They probably have colonic washouts as well, but that doesn't make them objective opinions.'

'Don't be stupid, darling,' he said, putting on his dark blue overcoat with the velvet collar, and picking up his Louis Vuitton briefcase. 'You know that the NHS is cheap and cheerful, but we've progressed way beyond that level now.' And he picked a stray blond hair off his lapel and closed the front door without waiting for my reply. Sophie cried, and I felt like joining in.

So Rupert was born in the luxurious surroundings of St Mary's private wing, surrounded by other infants of the rich and famous. And I languished in a private room, lonely and exhausted, and surrounded by flowers from his side of the family. My mother came to see me, but was intimidated and overwhelmed by a wave of joy and emotion from Richard's mother, who burst into my room without warning, like an avenging angel come to save her most precious hostage to fortune.

'Darling,' this to Richard, who was sitting beside my bed reading the Law Gazette. 'How amazingly clever of you. Isn't he beautiful? Just the same as you were!' And she picked up Rupert, who had just been fed and put down, and had gone to sleep. He retaliated with a milky puke down the front of her silk blouse, and started to cry. I was cheered by his response, and was brave enough, for once, to answer back to this deluge of possessiveness.

'I had something to do with it as well, Beatrice.' I muttered, pulling myself painfully up the hospital bed. 'And I'd be awfully grateful if you wouldn't disturb him when he's just gone to sleep.'

'I know, dear,' she gushed, patting my hand. 'It's just the hormones talking.'

I tried to catch Richard's eye, but he studiously avoided mine. I could have cheerfully hit them both. The visit was not a success.

But we plodded on over the next year or so. I went back to work again, which was a relief, and I found an au pair who I liked and trusted, and she became a friend and an ally. The separation between professional life and home and children, though, became harder and harder to demarcate, as the calls of the children on my time and emotion increased, and Richard's seeming commitment to the domestic scene became less and less. His tendency to have important case-conferences on an increasing number of evenings every week could have been just a normal part of his success, even though there was sometimes wine on his breath when he eventually came to bed long after me. And of course the cases in Manchester, where the General Medical Council was based, meant that he was often away for several days at a time, staying in hotels. I wondered, vaguely, once or twice, what he got up to in the evenings up there. So much time on his hands to have fun.

He was specialising in medical negligence, like me, but he

was always the prosecuting barrister, never defending. Perhaps it was this that gave him such a jaundiced view about doctors and their competence. Or, as he saw it, lack of it. We regularly argued about my perspective of doctors doing their best, often in difficult circumstances, and his of them being self-serving technicians. The concept of someone making an honest mistake under pressure was not one he was prepared to contemplate or make allowances for. Any more than the idea that judgement could only turn out to be wrong in retrospect. I began to think that he was a hard and judgemental man, without much kindness, and wondered what he would say or do when the children made mistakes. It took me some time to realise that we thought in very different ways, and it worried me.

*

It came to something of a crunch over a Christmas, when Rupert was nearing his second birthday. We'd spent the last Christmas at home, and I had nearly enjoyed it – the Christmas stockings, Sophie's excitement, presents, doing the Christmas dinner; all the things that I had imagined a proper family doing together. But the year after it wasn't the same at all.

I mentioned to him at the beginning of December that I had ordered a goose for us this Christmas, instead of a turkey. His face froze.

'But we're going to my parents.'

'Are we? I hadn't heard about that. Do you think you might have consulted me first?'

'Sorry. I rather assumed you'd be happy to go. Mother rang me a fortnight ago to say they were expecting us, and I just went along with it.'

I was suddenly furious, seething.

'There are two of us in this marriage, Richard, for Christ's sake. It's meant to be a partnership.'

His face was expressionless. 'Of course. But I thought that you'd enjoy it. Less work for you, and the children will love being made a fuss off.'

'Like the fuss you make of them every evening at bed-time, I suppose. Can you remember when you last put them to bed?'

He looked at me consideringly, his eyes cold. 'If you'd wanted to marry a house-husband, Antonia, you should have chosen someone else. I'm off to an Inns of Court dinner at the Temple – can't remember if I mentioned it. Don't wait up for me.' And he sauntered out of the house.

I turned away. I felt that if I had taken that confrontation any further, it would lead to irreparable damage. So I took my anger away, and internalised it. I noticed the looks that came my way at work over the next few days, and the way colleagues skirted cautiously around me, and felt a sort of vicarious pleasure from being treated as a storm centre.

Christmas, when it came, was a turning point. I made myself a promise to behave as a dutiful daughter-in-law should, as we drove through the foggy roads towards the Cotswolds late on Christmas Eve afternoon. The children in the back of the Volvo (why did he always buy conventional bloody Volvos?)

were excited, Rupert gurgling in his car seat. We arrived at the Cotswold manor house just as dusk was settling in, and the warmth of the welcome, the familiar old-fashioned Christmas decorations, and the crackling open fire went some way to calming my heightened suspicions about the invitation. We were enveloped in the middle class atmosphere of carols and mince pies and mulled wine, and I felt the stresses and anger seep away from me.

After supper ('we always have smoked salmon on Christmas Eve, dear'), we relaxed in front of the fire. At ten thirty, I was yawning for the third time, and the big bed in the chintzy spare bedroom beckoned.

'It's been a long day. I think I'll go up then.'

Richard's mother sat up with a jolt

'Aren't you coming to midnight Mass, then, dear?' she said, with a hint of sharpness in her voice. 'We always go to midnight Mass at Christmas.' She pronounced Mass to rhyme with arse.

'You know that religion and I parted company a long time ago, Beatrice,' I said. 'I would fall asleep half way through, and be bad company. You'll enjoy it much more without me.'

'But you must come.' There was a wail in her voice, and a demand. 'We won't be a proper family if you don't.'

"Don't bully her, Bee,' her husband said from the depths of his armchair. 'Why shouldn't she go to bed if she wants to?'

'It matters to me if she won't come,' defiantly, from Beatrice.

I caught Richard's eye. He knew how irritating I found the conventions of religion. But there was a look of defiance in his glance.

'Of course, you'll come, darling,' he said brusquely. 'We're mother's guests, and it would be rude not to do what she asks. It's not such a big thing, anyway. Come on; buck up. You might actually manage to enjoy it.'

So the battle lines were drawn, and I went to midnight Mass to rhyme with arse. Much later, exhausted and still furious, I was getting ready for bed in the chintzy bedroom when he came in. He smelled of whiskey.

'Why do you have to be such a misery, darling?' he said. 'It wasn't so bad, was it? And it made Mum very happy. You should remember that.'

'I'm too tired to argue, Richard,' I said, stumbling over a useless decorative footstool by the bed. I kicked it out of the way. 'You may remember that it was me who got up twice last night to Rupert, and then got your breakfast, and then fed the children, and then went to work myself. That seems to have escaped you in your desire to please your mother.' To my surprise, I found that I was shaking with anger. 'You need to decide on your loyalties in this marriage. You obviously feel that her sensibilities are more important than mine.'

He didn't reply, but his silence made it very clear which way his loyalties lay. We lay beside each other, rigid and untouching, throughout the night.

And so the battle lines were drawn, and the slow, long-drawn-out decline in my marriage became steeper. Both of us realised that a line had been crossed. The journey back to London three days later was miserable. The traffic was awful and the fog was thick. The children were restless and miserable too, and grizzled for no reason, and we snapped at them. When we finally got home to the smart terraced house in Islington, to which we had moved to confirm his rising status, it felt cold and unwelcoming, the Christmas decorations tawdry. The cat sensed the atmosphere, and slithered round our legs to escape through the cat flap unfed.

The decline in our relationship over the next few weeks was as predictable as it was unpleasant. I think we both realised that we had fallen out of love with each other a long time ago, and now didn't even like one another very much.

'Daddy doesn't love Mummy any more,' Sophie said one morning, when he had left without kissing me goodbye, or, if truth be known, even acknowledging me.

'No,' I said, hugging her too me. 'I'm afraid he doesn't.'

Three weeks later, about the same time that I first met Nick Malenkov, he moved out to one of the small flats above his Chambers, and we started the long, slow and expensive process of divorce. Our respective parents flapped round the fringe of our private hell, helpless to intervene or console. We made it, and we broke it, so we should have to sort out the consequences.

CHAPTER 5

I was coming back from my first interview with the solicitor I had chosen to represent me in my divorce when Nick Malenkov came on my horizon once more. The solicitor was a calm and competent woman, and I felt I was in good hands. So as I sat behind my desk back in the office, I was feeling better than for ages, and didn't even feel irritated when my secretary came in without knocking.

'It's that Dr Malenkov on the phone,' she said. 'You know, the one with the eyes.' I did know . There was only one client with eyes that both of us would have noticed, despite all the others who passed through the office. But that was ages ago, it seemed.

'What does he want?'

'To see you.'

'Why? Nothing has happened, and it has been – what? – six months since we last heard from him. And I've heard nothing from the claimant or his solicitors.'

'He didn't say. But I thought you'd probably want to see him.'

I looked at her hard. She didn't know anything about my impending divorce yet, but the rumour mill was as active in a solicitor's office as in any other, and I wondered if she was making a snide comment. She looked back at me without blinking, and I couldn't detect any sneer. Perhaps she was just sharing that womanly thing of acknowledging that an attractive man was attractive.

'Better tell him to come', I said. 'Maybe it's urgent'.

*

He came to see me the next morning, squeezed in between two existing appointments. My job, like a doctor's, consisted of a lot of routine work interspersed with things that were considered urgent by the patient or client. Often they were nothing of the sort, but the very fact that the person on the other side of the desk was fearful or worried or panic-stricken or angry made their demand for an instant solution impossible to refuse.

When it came to it, there was no pressure, as my first appointment was a no show, and I had time to sit and enjoy a coffee before he arrived. I swung my chair round to look out of the window. It was another lovely spring day, with the trees in Covent Garden covered in blossom. The early tourists were pottering about, and the first of the street performers were just getting into their stride. The human statues were standing immobile on their boxes, painted silver, waiting to startle children by sudden movements. A juggler was well into his first set of clever patter, and was getting a Japanese tourist in a baseball cap to help him mount the unicycle, which would make his juggling act seem even more skilful. I thought, as I always did, how brave these people were to stand up in front of a crowd and expose themselves to ridicule or applause. What extraordinary self-confidence you must have to do it. Rather like politicians, so convinced of their own rightness that they seemed immune to criticism. On the surface, at least.

And talking of criticism, it was ages since I had been down to Sussex to see my mum. I always felt slightly guilty that I had neglected her since my father had died. I must give her a ring. She hardly ever bothered me, and had lived alone in Sussex, in a pretty village just outside Chichester, in a fold of the Downs. I wondered if she was lonely, and then felt even more guilty about not seeing her more often and doing something about it. Things always seemed to get in the way, and my marriage mess didn't help.

My meandering thoughts were interrupted as Nick was shown in. I stood up and shook his hand. The eyes were just as remarkable, but the brow above was furrowed.

We went through the usual process of meeting up after a gap, the 'how have you been' chitchat, and 'what kind of journey up did you have?' But he was anxious and nervous. We sat down in the chairs on each side of my big desk.

'What's up?' I asked without further preamble.

'This'. And he passed some paperwork across the desk.

'This' was a Notice of Hearing. The official document that sets in train a hearing at the High Court, the first real shot in anger. I was very irritated. None of the proper procedure had been followed by the complainant, by his lawyers, or by the Court itself. This was a cheap shot , an underhand move. If justice is to mean anything, it must mean fairness of process, and this ploy was manipulating that.

'This is just a dirty trick', I told him. 'A dirty devious underhand move. It tells us more about the type of lawyers who are representing your client than it does about the strength of their case. They are using a technical trick to try to get us into court without proper preparation, so that they can hit us with allegations and expert opinions that we cannot refute. In effect, they are going for a quick win. It is a rarely used technique, and one that goes against all the tenets of natural justice and due process, but the loophole still exists because the process of changing the law is hopelessly slow and lugubrious. The default position of the Department of Justice seems to be to stall, to prevaricate, to defer. Idiots', I said, feeling hot under the collar. 'Idiots. What is it about some civil servants that makes them so obtuse?'

'It's no different in the health business', he said. 'When I last spoke to a Minister he gave the Irish answer; he said that if we wanted to get somewhere different, we shouldn't have started from here. I pointed out that was of not much help to those of us who have to deliver a service. '

'Roll on the revolution', I said, and we smiled at each other. A thought struck me, though.

'Do you often speak to Ministers?'

'Well'. A thoughtful pause. 'I had the privilege of an expensive education. That means that now I have many friends and contacts, one or two in high places. It's an interesting position to be in,' he went on reflectively. 'One that is open to abuse. But it gives me the ability – some might say the right – to tell it like it really is to some of the powers that be, especially if they are making fools of themselves.' And he smiled, and the smile softened the creases in his drawn and anxious face.

'So you are a rich man doing a poor man's job', I said, trying to be funny, and failing.

The smile disappeared. 'I wouldn't put it quite like that. And my choice of career definitely hasn't made me rich.'

I felt a little stupid. I had made a faux pas. There was a slightly uncomfortable pause, and we could hear a smattering of applause from outside, as a street performer finished his act. I did my 'I'm in control' act to fill the silence. 'Listen. This is what we'll do. I'll come out all guns blazing at both his lawyers and at the High Court. They have bent several rules to get the hearing listed like this, but there is absolutely no doubt that we can defer it. But it does mean', and I put on my 'now the bad news' face, ' that they feel confident enough to keep blaming you, and we must do some hard work on your defence. That gives us two tasks.'

'Right,' he said, a little uncertainly. 'What do you want from me?'

I paused and thought. ' First and foremost, we must get hold of his medical records. They are critical. If, as you said, you kept quite good notes, they may stop the whole thing in its tracks. So search every nook and cranny, chase the NHS medical records people, and anyone else you can think of. But find them. For the rest of it, let me think of all the options. I'd rather not give you an off the cuff answer until I've discussed this with colleagues and worked out a proper plan of campaign. We've got to be prepared for all eventualities, expected or unexpected. And in view of the behaviour of his lawyers so far, I fully expect the unexpected.'

Another crinkle round the eyes. 'You obviously know exactly what you are doing'. He said. 'Thank goodness for that. I got slightly near panic yesterday. Thank you.'

'Right', I said, resisting the urge to pat his arm. 'Let's get a few details out of the way. Are you staying in London? Have you got good professional and personal support to lean on through all this? What does your wife feel about it all?'

'I'm staying at the Royal College, and there are a few friendly faces there. But,' and there was a pause, 'my wife left me quite soon after I first came to see you. It was a bit of a hard time.'

There was a long silence.

'Why?' It was absolutely none of my business, but I could not stop myself.

'Well, she had difficulty coming to terms with a whole series of things. It probably started when our son died. Such a huge thing for a mother to come to terms with. She had been an extrovert before that – the life and soul of the party, cheerful, funny, happy. But she became depressed, angry, bitter. She felt life had let her down, and the doctors had failed her by not saving Paul, and I, of course, represented doctors, so came in for blame as well. The way of life of a GP didn't help either, the commitment, the time...' His voice trailed off, and his eyes looked inwards at an episode that had changed so much of his life. I suspected that he had been deeply hurt by it. Quite different to my situation, I reflected, where we just didn't like each other any more.

He looked up again. 'Life goes on'. There was a smile – wistful. 'I'm beginning to get the hang of ironing my shirts'.

We were silent for a moment longer.

'So who is looking out for you? Who do you talk to about all this? You should – you must – have someone to share it with. Carrying all this by yourself is a disaster in the making. And we will need you on top form if and when this finally comes to court. '

'Do you think it will?'

'Don't know. Possibly. Probably, in fact. It looks as though this lot are going to go for your throat, whatever the strength and weaknesses of their case. So we need to do the hard graft to make sure we're completely ready.'

His face fell again, and once again I wanted to reach out and touch him. He reminded me of me. Alone. Loneliness is such a sad thing to observe. But the professional in me straightened my shoulders and went back into action mode.

'Right. Leave nearly all of it to me. I will find a good barrister, the right one for your case, and discuss our strategy with him. We'll chose the experts who will be best at rebutting their line of argument, which will be hidden in the small print of the Notice. Then we'll meet to discuss tactics. OK with all of that?'

'Yes. Anything else you want me to do?'

'Get your story absolutely clear in your mind. Try to strip it of all emotion and concern about what you did, and what happened to him. Get the facts completely clear in your mind, so that you come over as a calm sensible, competent doctor, not a self-questioning doubter. And find the notes'.

'OK'.

'And talk to people. Unload it onto friends, colleagues, anyone you can trust. You cannot carry the stress of this by yourself. We all need shoulders to cry on.'

'Right. I'll try'.

'You'll do better than that. You'll actually do it,' I sad brusquely. 'I'm not going to waste my time defending someone who turns into a gibbering wreck under pressure.'

A final smile. 'OK'.

And he went out into the spring sunshine, back to his busy surgery and demanding patients and his lonely life. And I went back to my desk, strewn with piles of paper, and the details of the next doctor in trouble, and my sterile failure of a marriage.

CHAPTER 6

The process of dealing with a High Court writ is, in theory, straightforward.

You start by analysing the allegation – the thing your client is said to have done wrong . That leads to the first fork in the road. Either he (or she) did make some kind of cock-up that had a consequence for a patient. In which case you explore all the reasons for the failure, and try to get evidence that it was understandable given the circumstances, didn't amount to much in the grand sum of things, and had no real or lasting consequences for the patient. Or, the other fork, that you genuinely feel that your client did not make a mistake or cause a problem, and you proceed to prove just that.

In this instance, Keith Harrison, the litigant, had to prove that Dr Malenkov hadn't come up to the standards expected of a competent doctor. That meant that there needed to be some kind of definition of what competence was. The claim said that he should have been re-admitted to hospital, but that Nick failed to do that. In defending him, we had to prove that there was good reason not to do that, and that he had still done what any normal doctor would have done in the circumstances.

The critical word in all of this is, of course, 'proof', and the definition of that is a moveable feast.

Put simply, there are two standards of proof. The first one, the criminal standard, is the one which most people are familiar with. It is the one that criminal trials use and depend on, working through the so-called jewel in the crown of the British legal system, the jury. It is defined as being sure that something happened 'beyond reasonable doubt', but that, of course, raises the issue of what is reasonable. A much better definition is to say that a jury member 'must be certain so that he is sure' that an event took place. That removes the element of doubt from the decision; it means you must be absolutely convinced that something happened or is true. If there is any doubt at all, you are duty bound to find the accused 'not guilty'.

There are lots of question marks surrounding the consequences of this, but the tenet that 'it is better that ten guilty man go free than one innocent man be convicted' still underpins the certainty required by the criminal standard.

The civil standard of proof is much less easy to get your head around. Its principle is that a judge alone (and it is always a judge or judges sitting alone in civil cases, without a jury) decides that 'on the balance of probabilities it is more likely that an event happened than it did not happen'. So that means that if the judge decides that it is a bit more likely that something took place than it did not, then someone is guilty. This does not mean not that someone definitely did something and is therefore liable for the consequences, but that on balance, it is more likely than not that they might have done whatever it is that they are accused of. Then, of course, they are responsible for the outcome, and any damage if it has been done. I always viewed the balance of probabilities as a see-saw, and imagined that it only took one small fact or bit of evidence to tip the see-saw one way or the other. The scales of justice.

Fair? You tell me. But it is the system we have arrived at over centuries of legal evolution, and is probably the least bad way of arriving at decisions about responsibility. Solomon would probably have gone along with it; at least it would have got him off the hook. And it is the system by which allegations against any professional are judged in the High Court, be they architect, engineer, or, as in my case, doctor. Of course, there are lots of subtleties and nuances around the balance of probabilities judgement. One states that 'the more serious the alleged offence, the more certain a judge must be of the probability'. In other words, there is a sliding scale of guilt. If you are accused of failing to treat a cut finger properly, and the patient loses a week's work, the balance may be little more than 50:50. But if you fail to do an operation that needs doing, and the patient dies, the court may require greater certainty that not doing it was negligent.

All interesting stuff that law students learn at their mothers' knee, but a concept which most people find new and contrived and confusing. Nearly all the doctors that I represented were furious to find out that their guilt or lack of it was judged on the balance of probabilities scale. Most of them used the same phrases: 'Real life's not like that. We make dozens of judgements every day, sometimes under great pressure, and it is only hindsight that proves them to be wrong, or at least not perfectly right. And that is the very nature of making a judgement'. I could only agree. I spent much of my time making judgements, and knew only too well how often I was wrong. Luckily, not many of my clients died as a result, although they could be very damaged by my error. It was my good luck that not many clients sue their lawyers; not nearly as many as those who sue their doctors.

*

So I set about listing the things I needed to do to defend my doctor. Barrister – a good one; experts – sensible ones; character witnesses - reliable, and so on. And I started to sketch out a narrative that would read well in court – the barrister's 'opening submission', covering the sequence of events that had led us to this point. High Court judges are notoriously prone to being bored by verbiage, so it had to be short and to the point, but could not omit the salient details. The barrister would add his own polish to this; my job was to do the preparation, what in rugby is known as the hard yards.

About three weeks later, I rang Nick. He was between patients, and I could hear the noise of the waiting room in the background.

'Hello. How's it all going?'

'All right, I suppose. Busy. What can I do for you?'

'Well, I've got the skeleton of our case together, and we need to run through it with the barrister I've chosen to represent you. I've fixed up a case conference with everyone for Thursday week at 6.00 o'clock in his Chambers. Can you make it? It's important that you do.'

'It's my on call day. Hell. I'm sure I'll be able to swap it, though. My partners are a supportive lot. By the way, I still haven't managed to track down the medical notes. I've searched every place I can think of, the 'lost' depository, his previous GPs, even the Department of Health death file, which is notorious for having the notes of healthy patients hidden away. Nothing. Not a hint of them.'

'That's a pity.' I chewed the top of my pen in irritation. The cornerstone of any good defence is contemporaneous records. They are almost irrefutable, as they are – or should be – a record of what happened, made at the time. They are not just a recollection, as most witness evidence is.

I made reassuring noises: 'Don't despair. I'm sure we'll be ok without them.' But I didn't really believe that. Without the notes we were navigating without a chart. It becomes one person's word against another, and the sympathy of the court, of any court, always tends to go with the sufferer. I cursed under my breath.

'Anything else I should bring to the case conference?'

'Just your wits. See you then.' And I rang off. A picture of the slightly puzzled look in those blue eyes flashed across my mind.

*

Choosing a barrister for a specific case is quite an arcane skill. You have little idea which judge you are going to get, but you know which way judges as a breed tend to think and behave. They don't fall for the histrionics that so impress juries. Rather, they are impressed by clarity, and by the avoidance of any attempt to manipulate fact or emotion. Some actively dismiss any attempt at dramatics, and hold it against the dramatist and his case. On the whole, they are highly intelligent. But it is important to remember that intelligence and wisdom are not the same things.

The barrister I eventually chose was a thoroughly nice man, and dependable. Calm, clever and very competent. I had sent him several medical defence briefs in the past, and he had never let me or the client down. He wasn't a Silk, a Queen's Counsel, – that accolade of success for barristers that indicate seniority, skill and a greatly enhanced income, but he was a past master at dissecting a case down to its basic elements, and I enjoyed watching him in court. A true craftsman at work.

The expert witnesses were rather different. They had to be at or at least near the top of their specialist trees, otherwise they would not carry enough weight to impress a court. But they must not be too clever. There is nothing like a brilliant academic who can be made to flounder when confronted with the real world of medical practice. So they needed practical experience as well as gravitas. It had taken me some time to work this out. Early in my career I had used experts with long lists of research papers behind them, some of them professors. It was only after disasters with experts who I can only describe as very clever fools that I learnt that being expert in theory is not the same as being wise in practice. There is a move afoot to ensure that expert witnesses meet proper criteria and follow defined processes in giving their evidence. Not before time, some of us think.

The other thing that not all experts really understand is that their primary obligation is to the court, not to the client. Their duty is to make a judgement about the performance of a doctor in the light of their expertise, be that performance good or bad, and be able to justify that judgement. They are definitely not there to be a hired gun, to stack the cards against a doctor so as to ensure that he is found guilty. Not all experts have taken this on board, and there is a hard core of so-called experts who will say almost anything under oath in order to collect their fee. Luckily, most High Court judges are wise to such characters.

I hummed and hawed for a long time, tapping my teeth with a pencil, and leafing through my notebook that contained the details of experts I had used in the past, with their strengths and weaknesses. As the accusation against my doctor was about how he had managed – or mismanaged – someone with a gut disease, I came up with a gastroenterologist from a peripheral teaching hospital. Not one of the Harley Street high flyers, but a sound, experienced and wise individual. I had not used him before, but he came with strong recommendations from a colleague.

*

We met at six o'clock ten days later, in my barrister's room in his chambers. My soon-to-be ex-husband had agreed to have the children for a few hours before going back to his so-called bachelor pad just round the corner from where we were meeting. I had my suspicions that the 'bachelor' label no longer strictly applied. There was a long blond hair on the shoulder of his smart coat when he came to Islington to pick up the children, and I'm sure I caught a faint whiff of Chanel as he kissed me on the cheek. Had it really come to this? Had he moved on already? I had not seen him for nearly a fortnight.

'How are you?' I asked.

'Chipper'. He knew the word irritated me. 'Mustn't grumble'.

I left him in charge of the children with some reluctance, and caught a taxi to the meeting with the barrister. The children sensed my mood, and watched me go with glum faces. I'm not sure that they trusted him now any more than I did. Was what we were doing just a way out for two rather self-absorbed adults, without thinking through the consequences for the children? Didn't every couple go through bad patches, just as we were? Why couldn't we muddle through like so many people did, grit our teeth and cope with the normal frustrations and irritations of a marriage? I had loved him so much, and I really think he had loved me. So his mother was a pretentious cow. What of it? So he had had a fling with some blonde. So what? Wasn't that just a man thing, the primitive hormone-driven need to win, possess and dominate? And was I just being a self-centred career woman, adding to the stresses that all relationships have by insisting on my right to have a career as well as to enjoy motherhood? And did I risk missing out on both? Quite suddenly another emotional abyss opened up in front of me, and I found my mind overwhelmed by all that was confronting me. The rain on the taxi windows, or perhaps it was tears, blurred the streets outside, and I felt all my resolve and my courage and my certainty blur in sympathy.

With a huge effort, I dragged myself back to the present, and the job in hand. It wasn't part of my role to be a weak and feeble woman. Like Elizabeth the First, I had to have the heart and stomach of a man. Other men, and in particular a doctor called Nick, depended on me.

*

Our barrister's room in the Middle Temple was like a stage set; how a theatre designer might visualise a barrister's room to be, I thought. A gentleman's club snug, the walls lines with shelves of sonorous tomes, an Adam fireplace, a beautifully polished table that might have once graced a grand dining room, and dominating everything, an imposing partners desk with a leather swivel chair behind it. This room would be replicated in chambers all over the Temple, and in other chambers in cities up and down the country. It was part of the uniform, the camouflage with which all groups of people with a common purpose cover themselves. The doctor's white coat; the vicar's dog collar and vestments, the banker's pin-striped suit. It is partly protective – it shows that you are part of the club, and it is partly for show, to proclaim to the outside world that you have made it in your chosen role. The characteristic room in chambers is just as much an identifying stigma of the successful barrister as his wig and gown.

I let my eyes wander over the high coved ceiling, with the delicate plasterwork cornices, and the tall sash windows letting in the light from the beautiful gardens of the Inner Temple. I could just see the top of the curious round tower of Temple Church above the buildings on the far side of the garden. It was a royal peculiar, one of those hangovers from the early middle ages that we are so adept at maintaining in England. That meant that it was under the direct control of the Monarch, and no one else had a say. Almost nobody knew about this anachronism, or cared about it, but the sense of history that is so deep in our national genes seemed to need to maintain it. And such history in a single place. The Knights Templar had walked and talked here before they set off to the Crusades.

James Brooks the barrister bustled in and sat us all down, and made small talk for a few moments. Tall, with a kind face and a clever way of putting clients at their ease, almost as though he was welcoming us to a drinks party at his home. I watched the doctor relax.

'Hello Antonia. Hello everyone.' We pulled up the elegant Hepplewhite chairs and sat around the big table, the four of us; myself, Nick, the expert gastroenterologist and Brooks, and introduced ourselves.

After saying who he was, Nick said 'I'm afraid I'm the cause of all the trouble.'

'Nonsense,' said Brooks cheerfully. 'Trouble is quite the

wrong word. And if anyone is causing trouble, it is your difficult patient and his lawyers.'

I made an encouraging noise of agreement, and saw that it had an effect.

'Right. Let's get to it. Antonia, you are the best person to give us a summary of the current state of play.'

So I took us through the story so far, summarising the background and the things that my doctor was being accused of, and finally my plans for rebutting them with our expert.

'Fine. Any questions before we go into the detail?'

None.

So we went through the sequence of events day by day and line by line, so that Brooks had it absolutely clear in his head. One of the skills barristers have is the ability to memorise a sequence of events in great detail, so that they can spot weaknesses or errors when it is retold in court, and undermine a witness. Brooks was clever at introducing the expertise of Professor Long, the gastroenterologist, and using it to demonstrate that the errors had taken place in the hospital before Harrison was discharged. As he said, this had left Nick holding a particularly toxic baby.

'I like that phrase,' said Brooks, amused. 'May I borrow it for use in court?'

It took well over an hour for us to do this, but finally we seem to have covered all the points. Brooks rubbed his hands and sat back.

'I think that covers everything. Thank you, everyone. Any questions before we all go home for a well-deserved drink?'

I was putting my papers into my briefcase when Nick Malenkov cleared his throat.

'Er, well, there is just one thing....'

Brooks smiled at him. 'And what is that, Dr Malenkov?'

'I may be speaking out of turn, but I just wonder if we might be using the wrong expert.'

The gastroenterologist shifted in his chair, uncrossed his legs and leaned forward. I stopped what I was doing and sat up straight. What on earth was he on about?

'I don't mean to be rude, Professor Long, but I feel we may be looking at the wrong issue here. This isn't about gut disease and illness.'

'The chap had Crohn's disease', said Long, a little crossly. 'If it's not about that, what is it about? That's what he is accusing you of making a mistake over.'

'Sorry'. Nick fumbled with his pen in embarrassment. 'Sorry, Professor Long. The last thing I want to do is seem rude. I'm definitely not querying your expertise, on the contrary, if I had Crohn's disease, I would definitely come and see you.'

He paused to collect his thoughts, and we all watched his face.

'I just wonder if we are shooting at the wrong target. We have spent a lot of time and effort thinking about how we could defend me against an accusation that I mismanaged this man's bowel disease. That is why' and he nodded to the professor, 'we have asked Professor Long to give us his opinion. But is it really that which I am accused of failing to do? In the event, I managed the onset of the illness reasonably well. I did nearly all the right tests, made a good stab at the correct diagnosis, and admitted him to hospital when he needed it. The only thing I might have done differently is find a hospital where the relevant specialist wasn't on holiday, and that was hardly in my gift. So the problem lies entirely with the events after his discharge, when he refused, against my strong advice, to be readmitted. So the crux of the matter is not about the management of Crohn's disease. It is about the rights of the individual to accept or reject medical advice, even if rejecting the advice may have bad consequences.' There was a short silence while we digested this. James Brooks face remained impassive, but I could see his mind turning over the options. Professor Long took more time to think it through, and his frown and irritation told of the age old barrier between specialist and GP. I could almost hear him thinking 'what does on earth does a GP know about a complex illness and how to manage it.'

Brooks was the first to break the silence.

'That's a very interesting take on things, Doctor. I must admit that I hadn't thought of it in those terms. But where does it take us?'

'In an entirely different direction.' Nick was less uncertain now. 'If we agree that it is nothing to do with the illness itself, it has to be about human rights, the right of an individual to make decisions on his own behalf, whatever the consequences. That is what the law of consent is all about. All patients have to agree to a treatment, even if it's taking a pill or having an ingrowing toenail removed. If they don't agree to a treatment, the doctor is guilty of assault. The only caveat is that the patient has to be in their right mind.'

'I'm with you so far.' Brooks sat back in his swivel chair. 'So what do we do next?'

'Change our experts.' The doctor glanced at Professor Long again. 'I have no doubt at all that the Professor would run intellectual rings round me and all other GPs on how best to treat Crohn's disease, but I wonder if he is the right expert to expound on the Human Rights Act, and the balance between a doctor's obligation to do the best for his patient, and a patient's right to reject that advice.'

'So?' Brooks was obviously intrigued.

'So our expert must be a specialist on the law of consent. I don't know who, or even if it need be a doctor at all. But we need to prove that he was within his rights to reject my advice, and that I was powerless to force him to accept it.'

Long made no attempt to hide his irritation. 'We are both doctors', he said forcefully, addressing my doctor directly. 'We are trained to recognise disease, and to do the best for our patients in the light of that recognition. You are suggesting that we can hide from that if the patient doesn't like the treatment we offer. If we follow that principle, no child would ever have a vaccination because they didn't want to have the pain of the injection.' He sat back and folded his arms in the classic defensive pose. I could almost hear the unspoken 'You're just a GP; what do you know?'

My doctor glanced at me, worried.

'I don't want to make a thing of this. It was just a thought.'

'And a very interesting thought.' Brooks' interest was apparent. 'And one that bears thinking through.' He turned to Professor Long.

'Have you ever had a patient discharge themselves from your hospital, Professor?'

'Of course. It happens in every hospital.'

'And what is your responsibility in that situation?'

'To explain the consequences.'

'And if that doesn't make any difference to the patient's decision?'

'Well, that's it, then. It's up to the patient.'

Brooks paused, and I could see him thinking how to prevent this becoming confrontational. 'I think you are both saying the same thing, but coming at it from different angles. What would you like me to do, Doctor, if they call an expert gastroenterologist to take Professor Long's line, and state that this is all about management – or mismanagement – of his bowel disease?'

'Ignore him,' said Nick immediately. 'Make it very obvious to the court that he has no experience at all in the problem we are discussing. He may be brilliant at managing bowel disease' – here a smile at the Professor - 'but he will almost certainly never have been a doctor on call in the community, faced with a dilemma like this.' He glanced at me. 'Antonia and I have chatted about this, the difference between consultant and GP roles. The functions should be complementary, but they are very different jobs in very different settings. So if you really want to undermine him, ask him how many patients he has seen in their homes, and if he ever has, how many refuse to follow his advice. The chances are he will not have seen any.'

'I can see exactly what you are saying, Doctor, and it ties in with what Professor Long is describing when a patient doesn't take his advice.' Brooks was the calm voice of reason.' May I think this through and talk about it with Antonia?' He gave a nod to me.

Long made harrumphing noises that I took to be agreement, but I could see that he was still irritated. Would we ever grow out of the arrogance of hierarchies, I thought. Every profession, every government, every business, every religion has them, structures that place one individual above another in a pecking order that gives power to the one above you. The more junior you are, the less likely your opinion is to carry weight. And the corollary, of course, is that the more senior you become, the more you are surrounded by people who think and behave like you, and who don't challenge you. So the status quo is maintained, however ineffectual that is.

I was jolted back to the present. 'Antonia?' Brooks had asked me a question, and I hadn't heard it.

'Sorry. I was miles away.'

'Well, get back here, please.' A brusque rebuke. 'I asked if you had anyone in mind who was a specialist in this area.'

'Off the top of my head, no. I'll need to do some research.'

Professor Long stood up. 'You obviously don't need me any more. The proper way to treat a disease has obviously become a secondary consideration compared with bloody management, as in just about the whole of medicine. I can be more useful seeing patients'. And he walked out of the room, the ruffled feathers clearly visible.

There was a pause after the door closed softly behind him.

'Sorry,' Nick looked crestfallen. 'That was my fault.'

'Not at all,' said Brooks. 'In fact, I think you are entirely right. The Professor has merely shown us how the other side may run their case. It is helpful to have had it pointed out so clearly. Antonia and I will do some research on how best to make your point in court, and who we should get to support it. Anything else on your mind? You obviously have a clear grasp of the principals involved here.'

'Well, yes, there is one other point'

I was collecting my papers again, but paused.

'Go on.'

'The only way they have of proving that I have a responsibility to over-rule his wishes is to demonstrate that he was bonkers. Sorry about the word, but you know what I mean – 'not of sound mind' is the technical term. They will need to show that he was so ill that his judgement was affected, that he was unable to make a rational decision. That situation happens commonly when people have acute psychiatric illnesses, schizophrenia of instance. They can then be 'sectioned' under the Mental Health Act. Their right to make decisions on their own behalf is temporarily removed for their own good. It is much less common in physical illness, and there is a grey area between the psychiatric effects of a physical illness, and the illness itself. When you have an acute infection such as septicaemia, you can get a thing called a toxic confusional state, which can make you very confused, even aggressive. So they might use a psychiatrist to try to prove that he was not aware of what he was doing, and we will need one to say that he was.'

This man should have been a lawyer, I thought. His grasp of the big picture was rare in a client. Of course I should have thought of that possibility. Why the hell hadn't I? Was I losing my grip? Becoming distracted? And if so, why? I caught Brooks' eye, and he nodded. I could see he was thinking the same. Why hadn't I thought of that?

'Antonia?'

'I'm sorry. I should have .....'

'Yes, you should. Or we should. Organise it please.'

As we left Brooks' chambers, I felt that stupid female tendency for tears threatening me. I could feel Nick looking at me as we walked out into the spring sunshine.

'All right?'

'Fine, thank you. But I think I've got a cold coming on.' I struggled in my handbag for a tissue, and he stood beside me, holding my briefcase.

'Thanks.' A big sniff.

He smiled at me. 'Take care of yourself.' And he turned and walked away.

And so we went to Court.

CHAPTER 7

The first day of any court hearing is exciting, sometimes a little frightening. It brings that frisson of fear to the fore, the fact that you are going to be tested, and tested in public. And your performance will be judged, and judged by people who you hold in awe. It is what all the preparation and hard work is aimed towards: to arrive in court with every avenue covered, every eventuality checked.

It is normal practice to arrive early at the High Court in the Strand on the first day, to gather one's wits and to check that everyone is present, correct and on the ball. Brooks and I had arranged to meet our doctor in a rather seedy café just across the road from the imposing Gothic court building with it's statue of Liberty holding the scales of justice. To my utter fury, I was late, and flustered. Richard had promised that he would come to the house and do the school run that morning, so that I could leave early and arrive serene and calm. But he was late, I suspected deliberately, and the children whined as we waited at the front door. I snapped at him when the Volvo finally pulled up in front of us, and he ignored me with that supercilious air that drove me mad. Why on earth had I married such a manipulative bastard?

So Brooks and Nick were waiting for me in the café, drinking milky coffee and looking at each other anxiously, when I finally flung myself out of a taxi and pushed my way inside. Not a particularly good start.

'Everyone OK?' A neutral opening gambit. They nodded glumly. Even the barrister, who was used to this scenario, smoothed his silk tie without looking at me, and finished his coffee. He glanced out of the window.

'Here comes the opposition,' he said. We watched as a little posse of well-dressed people marched through the gates of the High Court and on up its imposing steps. Leading them was someone I knew well, a small and very assured female figure with a formidable bust. The gaggle of onlookers automatically stepped back before her, rather as small boats scatter before the bows of an ocean liner.

'It's that damned Gwen again,' said Brooks. 'Damn. Damn and blast.'

'Why?' Nick looked anxious. 'What does that mean?'

'It means,' Brooks frowned, 'that they are well prepared and confident to the point of cockiness. Gwen Richardson is a solicitor who is notable, some might say notorious, for pulling rabbits out of hats and for twisting judges round her little fingers.' And he stopped speaking suddenly, aware that he had said too much.

I jumped into the breach.

'That is not to say that she is any better than any of us, or that her case is any stronger. Just look at who she's got as a barrister.'

We looked. Climbing the steps of the High court behind her was a small man, almost as round as he was tall. He was already out of breath and perspiring heavily even though it wasn't particularly warm. His suit jacket was unbuttoned, revealing a large belly, and as the wind caught the fabric, there was a flash of crimson. It is part of the uniform of the successful QC to have beautifully cut suits with exotic silk linings, even if these are not visible under robes in court. His trousers were held up by matching crimson braces; I could see how hard they had to work to do their job.

'Who is that?' asked the doctor.

'That,' I replied, 'is Henry Doggart. A silk of dubious renown. One of the patron saints of dodgy causes and ambulance chasing solicitors. I wouldn't touch him with a barge pole if he was the last barrister in the taxi rank. But,' I conceded, 'he's competent. Greasy, but competent'.

The third member of the group was a tall man with sandy hair, thin to the point of emaciation. He walked with a stoop, and there was an aura about him of – what was the word? – unwellness. That, I thought, must be Keith Harrison, the man who this was all about. The man who wanted to blame someone for his ill health. And Nick, my doctor, happened to be first in the firing line.

The posse disappeared through the imposing Gothic doors of the High Court, and he looked at me, worried.

'Does that mean they have a good case? Or at least think they have?'

'Possibly. But they have no idea how good ours is, and we,' I said confidently, 'have a very good case indeed.'

I watched his shoulders go back and his face relax a little. My job, I thought, was quite like his. You can't be certain that you'll cure the patient any more than you can be sure that you'll win the case, but at least you can maintain morale throughout the process. A quote from Tolstoy, one of my heroes, sprang to my mind. Natasha, when she was very ill after breaking with the Count in *War and Peace* was seen by many doctors, all of whom failed her. Perceptively, Tolstoy points out that the doctors did not realise that 'every patient had an illness that was unique and personal to them, and required a treatment that was unknown to medicine'. He was saying that every illness has a psychological component as well as a physical one, and that many doctors ignored that, because they couldn't treat it in the conventional sense. I knew the illness that was affecting my doctor, I thought. It was grief; grief for his wife, who had left him, grief for his dead child, and now grief for the loss of his professional innocence. All these weighed him down, and suffused him with a sadness that, unless I found the cure for it, might overwhelm him.

I looked at him again, seeing for the first time that his shoulders were a little stooped, his shoes a little scuffed, and realised how much control he had to exert to maintain a front. I felt a sudden urge to give him a hug. But then – stupid woman. Never confuse sympathy for a client with anything else. Help him, advise him, do your best for him, but never, under any circumstances, feel anything more for him. Down that road lies disaster.

And with that thought spinning in my head, I gathered my little team together, and marched them across the road and into battle.

*

As you go up the steps of the Royal Courts of Justice in the Strand, you are immediately confronted with the gravitas of the law. The outer entrance is decorated with busts of eminent Victorian judges. Their disdainful and arrogant expressions are enough to put the fear of god into anyone, be they guilty or innocent. At the apex of the arched portico is the figure of Christ, and to his left and a little lower, reflecting their relative status, are Solomon and Alfred the Great. Solomon, of course, is there on merit, but quite why Alfred should be up there has never been fully explained; perhaps it is more a reflection on his imposition of the rule of law than on his culinary skills.

As if the visitor isn't already nervous enough, he or she is then confronted by an enormous echoing hallway, populated by people walking briskly in all directions. Some are wearing the wigs and gowns of lawyers, others are carrying bundles of important looking papers and looking busy. Interspersed with these are the litigants, defendants and witnesses. They are there to obtain their rights for a perceived wrong, or to defend themselves against the slurs on their reputations presented by malign and biased accusers. It is easy to recognise them as they all look anxious. Unless you know where to go, the whole area presents a sea of confusion, specifically designed to further terrify the already frightened. 'Bloody hell,' said Nick. 'This is terrifying. I never in my worst dreams thought it would come to this.' He looked at me for reassurance.

I watched his eyes take in the surroundings, the echoing hall, the robed figures strolling past, and the sheer gravitas of the place. Finally the eyes came back to me in an unspoken appeal for reassurance. I had seen this appeal from clients before when the reality of arriving at the High Court hit them, and had my reassurance ready.

'Think of it this way. If you were a patient – me for instance –going into hospital to have an operation, I would feel exactly as you feel now. You are in an alien environment, somewhere where you have no control over what happens to you. Keep in mind that everything about this place and what is going on here has a single purpose – to deliver justice. Just as everything about a hospital has the single purpose, of delivering health. So put out of your mind all the things that intimidate you. Don't worry about the wigs and gowns and the frightening courtrooms, just as I shouldn't worry about the hospital scrubs and the operating theatre. Concentrate on one thing, the only thing that matters – that it is all about proving that you are not at fault. Let everything else go by on the other side. Ignore it.'

It was a spiel that I had used – with variations – with previous clients, and it had the right effect. I watched as the hunched shoulders relaxed a bit, and the furrows in the forehead smoothed out.

'Thank you', he said. 'You'd have made a good GP'. And he reached across and touched my arm, and smiled.

'Concentrate, woman', I said to myself. 'Don't go there. Do not get distracted'.

But I was.

*

Brooks caught us up. He had stopped to have a quick word with a colleague.

'All OK? Which courtroom are we in, Antonia?'

Having taken part in this ritual dance before, I knew what to do and where to go, and shepherded my little flock to the grand staircase that led towards the courtrooms of the Queen's Bench Division. This is the branch of the High Court that deals with all the personal injuries and negligence cases, and the disputes over contracts.

As the senior division of the High Court, headed by the Lord Chief Justice, it is the first port of call for all appeals arising from the lower courts. The other divisions are Chancery, dealing with trusts and probate, and the Family division, which makes decisions on personal things like divorce, custody of children, and so on. I had a lot of admiration for the judges who had to adjudicate on difficult things such as awarding custody, or withdrawing medical treatment from children against parents' wishes. No winners there, and a lot of losers. As I walked past the sign pointing to the Family courts, I reflected a little cynically that my marriage would soon be on the list of cases there. But our business lay in the Queen's Division, and it was to its Number 3 Court that I led my little group. Opposite the imposing double doors of the courtroom itself there were a few cubbyholes that acted as offices for the various protagonists, and we laid claim to one of these and unloaded briefcases and coats.

Brooks shrugged on his robe, and took his wig out of the little box which these anomalous gestures to the past live in. He straightened it on his head, and I was intrigued by the change that it brought about in him. Gone was the individual, the man, and he was transformed into the anonymous barrister, the advocate, who existed to represent his client's best interests, be he guilty or innocent. Perhaps wigs weren't such a bad thing after all.

'Right. Into battle. Let's see which judge we've got.' and to Nick, 'Don't forget that there is no jury in a case like this, It is down to the judgement of one senior member of the judiciary.'

The Doctor nodded. 'Yes. Antonia explained that to me.'

We trooped into Number 3 Court, and took our places. I sat next to our barrister on the lawyers' bench at the front of the court, and the Doctor sat next to me. Only in a criminal court does the accused sit in the dock; in all other courts they sit with their lawyers. A rather podgy middle-aged woman edged into the bench behind us, and leant forward and made wittering noises of greeting to him.

'Who on earth is that?' I whispered into his other ear.

'That' he whispered back 'is Joan Withers. She's a retired GP who has been sent by the BMA to support me in my hour of need. A shoulder to cry on'. And he grinned at me and shrugged his shoulders slightly.

Dr Withers reached forward and presented a rather limp

hand for me to shake. I touched it briefly, and turned back, feeling surprisingly put out. I was vaguely aware that the BMA, the doctor's union, often provided support for doctors who were in trouble, but felt that if any shoulders were going to be cried on, they were going to be mine, not the narrow and tweedy shoulders of Dr Withers.

There was a stir and a bustle at the double doors of the court, and the opposition made its entrance. Henry Doggart was in the lead, in robes that looked several sizes too big for him. Just behind him was Gwen Richardson. Despite her diminutive size, she dominated the group. A small man trotted behind her, her bag carrier, laden with files and briefcases. A good way of making an impression – too important to carry your own baggage. The group sailed down the aisle between the benches towards the litigant's position, and arranged themselves.

Taking his seat beside Richardson was the tall, pale sandy-haired man who we had seen outside, the man who Nick had tried to help, and who now wanted his pound of flesh. It is a stupid mistake for a lawyer to like or dislike a client or an opponent. We are trained to be dispassionate. Anything else can produce bias and can cloud judgement. But I automatically disliked Mr Keith Harrison. Perhaps, in retrospect, that dislike was a measure of how far my emotions had been affected by my doctor, but I did not realise that then.

Harrison sat down next to Gwen, and I had an opportunity to observe him properly for the first time. It was hard to know what to make of him. He was one of those people who have an aura of coldness about them, almost as though they are encased in a thin layer of frost. There was not a single iota of warmth about his appearance, his body, his expression or his movements. I felt he was the exact antithesis of touchy-feely. The expression 'a cold fish' could not have been more appropriate.

He turned as I watched him, and, rather shockingly, looked directly at me, as though he had known I was watching him. His pale eyes with their sandy lashes were expressionless. After a long moment, he looked away, and I felt none the wiser about what was going on in his mind.

The muted chattering and rustling slowly subsided as all the players settled into their places, and the few members of the public who were interested in this apparently dull case shuffled into the public gallery. It always reminded me of that moment at the start of a theatre when the lights go down before the curtain rises and the action starts. I would have a careful look at the observers later. With any luck, this case was far too routine for the press to be interested in, but you never know. Any hint of scandal, anything that titillated, and the vultures would gather. Sensation trumped fact any day of the week for the more salacious newspapers.

The Clerk of the Court stood up, and we all followed his lead and creaked to our feet. A panelled door on the left side of the raised judge's opened, and the Judge in whose hands my doctor's future lay entered the courtroom.

CHAPTER 8

Not many High Court judges are female. Less than a fifth of the total of ninety or so judges. They tend to get to the top of their profession because of two characteristics. First, their sheer cleverness – obviously. And secondly, their remarkable tenacity.

For a woman to win in a man's world requires exceptional perseverance, and the women who made it to the top of the legal tree had that in spades. Those who held these positions now were heroes in my eyes. Their generation had had to break the glass ceiling. But in doing so, some of them had, of necessity, to develop a hard shell of flinty determination that could, sometimes, come across as lack of humanity. Some of them could be as hard as nails. A characteristic that could cut both ways.

Dame Isobel Nicholson was just such a woman. I had seen her perform as a QC early in my career, before she went on to higher things, and I could still remember her relentless efficiency in court, cross-questioning a police inspector in a criminal trial with such determination that she finally wrung from him an admission that evidence presented as fact was not all that it seemed to be. Even then she did not let up, and forced him to admit a dishonesty that ended his career. So not just hard, but determined, thorough, and very, very clever.

She bowed briefly to the Court, gathered her gown about her, and took her seat in the right hand of the three raised throne-like chairs behind the Bench. Small, shrewd, serious, she was alleged to be charming and witty in private life. Here, in her place of work, she had a presence and a stillness about her that commanded respect.

When the shuffling and rustling of everyone sitting down again finally stopped, she nodded to the Clerk of the Court. He rose, bewigged and beribboned, and intoned the opening words that set the whole procedure in motion.

'A hearing in the High Court, Queen's Division, of Harrison versus.....'

His voice droned on with the formal words that opened all cases of alleged negligence against a doctor.

'....that on July 31st he did visit the said Keith Harrison at his home, and failed to properly asses his clinical condition and to provide appropriate treatment. Furthermore, that on the same date he did fail to advice Mr Harrison appropriately, and that as a result of these failures, Mr Harrison's condition deteriorated so that he had to undergo major surgery such that his life was endangered. And that consequent to this, he suffered and continues to suffer physical and psychological injury, and also professional and financial disadvantage, the amount to be quantified by the Court, due to negligence on the doctor's behalf.'

I sat up and started scribbling. This was not the same

wording as the original writ that we had been working towards defending. That had said that the Doctor had not exercised a proper standard of professional behaviour in persuading Harrison to be readmitted. This went much further: it alleged that he had not examined him, and had not advised him to be readmitted at all, a far more serious charge, encompassing all the actions he had taken.

I dug Brooks in the ribs. 'That's not what the original allegation said at all'.

'I know', he said under his breath. 'I'll raise hell about it as soon as I can'.

I sat back, seething. It was a typical devious trick, just the kind of thing I should have expected from Gwen Richardson. Slight changes in the wording of an allegation of incompetence or negligence against a professional can seem innocuous at first sight, but can materially alter the implication of the charge. Judges tended to let small changes go through on the nod, despite protests, rather than stopping a whole hearing and having to start it again at a later date. Understandable but expedient.

But this was well beyond a minor change; it altered the whole accusation. I should have seen this coming. Damn.

The clerk finished, and James Brooks was on his feet almost before he had sat down. He had a presence that tended to impress a court. Judges, however, were used to that, and tended to discount it. They, after all, had been practising barristers themselves before they were elevated, and were aware that they must only be concerned with fact.

'With your permission, M'Lady, may I draw your attention to a significant difference between the allegation just read out, and the writ my client received? May I submit that this difference in wording materially changes the kernel of the case, and that we should revert to the original wording of the writ?

'How does it materially change it, Mr Brooks?' Dame Isobel was direct and to the point.

'The allegation now states that my client failed to assess Mr Harrison and to advise him appropriately, and that as a result he deteriorated clinically. The original writ alleged something quite different. It claimed that my client did not advise Mr Harrison strongly enough, and that consequences flowed from that. It made no mention of assessing him, appropriately or otherwise. There is an obvious difference between not advising a patient strongly enough, and not assessing and advising him or her at all. I submit that there has been a significant shift in the grounds against the doctor, and that the hearing should be paused until this is clarified.'

'Mr Doggart.'

Doggart hauled himself to his feet, and glanced at my barrister. He was a great one for the histrionic pause, I remembered.

'I suggest, M'Lady, that the change is of no consequence.' He had a plummy voice with a hint of roughness to its edges caused by the cigarettes I knew he smoked. He was sweating already. A prime candidate for a coronary, I thought unkindly. He went on. 'Advice is advice, and it can be inadequate because it is of poor quality or if, as in this instance, it is not given at all.'

'With respect, that cannot be true'. Brooks was sharp. 'A doctor has a duty of care to his patient which includes giving him advice, which will of course depend on making a proper assessment. If that advice turns out, with hindsight, to be incorrect, that is an entirely different matter from not advising him at all. One is an error of omission, the other a judgement call'.

The steely eyes of Her Ladyship looked at each barrister in turn, considering.

'Your point is reasonable, Mr Brooks. I do not like games being played with the wording of allegations. However,' and she paused to consider, 'it is largely academic. In disproving the allegation of inappropriate or inadequate advice, you will no doubt wish to demonstrate that your client did undertake a proper assessment. That is an inevitable requirement. Any advice that your client may or may not have given the litigant would, of course, stem from having made a proper assessment. The two are separate but equal parts of a continuum of good care. So I direct that we will continue with the new wording, but bear in mind the change from the original allegation.'

I was furious. As was Brooks.

''With respect, M'Lady, are you not setting a precedent that any allegation can be changed – tinkered with, for want of a better expression – at the last minute, thereby altering the main drift of any complaint?'

'That is a view, Mr Brooks. It only stands if the wording is changed so that a differing criticism of an action is implied. In my judgement, this is not so in this situation. So let that be an end of it.'

No point in pursuing it any further, she was saying firmly. Don't waste any more time on it. I have made my mind up. Brooks shrugged, and sat down, every fibre of his being showing indignation. And I could only feel the same. This was points scoring on a grand scale, and manipulating due process to the very limits of its flexibility. There is no way it would be tolerated in a criminal court, so why in a civil court? Once again, I was left chewing furiously on the apparent unfairness of our archaic legal system.

Mr Doggart shot Brooks a venomous and smug glance and turned for a muttered conversation with Gwen. The pale sandy-headed man looked across at me again with his expressionless eyes. I could see why my doctor hadn't liked him. There was something dispassionate, almost snake-like in his gaze. I wondered, in a vague sort of way, about the characteristics and personality that had brought him here, had led to this act of retribution against someone who had tried to help him. Was it resentment of status, of success? That doctors were held in higher esteem than teachers? Better paid? Or was it a deeper rejection of class differences? I remembered Nick's description of his conversation with Harrison, his anger at what he perceived to be middle class self-interest. He didn't look a well man even now, all this time after the events we were here to thrash out. Pale; thin to the point of emaciation; a little stooped. Perhaps his life really had been damaged by all this, his hopes and dreams put for ever beyond his reach. Perhaps it was that had made him take revenge on a man who was the most obvious target. It is human nature to blame someone for a disaster, and, sad to say, doctors were often first in the firing line.

I caught his eye again, and made an attempt to acknowledge him, but he looked away. Doggart and Gwen finished their discussion, and Doggart looked up at the Bench, nodded his agreement with the decision, and rose to his feet again.

He was one of those barristers who didn't feel comfortable unless he had all his props about him. He had brought his own little lectern with him, and he propped a blue legal notebook on it, and arranged a pile of papers on one side, and a ring binder file of references on the other. He opened the legal notebook and ran his finger down the crease on the first page to prevent it from closing. To make doubly sure, he took off an expensive-looking Rolex watch, and placed it on the page. He glanced at his notes carefully once more, grasped, Rumpole-like, the lapels of his gown in both hands, and raised his eyes to meet those of the judge. All this, I knew, was part of a well-established ritual designed to impress his audience, which was usually a jury. It would cut little ice, I thought, with Dame Isobel Nicholson.

'With your permission, M'Lady'.

Her Ladyship nodded. And Doggart launched into his opening statement.

Opening statements, or submissions as they are more correctly known, are comprehensive summaries of the case that is being brought against someone. They usually start with a background description of the main players involved, and the circumstances of the game. They go on to the specifics of the case, detailing the failures – or alleged failures – of the defendant, and the consequences for the claimant of those failures. Finally, they describe how wonderful the claimant's life would have been if the devious, incompetent and malicious defendant had not failed so completely, and what a huge sum of damages would be necessary to return the claimant to his hitherto charmed existence. Statements like this can take anything from a few minutes to several hours to deliver. They often combine a modicum of fact with a maximum of hyperbole. They set the scene for the ensuing three act play.

Doggart was a crafty lawyer, and he was instructed by an even craftier one. I knew Gwen would pull tricks out of her bag, and together, she and Doggart made a formidable partnership. He demonstrated this immediately by running his opening statement backwards.

'The plaintiff you see her today, M'Lady, is a broken man.' He paused, and with dramatic effect, gestured at Harrison, who played the role with consummate skill. His pallor, his gauntness, his whole demeanour indicated someone whose health was in serious jeopardy. 'I do not exaggerate when I say he is a dead man walking'.

Everyone's eyes swivelled towards the dead man walking, and I could see in my mind's eye the noose over his head. He sat slumped in his seat, staring at the floor in front of him, the picture of a life destroyed. Had he been coached, I wondered, to present such a pathetic picture? He was managing to look like someone just out of a concentration camp. Skinny, with prison pallor, dejected. His face was expressionless. Was he really as bad as all that? I knew that he had been working since his illness, but wasn't sure what he was doing now. I must check up on that.

Doggart went on, building up a good head of steam. 'His whole life, a life that held such promise, and for which he and his partner had such high hopes, is now a shattered memory. His future is clouded by the certainty of a life that is limited by ill health, and the likelihood of deterioration. His future, his career, his life in its fullest meaning was literally snatched away from him. And the person who snatched it away was the doctor who failed him, failed him in his hour of need.' And he pointed at my doctor, sitting just a few feet away from him at the other end of the bench.

Even for Henry Doggart this was well over the top. I watched Dame Isobel as she looked hard at Doggart over her glasses. Was there cynicism in that look?

'Good histrionic stuff' I hissed in a stage whisper to my doctor, just loud enough for most of the court to hear. That was rewarded by another look from Dame Isobel, this time at me. 'Don't push your luck', the look said. I busied myself writing notes.

Nick was sitting rigid in his seat. I had forgotten how wounding this kind of aggressive attack could be on someone whose default position was to care for others. It was all part of the rough and tumble for we lawyers, but for the people in the spotlight, to be traduced like this in public was a humiliating and shocking experience. I hastily scribbled a note and passed it across. 'Take no notice of that', it said. 'It was just a silly opening salvo, and bears no relationship to the real issues. The judge won't be taken in by it'. He read it, and nodded without looking at me.

Doggart launched into his protracted description of the sequence of events leading up to the fateful hospital admission, emphasising how my doctor had been difficult to get an appointment with, had seemed disinterested, rude, inconsiderate, incompetent, and a complete disgrace to his profession. The words flowed out of his unattractive mouth in a smooth stream, and I could sense that he was in default mode now, running on that finely tuned autopilot that all lawyers develop as part of the art of presenting a case. It always amazed me the way in which a good barrister could read a brief once just before a hearing, and then present the whole story, embellished and dramatized, as though they had lived through it themselves. An extraordinary skill, one that needed not just a first class memory, but also an ability to take on board technical detail very quickly.

Doggart droned on, and as I knew roughly what he would be saying, I let my attention wander. I always rather enjoyed the stark beauty of the courts here in the Strand. This one, like the others, was almost a film set of what a court should look like. High ceilinged, panelled, with tall frosted gothic windows that let in so little daylight that the chandeliers which hung on long chains were permanently switched on. I was faintly amused to see that there was a fine collection of cobwebs far up the chains, as well as in the corners of the vaults of the ceiling. It must be merry hell trying to dust this place, I thought. They'd need an extension ladder or scaffolding to do it properly. The detail of the linen fold panelling behind the judge's raised dais caught my eye. It was perfectly even in each of the panels, as though cut by machine, yet I was prepared to bet that it had been done by hand back in the mid nineteenth century when the Royal Courts were built. What anonymous craftsman had done such skilful and beautiful carving by hand? And did anyone congratulate him on the quality? Or even notice him?

I was brought back to earth by Doggart beginning his peroration.

'And so, M'Lady, we shall demonstrate to you how the failures of this doctor have directly led to the present situation for Mr Harrison, and how, had any proper degree of competence been shown, my client's quality of life, and, indeed, his life expectancy, would have been greatly enhanced. With your permission, I would like to call my first witness, Professor Emeritus Sir Ralph Gaunt, past president of the Royal College of Physicians of Edinburgh, and vice president of the Society of Gastroenterologists.'

Brooks and I exchanged glances. He smiled encouragingly; just as we had predicted. I turned to transmit the smile to my doctor, but he was looking at his hands in his lap, and did not notice. I suddenly saw how old he looked, and how careworn. I remembered that it wasn't just his reputation that was on trial here, but his whole career. A finding of negligence against him could have untold consequences. Damages would be awarded against him, sometimes very significant amounts. He was insured against that, as all doctors had to be, but there could be much more important consequences than that. His whole career could be jeopardised, and with that, his way of life. GPs work in partnerships, and, like many professionals, are self-employed. They succeed or fail depending on their reputations, and if a doctor is rubbished in court, his patients will read about him in the papers and think about moving to another practice. Lots of GP partnerships have a policy of getting rid of a partner who drags their name through the mud – understandably. Perhaps most damaging of all, though, would be his own loss of professional self-respect.

Quite apart from all that, the General Medical Council, the body which regulates doctors, starts to take an interest when a doctor is found to be negligent. And quite right too, I thought, with Dr Shipman in mind. Any incompetent or dangerous doctor should definitely be struck off before they can do any more damage. But it is very frightening for a doctor who makes an honest error of judgement to be called to account for it by two separate legal systems. My doctor knew all this, and it was bearing down on him.

Sir Ralph was a craggy Scotsman, with the kind of bushy eyebrows that could provide a home for a small flock of sparrows. They gave him a look of permanent mild surprise. He ambled up to the witness box in a tweed suit, and took the oath in an engaging Scottish brogue. I took a bet with myself that he was a staunch Presbyterian. Doggart took him through his qualifications and career. He had passed just about every exam that existed, and had subsequently been the chief examiner for most of them. He had been a member of most of the eminent scientific bodies in Great Britain,, several government working parties on bowel disease management, and had advised no less than three Arab countries on health care delivery. In short, he was pre-eminent on the list of the great and good in medicine. He probably hadn't seen an acutely ill patient for twenty years. I scribbled a note to that effect and passed it to Brooks. He nodded.

Doggart squared his shoulders, looked at the judge. Grasped his lapels, and began to focus his expert on the main issue.

'Sir Ralph, was the management of this patient's condition up to the standard expected of a competent doctor?'

The eyebrows flexed up and down, and several sparrows flew out.

'By no means'.

'Why do you say that?'

A pause while he collected his thoughts. A few sparrows returned to roost.

'A host of reasons'. The brogue was very broad. 'Firstly, when any patient presents to a doctor with the symptoms that this patient had, he should immediately be admitted to hospital. Second, it is incumbent on a practitioner of any kind to keep track of his patient's condition while he is in hospital. Thirdly, and most significant, when the patient was sent home – inappropriately, in my view – the doctor should have insisted on his readmission.'

I drew in my breath sharply, and glanced at Brooks again. So many holes to pick in this opinion, and so many inconsistencies to point out.

Doggart patiently took the Professor through each of his reasons in turn, exploring the logic that had led him to them. After forty minutes of detailed and technical evidence, Doggart drew to a conclusion..

'So finally, Professor, is there anything else of relevance that you would like to tell the court?'

The sparrows scattered from the eyebrows again, and the brogue became more pronounced. 'Yes, M'Lady'. He looked directly at the judge. ' No doctor can be deemed competent if he does not have his patient's best interests at heart. It is my clear opinion that this doctor failed in all respects. He failed to admit the patient when he should have done so. He failed to keep track of the patient when he was in hospital. And when the patient was discharged, he utterly failed to put the interests of the patient above those of himself, and just palmed the problem off onto someone else. Or so he says. There is no evidence that he actually communicated with the doctor who would be taking over the care of the patient. These actions are not just unprofessional, they are negligent, and in my view, contemptible'.

And he made to return to his seat in the body of the court.

James Brooks rose swiftly to his feet.

'Just a minute, Professor. Not so fast. I'm afraid the British legal system requires that however eminent you are, your opinion must and should be tested by cross-examination. And that is my job. So I have one or two questions for you, some of which you may find significant.'

The eyebrows twitched furiously, and the Professor reluctantly returned to the witness stand.

'How long is it since you were in full time practice, Professor?'

'I can't see that that that is relevant.'

The judge leant forward. 'That is not for you to decide, Professor,' she said, her voice as clear as ice. 'It is the Court that decides on the relevance of evidence, not the witness'.

The eyebrows descended into a frown. 'As you please.' Not a good way to endear yourself to the bench, I thought.

'I ask you again, Professor. How long is since you were last in practice?'

'Eight years.'

And before you retired eight years ago, how long was it before you were involved in an acute on-call service?'

The brogue thickened even further. 'I can't be certain. Some years.'

'Have an informed guess, Professor. Was it about two years, or ten years, or what? Did Professors do emergency work in your day?'

Crafty Mr Brooks. The phrase 'in your day' already implied he was out of date.

'My contract was principally for leadership, teaching and research. Only a few academics do on-call emergency work.'

'Ah.' Brooks was emollient. 'That helps us, but only a little. I repeat, when were you last on call for emergency admissions?'

'Well, I was appointed as Professor when I was forty eight.' The brogue was very quiet, so that I had to pin my ears back.

'So, Professor, does that mean you have done no emergency on call work since you were forty eight?'

'I have seen many acutely ill patients since then.'

'We're not talking about that, we are exploring your experience of being on call, of being the doctor who is first presented with an acutely ill patient. You have severely criticised my doctor for his performance while on call. So it is reasonable to suppose that you must have experience of it yourself in order to make such a judgement. Is that fair?'

'I suppose so.' Grudgingly.

'And that such experience should be reasonably up to date?'

'Yes.'

'So are we to understand, Professor, that you did no on call or emergency work for the last twelve years of your career – assuming, that is, that you retired at sixty?'

'Yes.'

'And you retired eight years ago?'

'Yes. '

'So your judgement is entirely based on experience that is now twenty years out of date?'

'No, no.' The sparrows erupted. 'I know what it is like. I talk to people'.

'But you have no personal experience of being on call for emergencies for twenty years?'

With great reluctance: 'No.'

The clerk of the court looked up at the professor quizzically. The clerk is a sort of major domo, who orchestrates the proceedings. I often wondered about them; they sat in court all day and every day, watching lawyers perform, defendants being convicted or let off, judges come and go. Did they make judgements themselves, or draw conclusions? Did they rate us, the lawyers?

'Thank you , Professor. That wasn't so hard, was it? All you have to do is answer the question.'

Dame Isobel leant forward 'Don't tease, Mr Brooks. I am not a jury to be shown off to.' There were smiles on several faces in the court. The picture of Lady Isobel, with her commanding presence, as a member of a jury, was incongruous.

'Of course not, M'Lady. It never occurred to me that you were. My apologies.' There was a faint twinkle in Brooks' eyes. He turned back to the Professor.

'So we have established, have we not, that your hands-on experience of emergencies is now twenty years out of date. Has the medical management of acute emergencies moved on in any way during those twenty years?'

'I suppose so. Things have changed.'

'In what way have they changed?'

'Well.' The Professor paused and collected his thoughts, and began to recite a list of the technical advances that had come onto the scene; the new blood tests and scanning techniques, the advances in drug regimes and in surgical techniques. He was on safer ground now, and I watched with interest as he became visibly more relaxed and enthusiastic about the subject he had made his life's work. Brooks let him ramble on for some minutes. I looked along the lawyers bench towards Doggart, and could see frustration in every fibre of his being. He could see only too well the garden path his expert was being led up.

'Fascinating, Professor.' Brooks said when he finally came to a halt. 'But what relevance has any of it to the matter before us today, the competence or otherwise of this doctor, a GP?'

A silence while the implications of this question were digested.

'Let me help you' said Brooks silkily. 'You have given us a comprehensive guided tour of advances in specialist hospital practice. How does this apply to the job of a GP in the community, away from the undoubted excellence of your specialist hospital care?'

'Well, he should know about these developments.'

'In general, or in particular?'

'In general, I suppose.'

'So he should know in general terms about the advances in management of this condition, as of all others, but not the detailed implementation? If he knew the latter, of course, he would, by definition, be a specialist, would he not?'

'Yes, I suppose he would.'

'So what exactly are you criticising him for, Professor? For not being a specialist?'

No reply. Silence. The Professor looked at his hands.

Dame Isobel rose. 'Time, I think, for luncheon.' We all rose, and she swept out.

I turned to pick up my papers, and found Nick looking at me. His eyes crinkled at the corners.

'That went OK, didn't it?'

'Yes,' I said. I would have to control this surge of tenderness that crept up, on me without warning. 'After the opening hiccough, it went very well. But it's only the opening shot in a long battle. Take things one step at a time. There are ups and downs in any hearing. Let's go and grab some lunch.'

As we walked down the imposing marble staircase of the Royal Courts, I caught the high heel of my damned court shoes on a step and stumbled. I felt his hand take my arm for a moment, his touch sending a tiny feather of sensuality through me. Drat the man. Concentrate, you stupid woman. This is work, nothing else. He was just being courteous. But it was unsettling.

We ate an unappetising sandwich in a café near the Royal Courts. Brooks did not appear. He was probably working on this afternoon's cross-examination. A cup of muddy coffee, a trip to the loo, and we hurried back across the road to the Courts. He took my arm briefly as we scurried in front of a taxi. Who, for heaven's sake, was supporting whom? Or were we both in need of support?

*

The Professor had a truly horrible afternoon. Word by word, phrase by phrase and opinion by opinion, Brooks dissected his evidence, led him up a path towards identifying his experience of situations such as the one my doctor had been in, and demonstrated over and over again how the professor was completely unqualified to make a judgement on a GP. He had no knowledge of how either acute or chronic care was delivered outside hospital, and no understanding of what the job of being a GP entails. He had fallen into the classic trap of assuming that academic knowledge was equivalent to practical experience, of believing that theory is the same as practice. It is the same mistake that academics have made down the centuries, and which has bedevilled the NHS since its inception. Specialists being put in charge of designing and delivering a generalist service. I watched almost sympathetically as his stature seemed to decrease as the afternoon went on, and his self-confidence ebbed away. He shrunk visibly as Lady Isabel watched and listened, her shrewd eyes on him.

Finally, Brooks came round to delivering the coup de grace, in bull-fighting terms, the cruzar, the lethal sword thrust between the shoulder blades.

'In conclusion, Professor – and you have been very patient today in helping us understand the relevance of your expert opinion – could you assist us on one last point?'

The tweed-clad shoulders slumped even further. He wasn't a fool; he knew the stiletto was poised. Everyone present knew it as well, and a sudden silence came over the whole court, as we waited for the final dénouement. Even the hacks and hangers-on in the public gallery were silent. It was an electric moment.

'My client, the defendant in this hearing, is very clear that he advised Mr Harrison that he should be readmitted to hospital; indeed, that his life was in danger if he was not readmitted. Despite this advice, and because of his previous experience in hospital, Mr Harrison refused. Have you ever had experience of such a situation?'

'Obviously not'. The professor was irritable. 'I have always worked in hospitals'.

'But assuming, for a moment, that you found yourself in such a situation…?'

'Well, I would try to change his mind. And warn him of the consequences'.

'And if the patient still refused to take your advice?'

The professor shot a poisonous glance at James Brooks. He had been on his feet for much of the day, and looked as though he was dearly regretting his decision to take part in what must have felt to him like a bull fight, with him as the bull.

The bull made a final fruitless charge. 'If he was that idiotic, then it would be up to him', he snapped.

There was a sharp intake of breath from the other end of the bench where Doggart and Gwen Richardson sat. I could see them transmitting flashing warning signals to their expert, but it was too late, the damage was done.

'So', Brooks was very gentle, 'a patient who does not take his doctor's advice is an idiot, is he Professor?'

'Yes'. Reluctantly. He could see what he had done now. Dame Isobel looked down at him from the bench with a quizzical expression.

'And the patient's human rights, professor? His right to decline to follow medical advice, however good that advice may be?' Brooks voice was silky smooth.

'Then he must live with the consequences of his decision.' The eyebrows were a fierce line now. 'Whatever those consequences may be.'

'Thank you, professor. I have no further questions'.

'Do you wish to re-examine?' Dame Isabel asked Doggart. It is the right of any one putting a witness on the stand to have a second go at making his point, a second bite of the cherry, so to speak. Doggart shook his head and remained seated. There was no point. Nothing he could do or say would undo the wreckage of the professor's self-destruction.

Dame Isobel gathered her papers and stood up. 'Until tomorrow, ladies and gentlemen.'

*

I congratulated Brooks on his performance as we trooped down the marble staircase and out into the late afternoon sunshine. There was a little crowd on the pavement in front of the Courts, and the usual gaggle of scruffy press photographers, ready to grab a picture of someone newsworthy. They snapped away busily, even though we were of no real interest to them. The doctor flinched away from the intrusive lenses.

'All in a day's work,' Brooks said. But both of us knew that the hard part of the job lay ahead, and that today's performance, satisfactory though it had been, was just the legal version of an open goal. The doctor was cheerful though, seeing today as a moral victory. He turned to me as we stood outside.

'I don't know if it is unprofessional to ask this,' he said, 'but would you like to go for a drink?'

'I can think of nothing I would like better.' The words came out without thinking. Think before you speak, you stupid stupid woman. You'll get yourself into deep water unless you're careful. 'But I've got a home to go to, and children to make supper for.' Damn. Damn and blast.

His face fell. 'Oh. Another time perhaps.'

'Definitely. When we've won.'

I watched as he walked away down the Strand, a lonely

figure with a lonely evening ahead of him. What would be so wrong with having a drink with him anyway? It would just be a friendly gesture, nothing more. But as I went home on the tube, my mind was full of silly girlish thoughts that were far removed from being a solicitor.

CHAPTER 9

Dame Isobel Nicholson dumped her briefcase on the floor by the door, kicked her shoes off and sank back gratefully onto the sofa in the lovely drawing room of their flat. It had been a long day, and the Number 34 bus had been crowded, so that she had had to stand all the way from the Strand to where she got off in Pimlico. It was only a short walk from the bus stop to their flat in Dolphin Square, but the two flights of stairs were, she thought, a step too far now that she was sixty. And she had a headache, one of those dull throbbing aches behind the eyes that wear one down.

Her husband looked up from the document he was reading.

'Hard day?'

'Yes. Interesting though.'

'Want to tell me about it?'

'Later perhaps. It's a case that has only just started, and there'll be lots to tell as it unfolds.'

She wiggled her toes to get the ache out of them, and put her feet up on a Moroccan leather pouf. Unasked, her husband put a gin and tonic on the side table by the sofa.

'I don't think I will tonight, thank you. I've got a bit of a headache.'

'I'll drink it then. Shall I get you some Panadol?'

'Thank you.'

They smiled at each other, the complicit smile of people who were entirely at peace in each other's company, and he went to find the pills.

They had lived in Dolphin Square for over ten years now, and it felt like home. At first he had felt uncomfortable rubbing shoulders with such demonstrably well-off people as the other residents were, in what was one of the most desirable blocks of flats in Europe. But the convenience of the place, and the ambience, soon smoothed off his rough edges. He could realise why so many MPs chose to live there, and it always amused him that their flat was just across the courtyard from the one Christine Keeler had had such fun in, with such earth-quaking consequences for the Establishment. The fact that Princess Anne had subsequently moved in just round the corner had made it even more amusing.

Isobel's husband was a tall man. If you met him in the street, you might guess that he was a country solicitor, or a successful gentleman farmer. There was hint of old money about him, the assurance that came with status, security, an expensive education and success. The brown brogues had the patina of many years polish on them, and were probably hand made by Lobb. The suit was immaculately cut – country gentleman in London for the day. You could imagine meeting him in the West Car Park at Twickenham.

In fact, he was different, very different. For several years, he had been a Labour councillor on the Borough of Newham

Council, and was now Leader of the Council He had worked his way up the local government hierarchy, starting as a trainee clerical officer dealing with housing benefits, then moving on to traffic and parking, then into the finance department. He learnt his trade at the feet of the grand old men of the Left, the died-in-the-wool socialists who devoted their lives to the Movement, in the constant hope that finally, inevitably, the voters would see sense, and that the people, workers and all, would live in a properly egalitarian society. He had become deputy leader and then leader of the Council, and this allowed him to wield more power and more influence than most backbench MPs could ever manage. The decisions he made could, he felt, actually change people's lives for the better. The lure of national politics had beckoned at one stage of his life, but the practicalities and the idea of climbing another ladder was, at that time, a step too far.

He was a clever and observant man, and quickly realised that people were classified not just by the company they kept, but by the persona they projected. He watched and learnt, and finally decided that power, the power that he wanted to hold on behalf of his fellow workers, had a uniform. And the uniform could be used as a disguise, so that if you dressed and acted as a member of the elite, then people automatically assumed that you were a leader of some kind or another, and deferred to you. And that by wearing the uniform of the opposition, of those that wished to preserve the status quo and the class divide that depended on it, he could insinuate himself into their company, and learn how they thought, and use that knowledge to undermine them. It was a useful technique that few senior members of the Labour Party could comprehend.

So he became a chameleon. He learnt how to dress like a conservative with a small c, and to speak as a liberal with a small l, and slowly, ever so slowly, developed the appearance and personality of being all things to all men. When he first stood for the Council, he spoke at meetings as a firebrand revolutionary socialist, but when he knocked on the doors of the million pound owner-occupied terraced houses in his borough, he was the emollient calmer of fears about the impending revolution and its consequence for house prices. And when he was elected with a huge majority (no Conservatives made much headway in Newham), he kept his powder dry and watched and waited.

The Party recognised a true one of its own, and offered to pay for him to do an Open University degree to broaden his knowledge base. He grabbed the opportunity. No one of influence could go far without a degree behind them, even if it was a useless degree in Greats. He chose Local Government Management as his degree course, and enjoyed the discipline of regular OU dissertations and reading. He was in his early thirties by then, and lived in a boringly anonymous bedsit just outside the Borough area. So it was a huge, almost visceral shock when the degree course required him to go for a residential fortnight to a Cambridge college, empty of undergraduates during the Summer Vac. The dreaming spires were far outside his experience, and his initial reaction – to sneer at the privilege they implied – soon gave way to fascination with the freedom of thought and expression that they encouraged.

And it was at the OU residential course in Cambridge that he met a short, dark, vibrant girl – woman, rather – who turned his head, and his world, upside down. Her name was Isobel, and she had been to Cambridge before. Ten years before, she had drunk and danced her way through a three year law course and got a bad third, and had returned through the OU to improve on this and get to the places she wanted to go to. She was calm, beautiful in a quirky sort of way, motivated, clever, and she captivated him. She made it very clear from the outset that she was here to work, not to play, and that the fact that she found him attractive was not going to allow her to deviate from the path she had set herself. When others on the residential course went out in the evenings to the pubs and clubs of Cambridge, and pretended that they were real Cambridge students, not just visitors, the two of them sat in the library, working on the tasks set them, barely speaking, but basking in the pleasure of each other's company. Their politics did not coincide, but that was no barrier to the inherent attraction that drew them together. 'Animal magnetism', Isabel had called it at first, a more polite term than 'lust', but they both knew very quickly that the animal magnetism was just the icing on the cake of two individuals finding their soul mates.

They stayed in touch after the summer course, quickly progressing to seeing each other nearly every weekend. When they passed their respective degrees, each with flying colours, it seemed only sensible as well as practical that they should move in together. They were both committed, she with her pupillage to become a barrister, and he with his ascent of the council and

Party ladders. Both had observed that hard work paid off, and so both worked hard, very hard. She made a name for herself in the field of medical negligence, and he also made a name as a safe pair of hands, someone who not only understood the system, but who could play it, controlling the more extrovert personalities who wanted to change the world at a pace that it could or would not accept. He developed a skill at managing and focusing their scatter-gun energies, and became known and respected as a fixer. They were both far too committed to their respective causes to find time for children, and neither of them regretted that choice. Each was true to their chosen career, and equally true to each other. So although they did not speak much about what it was that motivated them, they were both safe and sure in the secure knowledge of the other's commitment. They were entirely self-sufficient. And at the time, his personal assistant in his role leader of Newham Council was a tall pale red-headed young man who had been a teacher until ill-health forced him to resign. Isobel had never met him. Or heard of him. There was no reason why she should.

Later that evening, after supper (he still would not play the game of calling it dinner), they sat, as usual, either side of the decorative Adam fireplace, each doing their homework for the next day. He had a brief to read about how to tackle petty crime in the Borough. It all stemmed from the drug trade. He knew it, and the police knew it, and the owners of the houses which were broken into knew it. But none of them, himself included, had any clear idea how to solve the problem. The idea of making soft drugs legal, as the paper suggested, was, to his mind, simplistic.

He mulled over the alternatives for a while, and then put the document on one side.

'Would you like a coffee?' Isobel had nearly finished summarising her notes.

'I don't think I will. I've still got a headache. I'll do one for you, though.'

He got up and stretched while she went out to the kitchen. After a while he heard the glugging noise of the Nespresso machine, and walked towards the kitchen. As he passed her iPad, still open on the arm of her chair, he glanced at it. A name stood out at the head of the notes she had been making. 'Keith Harrison vs Nickolai Malenkov'. After a moment it disappeared and the screen went blank as it automatically shut down. He paused, his mind making connections. Keith Harrison. Tried and trusted Keith. The P A who was always efficient, always motivated, unless he was off sick. In fact, he was off now, he remembered. Perhaps off on holiday. Or was it sick leave? Or was it possible that he was in Court, pursuing the damage that had been done to his health by the doctors who had failed him? He had hinted at this after his appointment, when he had got to know him better, and understood his limitations. 'If only,' he had said, 'they had all bothered more. Perhaps I would still be a teacher, not someone who is labelled as disabled, only able to get a job to tick the employer's box of equality and diversity.' He certainly wasn't a fit man, as his regular absences showed. But he was motivated, that was for sure. An active member of the Party, with all the right principles.

Isobel came in with his cup of coffee.

'Finished?'

'Yes. Have you?'

'Just about. An interesting chap who says a doctor messed up his care. Don't know how it will go.'

'That sounds a familiar story. What's his name?'

'No one you know.' She smiled at him. 'And if you did, I wouldn't tell you.'

CHAPTER 10

The next day, something very odd happened.

I struggled into the Royal Courts, the weight of the world on my shoulders. It had been one of those mornings when nothing went right. I hated the crowded underground, I hated the rain, I hated taking my silent children to school, and most of all I hated my bloody husband for being the cause of all this misery. I hadn't yet reached the stage of recognising that I might have contributed to it as well. Only with an enormous effort could I summon up a smile for Nick when he came into the little meeting room outside Court Number 3. He looked at me, concerned, so my mood must have shown on my face.

'Problem?'

'Not really. Just that life gets a bit complicated sometimes. Nothing to do with the case.'

'But a bit of a battle?'

'Nothing that I can't cope with.' Brusquely, with a professional smile. It probably looked more like a grimace to him.

'Anything I can do?'

I almost said something I would regret, but my answer was forestalled by our barrister bustling in with his pile of documents.

'All set? Good.'

And he led us back into Court.

The opposition made their entrance at the same time, less dramatic than yesterday, but still a show of strength. With them today was a tall sallow girl, with a curtain of hair that covered her face. She walked in beside Keith Harrison, and they exchanged a few words. Neither of them smiled. The girlfriend, I though. The one who had called Nick after her boyfriend discharged himself. The one, the only one, who would have been a real-time witness to what had actually happened on the day he refused to go back into hospital. Why had I forgotten her? How had I failed to check if she was a witness that we could use, whether she wanted to be used or not? Was Richard getting to me, stopping me thinking clearly, making me lose my professional touch?

Think, woman. Think. How could I use her to support us against her boyfriend? It would mean a subpoena – getting an order to force her to give evidence against her own best interests. She would probably be what is called a hostile witness – someone who is uncooperative, who you are forcing to say things that they may not want to. And that needs very careful handling. I must talk to Brooks about it.

My thoughts were brought to an abrupt halt by the Judge coming in. We all stood up. She paused, a little bow in acknowledgement, took her seat, and we sat down again in our turn, like a badly performing chorus line.

Doggart stood up.

'With your permission, M'Lady, I would like to call my next

witness. I call him in the clear belief that he will enable the Court to obtain insight into how and why the state of mind of my client was such that he was unable to make a rational decision about whether or not he should be readmitted to hospital, and how, by not taking this into account, the defendant failed in his duty of care. I call Dr Marcus Brain'.

There was a pause while the court usher opened the double swing doors at the back of the court to admit this new player, but just as he was doing so, there was a slight noise from the Bench. All the heads in the court, which had been looking over their owners shoulders to catch a glimpse of Dr Marcus Brain, swivelled forwards again, rather like the heads of the Centre Court crowd at Wimbledon during a rally. Dame Isobel was sitting slightly sideways in her high-backed chair, leaning forwards. Her hand was raised to her forehead, as though she was perplexed, or concentrating.

'Could you give me a moment', she said, her voice as steady as usual, but quiet and a little unnatural.

Then, without warning, she slumped forward, her face hitting the Bench in front of her with a hard, ominous thud. The chair tipped forward, and she slowly slid downwards behind the Bench, disappearing from view.

There was a moment of shocked silence in the Court, and then several things happened at once. The new witness, stopped in his tracks at the door. The usher let the door swing to behind him with a thud, and after a moment he took two steps forward towards the Judge and paused. Gwen Richardson stood up with her hand to her mouth, mute and immobile. Doggert placed his notes on the desk in front of him and sat down carefully, as though he had finished a speech or submission. Brook, my barrister, took a step forward, and then he, too, sat down with a thump. I, to my shame, did nothing. Only one person did anything useful, and that was my doctor.

I did not see how he got there, but within a moment, or so it seemed, he was rounding the end of the Bench, and bending down behind it to tend to Dame Isobel. His face reappeared almost immediately, and he called to me directly.

'Come and give me a hand.'

And to Mr Brooks 'Call an ambulance. Now.'

I hurried up to the raised Bench with its dais of throne-like chairs. The one in which Dame Isobel had been sitting was lying on its side now, and she was in a tangle beneath its legs. Her wig had come off, and he face, pale and composed, looked peaceful, as though asleep. There was a small dribble of saliva at the corner of her mouth. I was struck by how deeply ordinary she looked without the panoply of the law to enhance her dignity, and then I felt ashamed for thinking that. Nick shoved the fallen chair off her legs in a single violent movement. It was large and heavy, and fell with a crash some way away from her. As I watched, he put one hand underneath her jaw, lifting it forward. The other hand lifted one eyelid, and, after a moment, went to feel for the pulse in her neck. He glanced up at me.

'Kneel down beside me.' I hoisted my skirt up a little, so that I could kneel down in the confined place behind the Bench alongside him. He took my hand and put it firmly under Dame Isobel's chin and pushed it upward.

'Hold it like that.'

I did so, uncomprehending.

'You're keeping her airway open. We'll see if she's able to breathe by herself in a moment.'

He lifted one of her eyelids again, and then the other.

'What are you looking for?' Whispered. I felt as though I was alone with him. The other dramatic personae in this play had receded into the background. I knew they were all watching, looking, prying, just as the occupants of cars driving past an accident rubber neck with such fascination. I could not see them or hear them. Everything was focussed on the woman lying in front of me, as though I was watching her through the wrong end of a telescope.

'Reaction to light.' He glanced at me. 'Whether she has had a stroke.'

'I thought it was usually old people who had strokes.'

'It can happen to anyone, at any age. A blood vessel just lets go. A collapse like this means that it's significant.'

He felt for a pulse in her neck again, and then lifted one of her hands and let it drop. It fell with a thump onto the polished boards of the floor. He tried the other one: it stayed up for a moment before relaxing down gently. He shuffled on his knees down towards her feet, slipped off her shoes, and ran his thumbnail up the outer edge of the soles of her feet. And grunted.

'What does that mean?'

'That something big is happening in her brain. One toe went downwards when I stimulated it, and one went upwards. Not good.'

I gradually became aware of a growing bustle of activity round the two of us, and the bubble of isolation surrounding us slowly dissolved. I could hear the usher clearing the court, his firm voice asking – telling – everyone to collect their belongings and leave as soon as possible. He said – with kindness, I thought, that no one should try to see what was going on behind the Bench, but 'we should leave the judge in the capable hands of the professionals.' 'Capable', I thought; 'it was just how capable he was that we, especially Lady Isobel, were all here to judge. What an extraordinary contradiction.'

In the distance I could hear the wail of an ambulance siren. So common to everyday life for we Londoners, and so meaningless. Unless, like now, it was coming for us. 'Come soon,' I thought. 'Come very soon.' Suddenly, Dame Isobel, and what was happening to her was very personal. The chin under my hand was heavy, and I must have relaxed my hand a little. My doctor pushed it firmly back upwards.

'Sorry.' I said quickly.

'Keep it there. She's not maintaining an airway by herself.'

'What does that mean?'

'That whatever is causing this, it's causing a lot of damage,' he said quietly, 'and her ability to breathe unaided is jeopardised. Most likely to be a bleed.'

'Where?'

'Into or around her brain. One or the other. Possibly a blocked artery.'

'What will happen to her?'

He shrugged, and glanced over his shoulder at the

courtroom door to see if help had arrived. 'Don't know. If she can get to a stroke unit very quickly, it may be possible to limit the damage. But it'll have to be quick.'

There was a bustle at the door, and two green suited paramedics hurried in. They took in the situation immediately, and looked to my doctor, who was obviously in control.

'Sudden collapse. No warning. Medical history not known. Not able to maintain an airway unaided. Left plantar going up, and right pupil dilating. Intracerebral bleed of some kind. Needs a CVA unit pronto.' He summarised the situation to them in quick staccato statements.

'You a doctor?' This from one of the paramedics as he took over controlling her jaw from me.

'GP. Used to be an A and E consultant.'

'Thanks, doctor. We've got her now.' And they calmly did all the things that paramedics do with practiced skill and speed. With a plastic airway inserted into her mouth and a drip in her arm, Dame Isobel was whisked away on a wheeled stretcher in double quick time.

'We'll go straight to Bart's stroke unit.' over his shoulder, the paramedic to my doctor.

'Thanks. Well done, guys.'

And suddenly the drama was over, as quickly as it had begun. There was a stunned silence in Court Number 3, and the people who had witnessed what had happened looked at one another. The speed of events, which had seemed to be in slow motion for the last few minutes, returned to normal. Without a judge present, no one seemed to be in charge. The two barristers glanced at one another, and Mr Doggart stood up.

'It would seem that, in view of what has happened, that the hearing should be adjourned until we are made aware by whoever is in charge of these things what happens next, and whether Dame Isobel will be able to resume hearing this case. If she cannot, then we will, no doubt, have to restart the hearing with a new judge sitting.'

He sat down, looking rather self-satisfied, I thought, at having assumed the status of ex officio Court official. Cocky bastard. I started to collect my papers and briefcase, but halted in surprise as Nick Malenkov stood up suddenly and addressed the whole court, turning to include all those on the gallery as well.

'I think all of us, whatever it is that has brought us here, would like to say that our thoughts and good wishes are with Dame Isobel and her family. What has happened is shocking in its suddenness, and we can only hope that she makes a full and rapid recovery.'

As we trooped out together, I glanced up at him.

'Thank you for saying that. At least someone showed some humanity as well as competence.'

Doggart, who was walking just ahead of us, half turned as he heard me speak. 'I agree. It was well said. But that doesn't alter the facts of this case.'

I bit back the angry retort that was on the tip of my tongue. Trust Doggart to get a dig in, whatever the circumstances. Trading insults would achieve nothing.

Nick smiled, a little grimly. 'Don't forget that this is what I do for a living – deal with crises as well as sore throats. And it is the effect on others that needs managing as much as the effect on the individual concerned. I hate seeing people, whoever they are, being struck down for no reason.' He smiled again. 'And besides, I couldn't let that arrogant barrister,' nodding at Doggart's receding back, 'get the last word in.'

'What will happen to her?'

'Well.' He stopped abruptly and looked at me; the blue eyes surprisingly hard. 'I think she has probably had a massive bleed in her brain. The chances of recovering from that and getting back to the condition she was in before are pretty slim. Even if she survives, she may well have considerable brain damage, however good the clever doctors a Bart's are at opening up her cerebral circulation again. Brain damage is brain damage. The computer will never be quite the same again. She may look like she did, but she may have motor damage – weakness - or personality changes, or inability to process information. Who knows? I'm afraid it is a waiting game, often for weeks or months. Assuming, as I say, that she survives. But that is all completely hypothetical as far as Lady Isabel is concerned. I could be completely wrong. It could be something entirely different.' A pause, and a wry smile. 'If it was me, and I had big brain damage, I would rather not survive than live on as a cabbage or be dependent. Especially as I now have no one to depend on. Or to depend on me.'

I digested all this. Everything had changed; the balls were all up in the air once more. And there was something about the case as well as about Dame Isobel that was niggling away at the back of my mind. Something – or someone - that I might be able to use to prove that my doctor had done nothing wrong and had not failed his patient. Someone that I had overlooked before. Someone who I had seen today. The girlfriend.

'Keep in touch,' I said as we walked into the Strand. 'I'm not sure when and how things will happen next, but I think I can say for sure that we won't be in Court tomorrow. So I'll text or ring you when I know. In the meantime, I've got work to do.'

And I turned and walked away towards the Tube. I glanced over my shoulder as I hurried away, and saw Nick Malenkov looking after me quizzically.

CHAPTER 11

Hospitals are very frightening places for the uninitiated. The people who work in them quickly forget this. Just as the cockpit of an airliner is merely the place of work for a pilot but to passengers it is fascinating and rather alarming, so too in a hospital, especially in the high tech bits like the intensive care units and operating theatres. These are the holy of holies of modern medicine, and can be terrifying. The acolytes watch the high priests going through their rituals in these places with fascination, glimpsing not just the skills exhibited, but the dependence of those being cared for, motionless on their beds or operating tables, tubes and wires and monitors often the only indication that they are alive. Sometimes, of course, they barely are, and the heroic battles being fought to maintain a flicker of life in someone overwhelmed by disease or injury are lost.

The laity who are allowed into these places, the friends and relatives who tiptoe in to see their nearest and dearest, are often overwhelmed at first. It can be very shocking to see the person who sat opposite you at breakfast that morning lying inert and unresponsive, machines breathing for them, monitors recording every parameter of their being. Those who care for the occupants of the beds often add to the impression of a different world. Gowned in anonymous green surgical scrubs, their hair covered, their faces often hidden by masks, they tend the machines and replace the drips, communicating in a jargon that only they can understand. So it is hardly surprising that a husband, visiting his wife for the first time after she has been admitted to such a place, is overawed and nervous. He is faced with such a huge range of unknowns that he has no idea where to start understanding what is happening.

The man sitting beside Dame Isobel Nicholson in the intensive care unit in St Bartholomew's Hospital in the City of London found himself in exactly that position. Although you would not have known, from watching him, what he was feeling. His face, which he had trained over the years to be impassive, betrayed none of the turmoil that was going on in his mind.

'She's gone again.' said the junior doctor standing beside him. She was young, and Indian, and very beautiful.

Dame Isobel's husband sat back. He had watched as his wife had, for a brief moment, opened her eyes and looked towards him. He did not know whether she was seeing him, but he had squeezed her hand and smiled at her, and felt the better for that brief moment. Then she had closed her eyes again, and gone back to the place where she had been before, a place where no one could follow her, a place where consciousness was lost.

'That's quite normal.' The doctor's accent was cut-glass Oxbridge. 'People who have had the kind of problem she has don't suddenly wake up as though they have been asleep, they emerge slowly from a deep dark place which we cannot understand. Unless, of course, we have been there ourselves, and even then we probably won't remember it.' She smiled, a friendly smile that suddenly made her more human. 'It can take many days or even weeks to return to what we would call full consciousness, so be patient. It'll probably be a long slow job.'

'But the fact that she has shown at least some brief awareness of her surroundings is encouraging?'

'Yes, very encouraging. The MRI scan showed that the damage is limited at the moment, and opening her eyes shows that her level of unconsciousness is lightening. We could check on that if you like.'

'How?'

'It sounds a bit brutal, but we could see if she reacts to pain.'

'Explain please.'

'Well, if you are deeply anaesthetised, or deeply unconscious, you don't feel any pain, however severe it might be. That is why we can do operations that would be agonising if you were awake. But if you are only lightly anaesthetised, or unconscious from, say, a small bump on your head, you can be only a little bit asleep, and so be aware of painful stimuli. So if I inflict a little pain on her when she is only just unconscious, her conscious brain won't register it, but she may react by withdrawing from the painful stimulus.'

'Show me. But be gentle with her.'

The junior doctor moved her beautifully manicured hand to Isobel's left earlobe, and squeezed it firmly between her thumbnail and index finger. Isobel muttered, a non-verbal complaint, and moved her head a little away from the fingernail.

'Excellent. She's not far off waking up, as you can see. I'll be at the nurses station if you need me.' She smiled at him – a reassuring human gesture - and walked off with a purposeful step towards a patient on a ventilator further down the ward, her surgical clogs clicking on the linoleum floor.

*

The chameleon in the suit sat on by the hospital bedside of the woman he loved, waiting. He never ceased to wonder at the disparity between them, not just in background and upbringing, but in ambition and political views and, for want of a better word, ethos. That two such different people, with such different perspectives on life, such variation in tastes and cultures, should find such kindred feelings and such closeness, was a marvel to him, and an unceasing gift. That she might have shared such closeness with any one before him was a constant cross he bore in silence, an image that he likened to a rotting corpse that still occasionally surfaced into his consciousness and hurt him anew, even though he knew, or thought he knew, that she felt about him as he felt about her. He knew that it was a childish jealously that triggered this intense possessiveness, and that he had no right to feel it. She, of course, had friends before him, and even lovers, but he chafed at the picture that she could have, might have, been as close to someone else as she was to him, have revealed her inner thoughts and feelings to another man.

The closeness they shared, the feeling almost of being a single being, was all-enveloping. That he could lose such closeness to the one human who really mattered to him was something that he could barely contemplate, let alone understand. Like many men, he had, over the years, got into the habit of supressing emotion, or at least of concealing it. The stiff upper lip was deeply engrained in English culture, if only as a defence mechanism against schoolyard bullying and adolescent hurt. So, as he sat by his unconscious wife, his face betrayed nothing of the churning turmoil that was going on in his mind, and the fears that he was furiously pushing to the back of his mind. No one would know, watching him, that the calm collected man watching the silent figure in the hospital bed was tearing himself apart.

*

At first, it sounded like a very faint, slightly irritating, distant echo, rather like noise of the sea heard when a sea shell is held to one's ear. Her head, in fact her whole body, felt as though it was encased in thick treacle, so that every movement and thought was slowed by a gelatinous syrup that dragged at her mind and her limbs. Through the syrup, she slowly became aware of the distant echo of her pulse. Everything was in a sort of sticky slow motion, and she watched, fascinated, as the thing that was her tried to struggle upwards towards the light, the surface of consciousness that lay above the treacle. For a while, she was quite unable to get anywhere near the surface, and kept sinking down again into the murky depths of thoughtlessness. But slowly, very slowly, she summoned up the mental strength to get to the surface again. The echoes got louder as she got nearer to the surface, and she could begin to distinguish sounds from outside. Presently, she could distinguish that the sounds were actually a voice. She assumed it to be a human voice, and that it was speaking to her, even though she had no idea at all what it was trying to say.

It was quite peaceful just below the surface of the treacle, and she was tempted to stay floating there indefinitely, in a sort of suspended animation that required no effort. But something deep within her knew that she ought not to do that, but should pull herself together and make the effort to break the surface. Her inner eye, the one which was observing her floating just below the surface, watched with interest as her body started to struggle once more with the effort of surfacing. Her body was not moving, of course. In fact, it lay quite still, so it wasn't her body that was struggling, her mind said to itself, but something else. Perhaps it was me, the mind.

She was instinctively fearful of what lay above the surface. Down here in the treacle, everything was safe and calm and smooth and peaceful. If only she could stay down here for ever, or perhaps sink deeper and deeper, so that she could forget that there was a thing called the surface at all. Sink towards oblivion. Perhaps that was what dying was like. But another bit of her, her mind, reminded her that she had a duty, an obligation to do what it was telling her, and to struggle upwards. Perhaps it was the echo that was telling her. Perhaps it was some deep internal imperative that was encouraging her to survive. Whatever it was, it was making her struggle on, and her inner eye watched fascinated at the internal battle going on within her. It seemed almost as though the eye was making bets on which would win; the desire to sink into nothing, or the drive to return to the surface. She watched with interest as the balance tipped one way and then another, not aware yet that it was she herself who was being fought over.

Then something changed, and the balance was tipped. She became aware that the sound, calling her name, was louder, more insistent. She began to distinguish the occasional word in between the jumble of unintelligible static.

'Isobel!'

Who was that? She was sure she knew someone who called her 'Isobel', but who she was, and where she had met them, was a mystery. Just below the surface of the treacle she lay motionless, pondering this. Could it be that Isobel was her? Impossible. She was someone, she knew that, but was her name really 'Isobel'? If so, who was the other her, the one trying to remember who Isobel was? It was all very confusing. But the voice was calling her, if that was her name. She was fairly sure that she had heard it before, but who the voice belonged to was quite beyond her.

'Isobel!'

With a sudden huge effort, she forced herself into a sort of frantic struggle that would take her to the surface. For a few moments she thought that she could not manage it, but finally, with a last explosive effort, her head broke through the surface of the treacle into the shockingly bright light of the world above. Her body remained encased below, helpless and immobile, but at least her head was free, and she could breathe again.

The light was intense, far too bright, so she screwed up her eyes and tried to turn her head away from it. And the noise, too, was startling. It was as though she had emerged onto a stage of arc lights and pneumatic drills. And she had a headache, such a huge headache. And the light and the noise were making it intolerable. Perhaps she could escape back into the treacle goo once more, and be at peace.

'Isobel!'

Surely she knew that voice? It must be someone she knew quite well. It was so familiar that she felt it must be someone who was part of her. It made her feel safe and comfortable, as though the voice, or its owner, was in control and would look after her.

Very cautiously, very slowly, she tried to turn her head towards the voice. At first, nothing seemed to happen, and the treacle seemed to try to envelop her once more. But with a huge effort, she turned her head a little towards the light and the voice, and began to be aware of the outline of a figure that seemed vaguely familiar. She could recognise it, but not define it. It was deeply familiar, but she could not, for the moment, connect the familiarity with a name or a function. Her address book seemed to have gone missing. She pondered this curiosity for a few moments, but it was beyond explanation, so she put it on one side for future consideration. That made her remember that she had a logical brain, something she had always found useful, and had been quietly rather proud of. Brain. That was the thing that ran us, that made us who we are, that allowed us to remember. Perhaps this strange state that she was in was due to something being wrong with her brain. How interesting. Well, the only way to find out was to test it a little.

She cautiously squeezed her eyelids open a little, still anxious that the light would make her head pound once more. The outline of the figure swam about, like an object seen through swirling water, but if she concentrated very hard (and oh, how that hurt), it began to come into focus. She tried again, and suddenly the figure became clear. It was a woman. And a man she knew well, with thick hair. What the hell was his name?

The man leant forward and kissed her forehead. He smelled reassuringly familiar, although she could not, for the life of her, think what he smelled of. Whatever it was, it was good, and felt safe.

'Hello Isobel.'

She tried to say something back, but there seemed to be a disconnect between her mind and her voice, and all that came out was a sort of mewing sound.

'Don't try to talk.'

She managed to keep both eyes open for a while, despite the fog in her mind, and looked into the kind, concerned eyes looking down at her. They must be something to do with the owner of the reassuring smell. Did eyes smell?

'Just lie still and be calm' the eyes said. 'Everything's OK.'

She shut her own eyes again. Think, woman. Eyes and voice. I know them both. They must be connected. But how? And suddenly it came to her, with absolute clarity; the eyes and the voice were part of the same person. And the person was.....? But the effort was too much, and she sunk gratefully back into the treacle, and watched from below the surface as the light and the noises slowly faded, and she was at peace once again.

*

Deep in Lady Isobel's brain, the pressure inside a tiny artery, smaller than the size of a pencil lead, increased fractionally, perhaps as a result of the painful stimulus to the lobe of her ear. The pressure outside, in the surrounding brain, fell a little. That small change was enough, and the wall of the artery developed a split, almost like a tear in a piece of wet tissue paper. It was a tiny split – only just over two millimetres long, but it was enough. Blood, just a few precious millilitres, forced its way through the split, and spread greedily, hungrily, into the surrounding neurones, distorting and disrupting them. They reacted in a panic, firing off irregular bursts of activity, sending confusing signals to the end-organs which they were usually so calm about controlling. Lady Isobel's breathing changed, and her blood pressure rose a little. Inevitably, the rise in pressure led to an increase in the leak of blood, and the process developed an unstoppable momentum of its own. Lady Isobel's life was ending.

*

Far down, far below the surface, in the deepest depths of the treacle which cushioned and supported her, Lady Isobel was dimly aware of change. Her awareness was not the awareness that you or I would feel – a pain if our arm is cut, or if a bee stings us. It was more of a sensation of change, of deepening, in the calm smooth peaceful inertia that enfolded her. It was as though a ripple or a current ran through the treacle, vibrating her and disturbing her equanimity. It wasn't unpleasant or painful. It didn't disturb or upset her. In the tiny part of functioning brain that was left to her, she was faintly aware of a deep subliminal thud, like a sack of potatoes being dropped on the floor. 'That's interesting,' the little bit of brain thought. 'I'd better see what that was,' and with a huge effort she tried to swim up towards the surface and the daylight again. But very soon, the little bit of brain realised that the effort was too much, and that it was more peaceful to lie where it was and relax. It – the little bit of brain – watched with disinterest as the surface seemed to recede, and the light become more distant as it did so. The thudding noise was repeated, and became a vague constant background beat. It didn't worry her at all, and quite soon, the beat became quieter and the surface more indistinct and the light dimmer. She lay there, relaxed and at peace. After a while, the little bit of brain could not hear the beat at all, and, as it could hardly see the surface now, the light was just a faint glimmer. Her last thought, if thought it was, was that it was lovely down here, calm and peaceful, and, as there was nothing else to do, she might as well go to sleep. After that, nothing.

*

Lady Isobel's husband became aware of a change in the figure in the bed beside him. She had turned her head a little when he first arrived, before the lady doctor pinched her ear, and he thought she had looked at him. Her breathing had been regular and even then, but now was slowly, progressively, becoming irregular. A cycle was developing. Whereas before, Isobel's breathing had been the slow breathing of a deep sleeper, it now came and went, like a tide ebbing and flowing. At the beginning of each cycle, the breaths were light and gentle, but then they slowly increased in depth and intensity, like a storm gathering. As they increased, they became deeper and deeper, until the last few breaths of a cycle were great shuddering gasps, racking her whole body with their intensity. Then, quite suddenly, her breathing stopped, as though brought up short, and there was a period of absolute silence. Shockingly, he thought she might have died, but then, after what seemed like an age but which was in reality probably only ten seconds or so, she took a small, slight breath, followed by another, and then another, and the whole cycle repeated itself.

He watched and listened to this for some minutes with a sort of horrified fascination. Finally, he realised that it must mean something was going on, either for the better or, more likely, for the worse, and that he ought to do something about it. He struggled to his feet, stiff and cramped after sitting for so long, and tried to catch the attention of the nurses who were collected round the end of the desk at the far end of the intensive care unit. After a few moments, when none of them looked his way, he walked towards the desk. A pretty girl in surgical scrubs who was working at a computer looked up.

'Yes?'

'My wife.' He indicated rather helplessly towards the bed at the end of the ward. 'Something seems to be happening to her breathing.'

'I'll come.'

The nurse walked briskly down towards Isobel. She didn't touch her at first, but watched her intently, and then looked at the bank of monitors that were arranged above the end of the bed, attached by wires and tubes that disappeared under the sheets.

'She's Cheyne Stoking,' she said.

'What's that?'

She avoided his eye. "It's a pattern of cyclical breathing that warns us that something has changed. I'll get the doctor.'

As he waited by the bedside, he felt the helplessness that all of us feel when we are faced with a situation over which we have no control. When the aircraft suddenly lurches just before landing, when the anaesthetist says 'off to sleep now', the same thought goes through our minds. 'How good is he? How often has he coped with this before?' We can only pray that the person in charge is good at his job.

A different doctor came down the ward, a tall man with a kind face and a sort of mature weariness in his movements. He drew the curtains round Isobel's bed, and gently suggested to her husband that he wait outside while he 'checked her over.'

Reluctantly, Isobel's husband took himself to a chair near the door, and waited, fearful. After a long pause, a pause that seemed endless, the tall doctor with the kind face came out from behind the curtains, and walked up the ward towards him. His face told nothing, but the fact that he had not drawn the curtains spoke volumes.

'Can we have a word in the office?'

Isobel's husband nodded, fighting back his anxiety, and followed the doctor into a small and crowded room behind the nurse's station. A couple of standard issue hospital arm chairs fought for space with a trolley bulging with hospital notes, a computer and printer, and, incongruously, an electric kettle and a jar of Nescafe. The doctor gestured to a chair, and sat down himself in the other one. He paused before speaking.

'I'm very sorry to have to tell you this,' he said gently, 'but I'm afraid your wife is dying.'

Isobel's husband stared at him. It took a moment for the meaning of the words to get though.

'What do you mean, 'dying'? Surely you can do something? What about resuscitation? CPR? She can't just die like that, without anyone doing anything! '

Shock, bewilderment, anger, confusion, all flashed through him in a chaos of emotion. 'It can't happen like that. The last doctor I spoke to, the Indian lady, said she was regaining consciousness! She can't, simply can't, just die. Do something! For God's sake, do something!'

The doctor let the words flow over him, and waited for the first intense surge of disbelief to die down. The quiet that he allowed to develop was something that he had learnt, over the years, went some way towards defusing the intensity of the reaction to sudden and unpredicted death. Only when the husband's breathing had returned to something near normal, and his eyes had started to focus on the room again rather into a far distant place, did he draw a long breath and lean forward.

'I'm terribly, terribly sorry. More sorry than I can say. You probably think I say that to everybody who is losing a loved one, but I feel it, feel it very strongly, especially when the person concerned has been fit and well, and when the events surrounding her collapse have been so sudden and catastrophic.'

'But how can she be dying?' Isobel's husband stared at the floor, dry-eyed. 'She was here just a while ago. She looked at me.'

The doctor drew another deep breath, and leant forward. Their knees were almost touching in the crowded little room. 'If you feel up to it, I'll try and explain what is happening, and why, and go through the reasons why I don't think there is anything useful we can do.'

Isobel's husband felt as if he had been thrown a thin life-line. 'So she's not actually dead? She can be resuscitated?' he said , and stood up. 'Why aren't you doing that right now?'

'No, she's not dead, but she is dying.' The doctor repeated, even more softly, and stood too. 'Would you like to go and sit with her for a while. She is completely peaceful. It might be a good time to say goodbye.'

Isobel's husband sat down again. He was a creature of process, of making sure things took place in such a fashion that they led to an outcome that he approved. Then, and only then, would he sometimes allow himself the luxury of emotion, of feeling pleased with the outcome. Because of this, he felt that he must understand exactly what was happening, must get an explanation for this tragedy that had so suddenly dropped from the sky onto him. Only when he was in command of the facts could he luxuriate – for want of a better word – in the distress he felt.

'Tell me what's happening to her first.'

The doctor with the kind face was tired. He had worked as an Intensive care consultant for nearly twenty years, and he sometimes felt that his batteries were getting a bit flat. He had been on call in the Unit for twelve hours, since seven that morning, and this was the third death he had had to deal with. The other two had been easier – old people who had reached the end of their lives, but who he had admitted to intensive care against his better judgement under pressure from their relatives in a last ditch attempt to stave off the inevitable. He had said to one daughter, about her elderly mother with end-stage kidney failure,

'I think that we may actually be prolonging her death rather than prolonging her life.' The daughter had stared at him angrily, and had accused him of 'wanting to let my mother die to save money.' But the death, when it came, was peaceful and quiet, a good death if ever there was one, despite the incongruous surroundings.

He sat down again opposite Isobel's husband, and paused to collect his thoughts and to think through the message he wanted to get over.

'The sequence of events was this, as I see it. Your wife, Isobel, was a fit, healthy woman. I gather that she was a highly intelligent individual and a credit to her profession. In court this morning she collapsed, and was found to be deeply unconscious. A doctor at the scene did all the right things, as she was acutely ill then, and probably saved her life by maintaining her airway and getting her sent to the right unit. When she got here, she had all the signs and symptoms of a moderate sized acute stroke, something we specialise in treating here. Such a stroke is caused by either a bleed into the brain, or a blood clot blocking the blood supply to it. In either case, the area of brain affected dies very quickly, unless we can dissolve the clot, or get rid of the blood.' He paused. 'Blood in or around the brain causes pressure on it, like a big bruise.'

'OK.' Isobel's husband, still dazed, nodded as he assimilated this. He was an intelligent man.

'When I first saw her three hours ago, I was fairly sure she had had a bleed, not a clot. We confirmed that this was the case by doing a scan. It was a smallish bleed, and we were about to discuss how best to manage it when something else happened. I don't want to give you a lecture on the anatomy of the brain, but it is basically divided into the thinking part of the brain, and the unthinking or subconscious part. The part that does all the things we don't think about, like balancing, maintaining blood pressure, breathing, temperature control, digestion, and so on. And the conductor of that part of the brain, the unconscious bit, is the brain stem, what is referred to as the primitive part of the brain. We share it with many animals, especially the mammals. All of us, whether we are capable of thought or not, have to have a brain stem that manages our bodies.'

'OK.'

'When Isobel's breathing changed so suddenly a short time ago, she was telling us very clearly that something had gone badly wrong with her brainstem. There are signs – changes in the body – that tell you quite quickly how bad the damage is, and whether it is ongoing. When I looked at her fifteen minutes ago, it was very clear that something catastrophic was happening. Her pupils were fixed – no longer reacting to light. Her voluntary muscles – the ones we can move consciously – were all in complete spasm. Her vital signs – things like blood pressure, pulse, oxygenation, breathing, were chaotic. From bitter experience, I was certain that she was undergoing huge damage to her brainstem. And from that there is no way back. She would be feeling nothing. She would have been completely at peace.'

'And there is no operation to stop the bleeding? Cauterising the artery? Resuscitating her?'

'No,' he said emphatically, 'I'm afraid not. To get to the brainstem, we would cause more damage than the bleed itself, cause damage that is incompatible with life. And catastrophic damage has already been done, and is beyond repair.'

Nicholson stared at him, and then put his head in his hands.

'And I'm also afraid there is huge misapprehension about resuscitation and CPR.' He smiled wanly. 'It simply doesn't apply to the situation that your wife is in. From that brain damage, I'm afraid, there is no medical solution.'

There was a pause. Isobel's husband stared unseeingly at his hands. After a long pause, he looked up at the tired face in front of him.

'You are sure, absolutely sure, of all that?'

'Yes. I'm very sorry to say that I am certain. When her heart stops, as it will, resuscitation might possible get it going again, but her brain would be gone, gone for ever.'

The doctor paused. He hated breaking bad news, but it was a significant part of his job. Sometimes personalising it helped.

'When my time comes, and let's faces it, it comes to all of us sooner or later, I just hope that there is a sensible doctor who is prepared to make the most difficult decision, the decision not to start treatment that is inevitably futile. The default position is to try to resuscitate everyone unless there is a clear reason not to. For better or worse, I think that such a reason exists in your wife's case. I will arrange a second opinion if you like, but I can honestly say that I think it is in her best interests to let nature take its course.'

There was a long silence. Isobel's husband looked at his hands again, his eyes far away. The bleep in the doctor's pocket trilled urgently, but he made no move to silence it or answer it. Finally, Isobel's husband looked up.

'Thank you, doctor, for telling me. It must take a lot of courage to assume responsibility for another person's life like that. If you hadn't been so frank, I probably wouldn't have believed you, and would be after your blood for failing in some way. But I do believe you.' He stood up. 'One other thing. The doctor who saved her life in the court room. He gave me the chance to see my wife before', and he choked on the word 'before she - she dies, and I'd like to thank him.'

The doctor smiled. I'm sorry, I can't help you there. As I understand it, he happened to be in court, I don't know why. Perhaps he was a witness in a case, who knows. But he did the right thing, and I'm glad for you that he was there.'

Isobel's husband shook the doctor's hand. 'Thank you. Thank you very much. I think I'll go and sit with Isobel for a while now.'

The doctor watched silently as Isobel's husband went behind the drawn curtains to say goodbye to his dying wife. Then he sighed, and went to answer his bleep.

CHAPTER 12.

INTERMEZZO

Spring is, or should be, wonderful. Hackneyed words like 're-birth' or 'renewal' fail to do any kind of justice to the deep, subliminal sensation that many of us humans experience at the extraordinary annual awakening which heralds the end of dark, gloomy, cold, miserable winter. Perhaps it is something very deep in our genetic makeup that triggers this sensation of waking up, of renewing energy. Maybe, aeons ago, long before we branched away from the Neanderthals and evolved into Homo Erectus and then into Homo Sapiens, we, like the bears and the dormice, hibernated, surviving the long dark time of winter famine by slowing our metabolism to a state of near coma, so that the need for sustenance became minimal, and we were able to survive for months on our store of fat, built up during the times of plenty. So that spring is literally a kind of reawakening, a starting anew and afresh, and perhaps our response to it now is based in some ancient subliminal genetic instruction, rooted far back in evolutionary time.

It is hard to get one's mind round the difference between biological and geological time. Very clever people have enabled us to work out roughly how old the earth is, give or take a few million years. Other clever people have explained how, over billions of years, the continents have formed and separated and reformed in a ritual dance that defies our comprehension. We know, or at least yet more clever people have convinced us, that life has only been crawling about on the surface of this earth of ours relatively briefly, for the last ten or fifteen percent of the time the earth has existed. And that life as we know it, the present biosphere, is right at the tail end of an evolution that has been churning out change for billions of years.

How many of us can actually visualise a billion years? A few astro-physicists perhaps, but even for those hyper-brains, the concept, and the imagery that goes with it, may be amorphous. It is hard enough to get your mind around the perception that dinosaurs dominated the world for forty million years, but died out sixty million years ago. So if that is hard to conceive, how much harder is the concept of a billion years. Maybe our reaction to spring, to the annual change in light and warmth resulting from the angle of rotation of the earth on its axis, is rooted deeply in the DNA from which we have sprung, and we are as unlikely to be able to understand how we feel about it or quantify it as is a bird able to comprehend why it has feathers, or how and why it migrates.

*

I love the spring. It has always produced a sense of joy and release in me even during the dark years of my teenage revolt, and when the mind-numbing years of work and motherhood that I had trudged through threatened to break me. However gloomy and miserable I felt, I could not deny the lifting of the spirit, for want of a better phrase, which a glorious spring morning produced. If I was even slightly religious, I would probably quantify it in terms of a gift from god. But I am not, not even slightly, so I was more than happy just to allow the sensation to waft over me like a warm breeze, and bask in the almost sensual sensation it produced.

So when I threw back the bedclothes on the Saturday after Dame Isobel's collapse, and saw out of the bedroom window of the house in Islington that the sun was shining, that the blossom was bursting, and that the birds, even in London, were shouting and yelling with excitement, I felt the same sense of exuberance that I imagined the birds were feeling, and the same urgency that I should join in their celebration.

I think this must have been infectious, because the children did not put up their usual barrage of whinges when I dragged them out of bed and away from children's television. Richard, the soon-to-be-ex-husband, was due to have them for the weekend, but I threw caution to the winds, and texted him to say that 'something had come up', and 'I would keep them here for now, and would next weekend be OK?' I got a brief reply: 'I suppose so', but even that was not enough to dent my spirits. I threw some cornflakes in front of them, waited impatiently while they cleaned their teeth afterwards, and bundled them into the car, with wellies and anoraks. They were a bit older now, and more capable of picking up the nuances of adult moods, and balancing their own wants and needs with those of people around them. I watched in the driving mirror, amused, as Sophie caught Rupert's eye in the back seat, raised her eyebrows, and shrugged. An unspoken question of 'what's got into her today, then?' He shrugged his shoulders back, but there was a smile on each small face, and that was enough to make me happy. When I dared think about it, happiness was a sensation that I had very rarely felt over the last few months. But today, spring was here, and things would be different.

I had no clue where we might go as I drove through the empty streets of the London, and then west towards the Kings Road and Chelsea, and over Putney Bridge. As the streets became less congested with houses as well as traffic, the children bounced up and down on the back seat, as far as their seat belts would let them.

'Where are we going? Where are we going?' A shrill chorus, containing excitement and impatience. 'Where are you taking us, Mum?'

'Where would you like to go?'

'The sea, the sea!' And once again 'the sea!'

'Right. It's a long way, but if that's where you really want to go, that's where we'll go'

'And a castle!' Rupert always wanted castles in adventures, whether the adventures were in stories or films or in real life.

That made me think a bit. Where was there a castle by the sea within reasonable driving time of south London? A distant memory stirred. Somewhere that my father had taken me one Easter, leaving my mother behind to her knitting and the church flowers and Woman's Hour. Where was it? A vague image of a pretty village and a wide river and an imposing manor house – almost a castle – glimpsed behind an ancient gatehouse floated into my mind. And then I remembered. A place straight out of times long ago, Beaulieu, with the hamlet of Bucklers Hard beyond it on the banks of the Beaulieu River, with the sea and the Isle of Wight in the distance. Bucklers Hard, with its row of perfect cottages running down to the waters' edge, either side of the slipway where the ships of Nelson's fleet had been built, the wooden walls of England. The place had been preserved, like an insect in amber, as a perfect example of Georgian artisan lifestyle. Calm, beautiful, unspoilt. I suddenly had an intense desire to see it again myself.

'I think I know a place which has got the sea and a castle, but you'll have to be patient. It's a long drive. OK?'

'It had better be worth it'. Sophie was always a realist.

'Well I liked it when I went there when I was the same age as you, or nearly. So let's hope it is still just as lovely'.

The children lapsed into silence in the back, and after a while I could hear the click of Sophie's fingers on her iPhone's above the drone of the engine as she texted friends played one of the dreadful games to which she was addicted. For all I knew, children found it easier to text each other than to talk, even though they might be sitting next to each other. We were making good time down the A31 in the direction of the New Forest. It might have been quicker to go on the motorway, but I had an unreasonable dislike of the intensity and speed on these arteries of progress, despite the statistics about their greater safety. Besides, going on the old roads allowed us to see the towns and villages and houses as we went by, to be part of them, not separated by crash barriers and embankments and crawler lanes. It was all part of the image of the day that I held in my mind, an image of escape from the grinding pressure of my life and a return to a happier, more carefree time.

Surprisingly, there was not much traffic, and we made it to the New Forest in double quick time, and wound our way past the town of Lyndhurst, the old capital of the Forest, with its ancient Agister's Court, said to be the oldest court in the country. Then along a winding road for miles through the old New Forest, populated with huge oaks which must have been teenagers in tree terms when the Georgian foresters took their axes to their parents, that were then dragged down to Bucklers Hard to build the ships of the line, the wooden walls of England. Then across the moorland that made up the open land of the Forest, with the gorse flowering, dotted with small groups of the hardy Forest ponies that lived wild there. Any Commoner, someone who lived within the confines of the New Forest, has the right to graze his ponies in the Forest, and all the animals are owned and identified by the way their tails are clipped, despite their freedom to roam unfettered.

The road swooped down from the moorland into the village of Beaulieu, with its quaint and now hideously expensive houses. Past them, the expanse of the huge millpond lying next to Beaulieu Abbey opens up, and we pulled over on to the springy grass surrounding it to take it all in. The children got out and stretched, and ran about in that pleasingly aimless way that carefree children have. In my enthusiasm to escape London, I had forgotten to pack any of the usual treats and bribes that I usually carry to keep small spirits and blood sugar up, so we walked the few yards back to the village, and found a shop that sold almost everything that a child, or a child's mother for that matter, could eat on a day out. I let them do all the choosing – fudge and Maltesers and sausage rolls and dreadful sugary drinks. Nothing healthy – for today was an escape, an aberration, and all rules could and should be broken.

We wandered back to the car, to find it surrounded by a group of ponies. One of them was nibbling tentatively at a wing mirror. Amongst them were a couple of donkeys, their grey coats contrasting with the bracken brown of the ponies. The children were entranced. Living in London had never allowed them to see wild animals close to, and they circled closer to them cautiously.

'Be careful, guys', I said. 'Don't forget that they don't know us'

Too late. One of the donkeys, the prettiest and most gentle-looking one, turned suddenly on Sophie and bared enormous yellow teeth at her, and made a grab for the paper bag she was holding.

'Ouch. She bit me! Horrible thing'. Sophie was more affronted than hurt, and the idyllic rural image that the donkeys had so craftily created was rudely shattered. With their ears back, their yellow teeth bared and their hind legs cocked ready to kick, they looked more like malevolent goblins than the sweet little animals portrayed on Palm Sunday. I clapped my hands at them, and they and the ponies tossed their heads disdainfully, and trotted off stroppily, making faintly disgusting snorting noises, as though they needed to blow their noses but didn't have a hankie.

'Yuk' said Rupert. 'I hate horses'.

I remembered that twenty five years later, when he was in command of a troop of the Horse Guards at the Trooping of the Colour, mounted on a superb black horse of over seventeen hands. But that is another story.

We recaptured the car, and drove slowly past the castle and into the grounds of the old Abbey. The original Abbey, founded by King John in the thirteenth century as a refuge for a group of peripatetic French Cistercian monks escaping a pogrom, was torn down three hundred years later by Henry the Eighth in his rampage of vengeful vandalism against the Church of Rome. What a despot. Sadam Hussein as a pussycat compared to him. In fact, much of the damage was done in order to recycle the demolished buildings at a profit, an early example of legalised asset stripping.

The original Mill still stood, though, a perfect example of the use of tidal power, still working as it did when the Cistercians built it eight hundred years ago, the mill wheel running in one direction when the tide came in, and in the other when it went out. I explained this to the children, giving what I thought was a rather witty potted history of the workings, but they interrupted me.

'Boring, Mum. Boring. Please can we see the sea? Now?'

So we drove the short distance down the tiny lanes to Bucklers Hard, and the children ran carefree down the close cropped grass slope which, two hundred years ago, had echoed to the sound of saws and adzes as HMS Agamemnon was being built from the oaks dragged by ox cart from the New Forest. The two rows of cottages where the craftsmen had lived lay on either side of what was once the slipway on which the ships were built. They were almost untouched, a perfect microcosm of an earlier life. There was a tiny chapel in one of them, where the shipwrights of old conformed to the mores of the age.

A wonderful place, unspoilt by the usual tat of modern life. Even the little stall that sold ice-creams was in keeping, and the peaceful atmosphere seemed to infect the tourists who were pottering about, so that there was a noticeable absence of transistor radios and litter. We wandered down to the waters' edge, and watched the swans' serene progress upriver towards the Abbey. The little marina that had been built in front of the old shipyard entranced Rupert, and he pottered about, asking questions of an elderly boatman working there, who seemed entirely unfazed by this precocious child. There were some very upmarket yachts and motorboats moored in it, one or two flying the White Ensign, indicating that their owners were members of that most prestigious of clubs, the Royal Yacht Squadron. Even princes of the blood had to join the queue to become members there. Other boats were ashore, having serious things done to their insides. The smell of tar and varnish and salt water was deeply evocative.

The warm afternoon passed in a dozy peaceful haze of tranquillity. Even though we hadn't made it to the sea proper, it was just down a bend in the river, and that was enough to satisfy

Rupert. The peace and history of this lovely place osmosed into our minds as the day wore on, and the shrill demands of electronic modernity faded into the distance. For the first time for many months I felt genuinely happy, and the carefree expressions on the muddy faces of the children showed that they, too, felt the same. If only all of life was like this.

I loaded them back into the car as dusk started to fall, and we meandered through the back roads, across the Forest and towards the arteries that led to London. Both children were asleep on the back seat, and for once I didn't find the increasing traffic and the inevitable roadworks as irritating as usual. We arrived back at the house in Islington just as the darkness of the spring night enveloped the blossom of the trees along the road, and I parked outside and pulled on the handbrake with a sense of fulfilment that I had not felt in ages.

Once inside, I saw that the message light on the answering machine by the phone was flashing.

CHAPTER 13

The voice on the message was only too familiar. It was my soon-to-be-ex-husband. It was abrupt, almost aggressive.

'Antonia, we can't let things drift on. We need to get things sorted between us. I haven't heard anything from you about what you want, so I've told my solicitor to make an offer to yours. That's all. Let me know what you think. 'Bye.'

That brought me down to earth with a bump. The peace of the day that I'd just spent with the children by the sea disappeared in a puff of irritation. Trust him to start calling the shots, doing things on his terms. And playing a crafty game. He had told his solicitor to contact mine with an offer, but asked me to contact him about it. A guaranteed way to confuse everything. Normally, if the participants in a divorce can't agree on a course of action between themselves, to divide up the spoils, so to speak, they get their solicitors to do the negotiating for them. Only if they then can't agree do they go before a judge in the Family Division who hears both sides, and arbitrates on who gets what, from the children to the books to the dog. Solicitors act as go-betweens between the warring factions, trying to get an amicable, or at least an acceptable agreement about the division, so that it does not have to go to Court, with all the inevitable blame and expense that that entails.

By getting his solicitor to contact mine, Richard was preempting any discussion that we might have had, adult to adult. At the same time, he was asking me to get back to him directly about it, thus confusing the role of the solicitors. If he had not been a lawyer, I would have thought this was just a confusion, a misunderstanding of how the system worked to achieve the best outcome. But he was a lawyer, a very clever and crafty one, and I had little doubt that there was method in this approach, and that the objective was very unlikely to be to my benefit. Manipulative bastard. I wondered what he would want from me. Would he claim that my earning power was potentially the same as his, so that he had to contribute nothing to me? And how about the children? And the house? Would he want me to buy out his share of the equity?

I drummed my fingers on the telephone table for a few moments, thinking furiously. Then common sense returned, and I recalled the old adage 'that someone who represents themselves represents a fool'. In other words, don't let the fact that you are a lawyer get in the way of getting objective legal advice, the key word being 'objective'. Managing your own divorce yourself is a recipe for disaster. In just the same way that a doctor managing his own illness is guaranteed to do it badly. Indeed, doctors are forbidden from treating members of their families, for just that reason. Emotion can destroy objectivity. So there was a simple response to the phone call: ask my own solicitor what to do. And that could wait for tomorrow.

So I suppressed my irritation, and tucked the children up in bed. They were tired and happy. Perhaps today would be one of the days that they remembered in years to come, days when the stresses of growing up fell away, and being a child in a care-free and cared for existence re-emerged as a sensation that became memorable. Perhaps, in a time many years hence, a sound of waves lapping, or a smell of the shore, pungent and evocative, would bring back a memory of that day. Who knows? But if, as a parent, I could give them just a few memories like that, combined with security and love, all the hard work would not have been in vain.

I made myself a mug of warm milk, and curled up on the sofa with the cat on my lap. I was aware that I was recreating the same sensation from my own childhood that I desired for the children, and I relaxed back into it, and allowed the concerns and stresses and anxieties about my life and my loves and my work, and in fact, my everything to recede into distant lines on the horizon. If I was patient, I could make the lines of worry disappear over the horizon and into the oblivion beyond it, so that they didn't seem to exist at all, and the things that made up the lines disappeared as well. . And so, for one night at least, I slept the sleep of innocence.

*

It never rains but it pours. Corny, but true. Or perhaps it is that when we have a lot on our plates, we cope less well with any extra stress, so that it feels as though everything comes together. There is a vanishingly rare chance that events, be they good or bad, will occur in a regular fashion, with a predictable time line between each, so that in real life they seem to occur in clusters. Inevitably, therefore, our minds tend to search for a reason behind these colliding problems. We search for a trigger or a cause. This leads to the widespread fallacy that association implies causation, that merely because one thing occurs alongside another, that one must be causing the other. Illnesses, real or imagined, have been blamed on power lines, mobile phones, diet, something in the water, mercury in amalgam, even sunspots; in fact almost anything that happens to coincide with the disease. It was the development of insight into this fallacy that led to the objective analysis of why things happen that is now known as scientific method. Sadly, it is hardly ever pointed out, let alone taught, as the irrational assumptions that are shouted so loudly in tabloid headlines so clearly demonstrate.

My inner picture of me and my energy is of a battery, perhaps like the little icon of a battery on a mobile phone that shows how much charge there is left. In theory, a day like yesterday and a night of sleep such that I could hardly remember should have entirely recharged the little battery of my mind's eye. But I knew, the minute the alarm went off, that it was barely half charged, and that any demands above the ordinary would deplete it quickly. The one thing I did not need was a whole series of problems, all at once.

So when the phone rang, just as I was opening the front

door to the soon-to-be-ex-husband who had come to pick up the children, I felt my tolerance sag, and my ability to deal with another worry to be limited.

It was my mother on the phone. Silly, ineffectual, charming, loveable. A feature in my life who had created such dependence, and occasionally such irritation, that I could never really understand what I felt about her. She had fussed around the periphery of my life for as long as I could remember, always worried about me and always completely unable to understand when I really needed help. Although she had the right motives, she did not have the insight or the empathy to know when to apply the calm and objective support that is the essence of parenthood.

Furthermore, she was torn between maintaining the exclusion zone round my father that he demanded, and providing the warmth and care that her errant children, or at least this errant child, had needed.

But for the last few years, since my father died, the role had been slowly reversing. No longer was she concerned about me, albeit without the emotional wherewithal to do anything constructive about it, but now she was the one fast becoming dependent, needing the help and support, although still unable to express what it was that she needed. A phone call was usually the cue for a long, rambling conversation about the story she had created in her mind about the past. She needed this image to justify her mirage of the ideal family that her memory had created. Lost in the long grass of the past were the difficulties, the arguments, the distances, the lack of love from a self-centred and iconoclastic man she had married. In their place was a rose-tinted story of an ideal happy marriage, with me in the supporting role of ideal daughter.

But the voice on the phone today sounded wobbly and frightened. That wasn't like Mum. She was, for all her verbosity, pretty self-sufficient. I couldn't remember the last time she had needed to see her doctor. I couldn't even remember his name.

'Darling, I don't feel very well.'

I waved to the kids as Richard wrestled them into their coats.

'Tell me what's up Mum. How long have you been feeling poorly?'

'Well….' And she went off into a long ramble about what she was doing yesterday and who she met.

I interrupted. 'Hang on a minute Mum. I'll just get the children organised. Be back in a moment. Don't hang up.'

I hugged Sophie and Rupert and shepherded them through the front door, trying not to notice that they were already entirely focussed on their father.

Richard raised a cynical eyebrow. 'Struggling, are we?'

'Not at all.' I found it difficult to be civil to him as he so obviously tried to irritate me. How on earth had I ever seen anything in him? What a bastard he could be when he wanted to. 'Just a bit of a problem on the Mum front that needs sorting. Thanks for taking the children. We've had a great time.'

'Did you get my message about my offer?'

'Yes I did,' through gritted teeth. 'Could we talk about later, when I'm not being pulled in three directions at once? I'll ring you.'

He shrugged, and I thought how his once handsome face had become puffy and sour when middle age and bad temper got the better of him. He ushered the children towards the car and I saw that it was new, and expensive. Two little faces turned towards me anxiously as they got in, and once again I was struck by guilt. I turned back into the house, and picked up the phone.

'Hi Mum. Sorry about that.'

There was silence for a few moments on the other end of the line, and I wondered if she had hung up. Then her voice came, rather distant and muddled.

'I'm not sure what's happened. I was all right yesterday, although I felt very tired. But today, when I woke up, I felt all wobbly and faint. I couldn't balance to put my things on when I got dressed, and I nearly fell down the stairs. Now I'm sitting in the kitchen feeling all weak and feeble.'

My heart sank. It was inevitable that something like this would have happened sooner or later; all old people get older, and with age comes the problems of a body that stops working so well. Sometimes it happens slowly, over weeks or months, and sometimes suddenly. I had wondered in a vague sort of way how we would cope when age caught up with Mum, but had never got round to actually thinking through a plan. I suppose that, even if I had, it would not have fitted the circumstances. Inevitably, it had happened at the least convenient time, I thought, as I checked my diary. She lived fifty miles away, on the far side of London, in the shadow of the Sussex Downs. The village which she and my long gone father had chosen to retire to was lovely but impractical. Miles from anywhere along twisty country lanes, the local shops had shut one by one as Amazon and Ocado made them unviable. The working population had moved away as house prices rose and commuting became more expensive. Not for nothing had this corner of Sussex become known as the geriatric corridor. Even getting someone to cut her lawn hadn't been straightforward.

'Mum, you know that I can't just drop everything and come straight away, however much I would like to. Do you feel well enough to call the doctor yourself? Or could you ring one of the neighbours to pop in? You know, nice Mrs Dickens from next door but one. Or do you think that if you have a good strong cup of tea and sit quiet for a bit that you may feel better?'

There was a pause on the other end. She was usually quite bright and brisk, so this slowness was something new.

'I'll try. If I ring Joan Dickens, she could ring the doctor for me. '

Too many ifs and buts. Joan D might not be in, and she was at least the same age as my mother, and even less sprightly.

'Ring Joan, Mum, and get her to come round, but I'll ring the doctor for you and get him to come and see you. I'll let you know when he can come, and when he's been, you can tell me what he said.'

'Thank you, darling. That sounds sensible.' She sounded tired and old. 'I don't think I could manage all those receptionist's questions just now.'

'Right Mum. I'll get cracking with that. I'll be in touch very soon. Don't worry; it'll probably turn out to be nothing. Lots of love to you.'

I put the phone down, but the sensitive antennae that we all have in our minds, the early warning system that warned us aeons ago that the lion was stalking us, was on full alert. She didn't sound like someone having a little turn. In fact, there was something about her voice of voice that was markedly different. She didn't sound very good at all. And it was unexpected. She was a tough old bird, and hadn't been ill for years.

I rummaged through the address book that lived on the sideboard in the kitchen for the address and phone number of her doctor. I knew I had it somewhere, but of course I couldn't find it under the D for doctor, or the M for Mum. Eventually I found it, folded in half in the E for emergency . Why on earth had I put it there? I vaguely remembered the doctor from the events surrounding my father's death, a rather weedy and unconvincing man. What was he called? Davies, I think. Yes, that was it, Davies. I rang the number of the surgery.

The first three attempts to get through resulted in the engaged tone. Infuriating. At the fourth attempt, I got a ringing tone, which, after an interminable number of rings was answered.

'Could I have a visit for my mother, please; Dr Davies.' Only then did I realise that the voice at the other end was a recording, giving the usual platitudes of welcome, and offering a menu of options.

'Press one for an appointment, press two to get your test results, press three if you wish to speak to a secretary, and press four for any other services'

I tapped my foot in impatience, and pressed four. The phone rang for what seemed like hours, and then was interrupted by the standard recording -'we are sorry to keep you waiting, but all our staff are very busy. We will answer your query as soon as possible.' The phone went back to tinny musak; infuriatingly, it was Vivaldi's Four Seasons, the standard musak in all lifts, hotel receptions and phone lines in the country. Didn't anyone have an ounce of originality in their stupid bodies?

Finally, after what seemed an age, but was probably only about three minutes;

'Good morning. Wisteria Surgery, Becky speaking, how can I help you?'

'Hello. I'm ringing for my mother. She needs a visit from Dr Davies. Soon if possible.'

'I'm afraid Dr Davies retired several months ago. Who does she see now?'

'I don't know. I'm sorry.'

'Oh dear. What's her name, and I'll see who she is under now.'

That always struck me as a stupid phrase. She wasn't 'under' anybody. Why not ask who cared for her, or who was responsible for her. If anybody. I gave her my mother's details and address.

There was a pause, and I could hear the click of computer keys.

'Ah yes. Here we are. She's under Dr Hussain now. He always likes to speak to anyone asking for a visit. It saves a great deal of time for him. I'll just see if he's free.'

Another long pause. I looked at my watch and saw with despair that it was nearly nine thirty, more than an hour after I usually got to the office. My irritating secretary would be irritated with me.

'I'm sorry; he's with a patient at the moment. Can you hang on or would you like to ring back?'

'I'm under a lot of time pressure myself. Couldn't you just put her down for a visit asap?'

'I'm afraid not. So many visit requests turn out to be unnecessary that all the doctors insist on speaking to the patient or the caller first. '

I bit back my irritation 'I'll hang on, then.'

But after five minutes I had had enough. I went through the whole painful process again, but I had missed the doctor, and he was now with another patient. There didn't seem to be a way to be sure of a call back from this doctor, and anyway that didn't guarantee a visit in any event. And I had to go to work. I rung off in a fury. What to do now? I paced up and down the hall, my mind in turmoil.

Suddenly, an idea came. Nick Malenkov lived in Sussex, and worked somewhere near where my mother lived. Could I, should I, dare to contact him? Why not? He had made the offer, although perhaps not in the same context.

Infuriatingly, I didn't have his phone number in my iPhone contacts. I rang the office, and got my officious secretary. She told me that my nine thirty client was waiting, and made an indeterminate noise when I asked her to give me my doctor's phone number; snooty bitch, I thought. But she found it quickly, and I dialled it as she dictated it to me. There was a pause while his phone rang, and I was surprised to find that I felt nervous. Don't be stupid, I told myself. This is just a professional call.

'Hello.' The voice sounded tired, even a bit irritable.

It's me. Antonia.' How stupid to think that he would know who I was without explanation. 'Your solicitor.'

'Hello Antonia.' His voice was warmer and friendlier. 'For a nasty moment I thought you were a cold call. Sorry if I sounded unwelcoming. How are you? '

'Fine. Well, not fine. In a bit of a mess, actually. That's why I'm calling.' I found that I was flustered, mentally all fingers and thumbs.

'Tell me.' His voice was calm and unhurried.

Ridiculously, I felt a sudden wave of emotion surge over me, and knew I was near to tears. Stupid woman. Pull yourself together.

'Take your time,' he said, as if reading me. 'There's no hurry. Don't forget, there is no problem without a solution, even if the solution isn't the one we expect or even want.'

He must say that to all his anxious patients. I took a big breath.

'It's my mother. I'm really sorry to bother you with this, but I couldn't get through to her doctor, and I couldn't think who else to ring.' I sniffed.

'Go on. What's the problem?'

'She rang me a few minutes ago, and said she didn't feel well, all weak and wobbly. She was a bit muddled, not herself at all. All my alarm bells rang, as she never makes a fuss or asks for help. I suggested she call a neighbour to check on her, but she's an old lady on her own as well, so I rang her doctor, but couldn't get through, and when I did he wouldn't do a home visit, and now the office is waiting for me with a client, and I didn't know what to do, and then I remembered that she lives near you and I wondered – well, I wondered if you might consider dropping in on her to see how she really is.....'

My voice trailed off, and I was aware that I had talked a bit incoherently, and given him a story that was only half of all the worries and fears that were blurring my mind. I felt the tears coming again. 'Sorry. I'm really sorry. It's unfair to ask you. And you probably can't see some other doctor's patient anyway. Ethics, and all that....'

'No need to be sorry.' The voice on the other end of the phone was reassuring. 'It's not a problem. We'll get her sorted out one way or another. Don't forget that dealing with this kind of problem is part of my job every day. So you did the sensible thing ringing me.'

I felt relief flood over me. 'Are you sure you don't mind? It won't break professional rules, or anything, will it?'

'Don't worry. Easily sorted. I'll get onto her GP and explain things, and get him to do a visit. If I can't get hold of him, I'll go and see her myself. Give me her details and the name of her GP.'

I dictated the information he needed, and I could hear him repeating them as he was writing it down.

'Fine. That's all I need. It's not far from here – in fact her GP is a partner in the next door practice to mine, and I know him. He's only just joined your mother's practice. I've got a quiet day anyway, so that it's no problem visiting her if he is not about. I'll ring you back in five minutes if there is an issue, and definitely when I know what is going on with your mum.'

I felt almost sick with relief. 'Thank you. Are you sure you don't mind? Thank you, thank you.'

'And Antonia....'

'Yes?'

'Go and sit down for a minute and get your breath back. Your peace of mind is far more important than rushing off to see a client. If you broke your leg, they'd cope without you, and cope better than having you there flustered and upset. So take your time. Don't carry the weight of the world by yourself; share it.'

I sniffled again.

'OK.'

'I'll ring you when I know what is happening. Goodbye.' and the phone went dead.

I sat at the kitchen table, and realised that I was trembling a little. I followed his advice and let the stress slowly wash out of me. I tried to remember the technique I had been taught by a counsellor at Cambridge when I had been in a state after my episode with the golden boy bastard. 'Picture the bad thing as a lump of blackness,' she had said, 'and watch yourself putting it into a box and locking it, and then putting the box into a big chest, and locking that with chains and padlocks, and then watch the chest being thrown into the sea, and watch it sink, sink out of sight, into the unfathomable depths where no one can go. See.... now the bad thing, the black lump, has gone, it's gone to the bottom of the sea, to the bottom of your mind, where it can't trouble you any more. If it does; if the chest tries to float to the surface once more, just wrap another chain round it in your mind's eye, and watch it sink without trace again. Sooner or later, probably sooner, the black lump of badness will be replaced in your mind by the image of the chest, and the picture of the chest sinking, will become manageable. And eventually, the chest will disappear completely, and never resurface.'

It had worked for me then, and I realised, with a bit of a shock, that I had several lumps of blackness floating round in my life at the moment, and that I had failed to see them for what they were. It had only needed one small final event for them to coalesce into an unmanageable mass, and it was this that had caught me so unawares this morning, and left me as weak and wobbly as my mother.

After a while, I squared my shoulders and stood up. I collected my bag and briefcase, re-did my eye makeup, which was smudged, put on my coat, and went out to brave the world once more. My mother was in safe hands now.

*

One of my partners had seen the client I was due to see first thing, and the office was calm when I got in, the staff solicitous and friendly. I got on with mundane things – going through the post, reading the Reports from recent Appeals, checking that some of the minor cases I was dealing with were all up to date and running smoothly. By early afternoon, I had almost cleared my desk, an unheard of event. I was just beginning to wonder what to do next when my mobile rang.

'Hello Antonia.' It was Nick.

'How is she?' I blurted out.

'A quick update. I couldn't get hold of your mum's GP, so I visited her myself. She was a bit suspicious, but let me in when I mentioned you. You were quite right to call, though. Something is definitely going on.'

My heart sunk as he went on. 'It would be silly to guess exactly what it is, as her state could be caused by any number of things. But top of the list are things like a mini stroke, or an infection somewhere, or a chemical abnormality in her blood, or one of several other things. Any of these could cause what is usually called a confusional state, when the brain doesn't work very well, and thinking and balance and movement are all affected. Unfortunately, it isn't possible to identify the cause while she is at home, so the sensible thing to do is to get her assessed in hospital. I hope you agree with that, as I've set the wheels in motion. She should have been admitted by now.'

'Right,' I said. My mind was working overtime, imagining Mum being carried into an ambulance, all on her own. 'You said she had a stroke. Do you think it's serious?'

'I said she might have had a stroke. It is just one of several possibilities. I honestly don't know what it is. Lots of people have episodes like this as they get older. The majority make a full uncomplicated recovery, but obviously that depends on what is causing it all. Until we've identified that, I'm afraid we'll just have to wait and see.'

'I think I understand. I'll get down to see her straight away.'

'Good. You may find her a bit muddled. Just being in the strange environment of a hospital can exacerbate the problem. Let me know if you need me when you come down, or if there is anything else that I can do. I must get back to my afternoon surgery now...'

'Thank you, a huge thank you. You can't imagine what a relief it was to speak to you this morning.'

'Think nothing of it. Just think what you are doing for me.' And the phone went dead again.

*

The hospital, when I arrived in the early evening, was so busy that I wondered if there had been a major accident somewhere. I asked the porter who was standing just inside the entrance to the A&E department what was going on, and he smiled wryly.

'Nothing's going on, love. It's always like this.'

Inside, people were sitting on rows of seats waiting to be seen, some apathetic, some irritated, some apparently entirely well. A harassed receptionist with a name tag round her neck sat behind the reception desk, trying to get details from the woman at the head of the queue in front of her. Behind her, an electronic sign said that the current waiting time to be seen was 3 hours. My heart sank.

A nurse came out of a door labelled 'Triage', and shouted 'Next!' and the patient sitting on the end of the row nearest the door got up and followed her into a cubicle. The other patients all shuffled along into the vacated chair next to them in a sort of caterpillar movement, making sure that they didn't lose their place in the queue.

A different nurse hurried through the reception area pushing a drip stand. I stopped her.

'Where can I find my mother?'

'You'll have to ask at Reception, love,' she said hurriedly. 'Sorry.'

I went back to the reception desk, and rather rudely pushed my way to the head of the queue, ignoring the muttered protests from those in line ahead of me.

'Excuse me. Could you tell me where my mother is? She was brought here this morning.'

'Name?' The receptionist didn't look up.

'Mine or hers?'

'Her's of course. It's not you I need to track down.' The stress of a long day was getting to both of us.

I bit back my stroppy reply, and gave my mother's details. She tapped at her computer for a few moments, while I tried to ignore the increasing grumbles from the queue behind me.

'I think she's still in the Department. She's due to be admitted to Care of the Elderly, but there are no beds, so she's still on a trolley somewhere.'

'So where can I find her?'

She pointed along a corridor that led out of A&E. 'Somewhere along there.'

I almost stamped with frustration. Surely a hospital should know where a patient is. 'And what is wrong with her?'

'Sorry, love. I don't know. That's up to the doctors. I just do reception.'

I thanked her, and after muttering an apology to the queue I had jumped, I turned away, frustrated. It wasn't her fault, or the A&E department's fault, or anybody's fault, as far as I could see. The whole system seems to be coming to a grinding, sclerotic standstill, and no one, from the very top of the NHS to the very bottom, was accountable. I made myself remember that there were lots and lots of people working in this hospital who had the most altruistic motives and ideals, and who were pleasant, friendly and caring. They just seem to have been submerged by the system.

I walked slowly up the corridor she had pointed to, which was painted in a Kafka-esque shade of institutional green, and had a scruffy linoleum floor. It was wide, but the width was restricted by a row of trolleys parked along each side. Each trolley had an occupant. Almost without exception, they were old. Many were asleep. Some were in their nightclothes, covered with a single hospital blanket. In many cases, the blanket had been thrown off, as the corridor was inappropriately hot, and they lay in attitudes of partial undress or abandon. Some had drips in their arms, others had their blue folders of hospital notes sitting on their tummies. Several smelt of urine.

I walked past an old man who was wearing a pyjama top and obviously nothing else. His wrinkled hairless abdomen lay exposed to every passer-by. He looked like a living corpse – pale and lifeless. Startlingly, he grasped at me with stick-like fingers as I came near him, and his skinny arm waved in an uncoordinated appeal for help.

'Can I have a drink, please nurse?'

His mouth looked parched, his tongue thick and fissured. There were little flecks of whitish dry spittle at the corners of his mouth.

'I'm afraid I'm not a nurse, just a visitor. I'll see if I can get someone to help.'

I turned rather aimlessly. This wasn't why I was here, to assist an old man who looked as though he was dying. I was here to find my Mum. But some instinct made me go and look for a nurse. When I found one, she was lifting an old lady onto a bedpan on a trolley near the entrance. I asked her if she could get the old man a drink, she tucked a stray strand of hair behind her ear, and shrugged.

'They should all be having drinks every fifteen minutes, but as they are not supposed to be here in the department, there are no staff rostered to look after them, so nothing happens. I was meant to be off duty an hour ago, but you can't just leave them, can you.'

'Can I get a drink for him then?'

'If you can find a cup. This is an Accident department, so there isn't a kitchen or proper crockery. Your best bet is the drinks machine in the reception.'

I walked back into the reception area, which was still heaving. The queue at the reception desk had got longer. I found the drinks machine in the corner, and searched my bag for a pound coin to put into it.

'Don't bother', said a voice. 'It's bust'. A very large lady was sitting two seats away from the machine. In fact, she wasn't just large, she was huge, spreading onto the chairs on either side of her. Her enormous belly stretched the fabric of her cotton dress to bursting point, and rested comfortably on her thighs. I could see the crease in the dress which was trapped in the waterfall of obesity of her tummy. Below the dress, her swollen legs were a vaguely bluish purple, and were crammed into surprisingly small shoes. Her ankles lapped over the edge of them. She smiled cheerfully at me, and I felt a small glow of warmth for her. Here, at least, was someone friendly.

'It's been bust for ages, weeks and weeks.'

'How do you know? Do you work here?'

'Work here! Give me a break. No, I'm up here regular, you see, with my diabetes. Can't get to see my doctor in the surgery, so I just come up here if I feel unwell or me rash flares up.'

Here rash didn't bear thinking about, any more than her diet or her blood sugar, but I sat down beside her. A friend in times of trouble.

'Is it always like this?'

'No,' she said, surprisingly. 'Sometimes it's fine. The staff are lovely, you know, always trying to help. It's just that there doesn't seem to be much flexibility in the system. So that when there's a rush, they get saturated very quickly. There's not much slack.'

How interesting, I thought. An astute observer, even though her appearance belied it. My bossy investigative solicitor mode reasserted itself unasked.

'So what would you do to improve things?'

'Well,' She looked down at her little feet. The toe of her left shoe tapped thoughtfully on the linoleum floor. 'I may look like a bag lady, but I used to be manager in a hospital in the Midlands. Mid Staffs. So I do have a bit of experience.'

'Really? How interesting.' I bit my tongue to stop myself saying 'what brought you to this?' We all have a background story that is best kept private.

'Yes. And I was quite slim then.' She smiled again. 'But the powers that be didn't like me. They never like whistle-blowers.'

'Wow.' The story of the Mid Staffs disaster was a byword in the medico-legal world, when the managerial desire to meet top-down targets had so distorted medical care that many patients died. No managers were held to account; in fact, no one was.

She went on. 'So I paid the price. And am still paying it.' She looked down at her belly, and smiled again. 'But I won't bore you with that, or with how to cure the NHS.' And she looked away.

I came down to earth with a bump. I wasn't here to have an abstract discussion about the NHS with someone I had never met before, however interesting that might turn out to be. I was here to see my Mum.

When I got back to the corridor of trollies, the old man was no longer there. I looked around. A bit further up, I recognised a crown of white hair, my mother's. I hurried up to her.

'Hello Mum. How are you? What's happening?'

She looked up at me, and I was shocked to see that this sickly little old lady was my mum, usually so upright and in control.

'Hello darling.' The voice was slurred and a bit hoarse. 'Sorry to be such a nuisance.'

'Not a nuisance at all. You mustn't think like that. But what have they said to you?' I smiled and gave her a hug, but she didn't seem to notice.

"I think….' a pause. 'I think they said I'd had a funny turn.

And that they ought to look after me for a few days. But that was ages ago. Can I have a drink?'

I held the cup of water which I had found to her lips, and she slurped thirstily. Some of the water ran out of the side of her mouth down her chin onto her nightie. I stroked her arm, which was cool and dry, the skin textured and wrinkled like someone very old. With a slight shock, I realised that she was very old. It was just that I never thought of her as such; she had always been the calm, rather distant presence of my childhood.

'Right.' I pushed my emotions to one side and went into bossy solicitor mode.

'I'll go and find out what's happening and who is in charge,' (if anyone, I thought), 'and get you tucked up in a proper bed.'

The next hour was frustrating. There seemed to be nobody, be they doctor, manager or nurse, who was in charge. The whole hospital seemed to suffused with a sort fire-fighting approach, in which staff did what they had to do to treat the problem in front of them, but then the next step, how the patient should be managed, disappeared into a black hole. It was self-evident that I wasn't the only relative battling with this problem; I came to recognise several faces, anxious and irritated, who were part of the same group who were directed from receptionist to nurse to junior doctor and back to receptionist again. All gave the same answer – 'we're full to overflowing; there are no empty beds; we're doing the very best we can.' And indeed they were, given the limited resource available to them. It became very quickly evident that two things were missing; one, enough beds, and two, a leader, someone in overall charge.

Eventually, several hours later, my mother was trundled on her trolley out of the hot-house corridor and into a four-bedded bay in the Acute Admissions ward. I sat beside her while she was examined by a tall and rather charming lady doctor. The name badge on her white coat said that she was Dr Truelove, and that she was a Staff Grade in the Care of the Elderly Department. As I watched her, I became aware how appropriate her name was. There was a gentleness as she spoke to Mum, listened to her chest and softly examined her tummy that told me that she was someone who cared.

After she had finished, and had spoken to the junior doctor who had watched her, she drew back the curtains from round the bed, and nodded to me.

'Are you her daughter?'

'Yes. I've come from London.' Not that it made any difference where I had come from.

'Come and have a word.' And she ushered me away from the noise and bustle of the ward into a side room. I sat down and waited.

'I'm not entirely sure what is causing your mother's problem,' she said sensibly. Much better someone who was honest, I thought.

'Her GP thought she might be having a mild stroke,' I said.

'There's no real evidence of that now,' the doctor replied. She's obviously very ill. There could well be something going on in her stomach. There is a suspicion of a mass in her pelvis, and I can feel her liver, which I shouldn't be able to. And she has some hard glands in her neck. Have you had any concerns about her recently?'

'Not really. I live in London, so only see her every couple of months or so. I ring her, of course, and she has sounded quite normal.'

'Not unusual. People of her age tend to be very phlegmatic. And feeling vaguely unwell can creep up on one very insidiously.'

'Oh.' I tried to think of any occasion when Mum had mentioned that she was feeling off colour, but couldn't remember one. Had she been keeping things from me because of my problems? Or had I been too wound up in my own issues to listen to her properly? 'So what will happen next?'

'We'll do the very best we can. We'll stabilise her – she is very anaemic, and her blood chemistry is all over the place. And we'll set in motion all the investigations that will help us identify exactly what is causing this collapse. What happens then depends on what we find.'

Then she leant forward and said something I would always remember with gratitude, and she said it with kindness, even though it didn't feel kind at the time.

'If she was my mum, I would try and think of it in these terms. She has had a long and good life, and she is now reaching the point when bad things happen. Modern technology can do wonderfully clever things to keep old people like your mum going, sometimes for years, but the problems accumulate, and sometimes, even though we get someone through an acute episodes, life can become a burden. She will be well cared for here, that I promise you. Even if we can't cure all the problems that come with old age, we can do a great deal to alleviate them, and make her life more comfortable. It can be argued that technology has exceeded wisdom in medical care. Sometimes we keep people alive with all our clever machines when their bodies have made it very clear that they have had enough, and are reaching the end of life. Sometimes what we do saves old people's lives, but condemns them to a long-drawn-out period of dependence and poor quality living, often in a nursing home or long stay ward. Maybe, sometimes, quality of life is more important than quantity. '

And she turned towards a nurse who was trying to catch her attention. 'Okay, I'll be with you in a minute.'

And then to me. 'Goodbye. I'll look after her, so try not to worry too much. See you.'

And she walked rapidly off to deal with the next problem.

My mind was a whirl. I realised that she was trying to tell me, as gently and tactfully as she could, that this was a big thing that was happening to Mum, something that might be life threatening. She was introducing the idea to me that medicine, even modern high-tech medicine, had limits. And that sometimes the cure could be worse than the disease or at least that the quality of life a cure produced wasn't necessarily for the best in the long term.

Such a lot to consider, to think about.

I had a sudden memory of a great aunt, a slightly intimidating old lady who always smelled of mothballs and lavender, who lived in an ugly bungalow outside Newquay. She was independent and self-sufficient until she had a stroke, and finished up in a rather seedy nursing home, dribbling, incontinent and profoundly unhappy at her loss of dignity.

She hung on for years, each chest infection being treated with antibiotics, each autumn a flu vaccine being administered on the orders of a caring government. Her quality of life became poorer and poorer. Eventually, she took control of things herself, and just stopped eating, and died a few weeks later, skeletal but finally at peace. Was it possible, I asked myself, that medical science really had exceeded medical wisdom in the way that it managed old people, people who were coming towards the natural end of their lives? Were people actually pleased to have lived into their nineties, with the infirmities that almost always go with that age ? Some obviously were, and had brilliant and productive old ages, But others definitely did not, as I knew from my training doing probate work. Was there a balance to be achieved between a few years less, and a better death? Was modern medicine sometimes prolonging death rather than prolonging life?

And another thing. Had I been a good daughter to her? Had I contributed to her isolation by being so wound up in my own ambitions and problems that I had not been there for her? The reasons I had neglected her were obvious – the school run, work, Richard, distance, and so on. But were these reasons, or just excuses? And was it too late now?

I wandered back to my car, feeling numb, and found a parking ticket on the windscreen. That returned me to reality. Just as I was getting into it, my phone warbled. It was Nick.

'Everything OK?'

I was tempted, oh so tempted, to pour out all the thoughts that had been running through my mind. But no, that would be stretching his good nature too far, and anyway, he was still a client.

'She's not good. They think there might be something going on in her tummy, and there is a lump in her pelvis, and that is why she is so ill.'

'I'm not surprised. I thought I could feel something there this morning, but I didn't want to push too hard. They are very good in St Peter's, they'll look after her properly.' He laughed, and I could visualise his eyes creasing, 'or I'll make sure they do. What about you? Are you OK?'

I thought of the doctor, and how I would do anything to do and relax in the reassurance of his company. But that was not an option. I was facing a divorce, and now my mother was probably dying.

'I'm fine. But I must get back to London. The children....'

'Ring if there are problems or you want me to do anything. The boot will be on the other foot, I expect, when we next meet, and you'll be looking after me.'

And the phone went dead, but I was aware of the warmth that his voice had left behind in me. Stupid woman.

CHAPTER 14

Four weeks later, I met Brooks entering the lobby at the top of the steps into the High Court in the Strand. He was cursing voluble under his breath.

'Bugger, bugger, bugger.'

'What's up?'

'Our new judge. We've got Harrap. Nasty devious little shit that he is. Can't be trusted to be either fair or objective. I overturned one of his judgements in the Appeal Court him six months ago, so he dislikes me already. His cousin was a doctor who was had up in front of the GMC for a variety of things and struck off, so he doesn't like the medical establishment, and tends to gun for them.'

I had heard about His Honour Mr Justice Harrap, but never seen him in action. His reputation was said to be that he ate lawyers raw for lunch, and sometimes for dinner as well. Apparently a humourless and cynical man, whose behaviour was often a throwback to of some of the statues on the staircase of the High Court. In the medical profession, the archetypal bullying surgeon, as portrayed by the fictional Sir Lancelot Spratt, had been managed out of existence a generation ago.

However brilliant such people were technically, their behaviour could be hugely destructive. If a senior doctor behaved like that today, he would be summoned to appear in front of a tribunal and given a bollocking and a last warning. Sadly, the law lagged behind medicine in this respect, and judges could get away with behaviour that would be unacceptable in almost any other walk of life.

I learned later that Harrap's father had been a left-wing bishop, a co-founder of a popular movement to give power to the people, based on the naïve kind of socialism so prevalent in the Church of England in the seventies. So Harrap himself had been brought up in an atmosphere dominated by religion and the Labour party, and it had left a mark on him. His elevation to the High Court entitled him to be called 'My Lord' in Court, but he was often referred to as 'My Cynical Bastard' behind his back. Like all judges, his word was – literally – law in his own Court, and he very obviously enjoyed laying it down.

But that cynicism could cut both ways, I thought. The use, or abuse, of the law to perpetuate a vendetta against someone or something was frowned on, even by the likes of Mr Justice Harrap. I said something like this to Brooks, and he nodded in agreement.

'If we were to push the line that the litigant is the manipulative individual, out for what he could get from an innocent and well-meaning doctor who was just trying to do his best, perhaps Harrap might turn his cold wrath on to florid Mr Doggart, rather than our doctor.'

We discussed tactics for a time, and decided that injured

innocence was perhaps a better line to take with this judge. But forensic dissection of a prosecution witness, and pointing out his irrelevance, as we had done with Professor Craig, would still be necessary. Brook straightened his shoulders.

*

Nick Malenkov came up the steps into the lobby at that moment. He caught my eye and smiled.

'I popped in to see your mum last night. She's not too bad. They are still waiting for some test results.' He couldn't explain this any further, as we were called into court.

Brook raised an eyebrow, but didn't say anything. As we walked into Court Number 3 he whispered to me out of the corner of his mouth.

'Never a good thing to mix business and pleasure.'

'It's not like that,' I whispered back, so irritated for a moment that I could hardly get the words out. Mum was on my mind all the time, still stuck in a ward in St Peter's, and now this bloody man was jumping to conclusions. 'He's just helped my mother, who's poorly.'

Brooks didn't reply, and we took our places.

Richardson and Doggart made their usual dramatic entrance, accompanied by their numerous acolytes and bag carriers. With them was the tall sandy-haired plaintiff, as distant and untouchable as before, avoiding all the eyes that looked at him. They all took their seats at the other end of the advocate's bench in the well of the court, spilling over onto the bench behind. It made our small group at our end of the bench look inadequate and besieged. Perhaps, I thought, that was a good thing. It made us look like as though we were being assaulted by aggressive superior forces, and were bravely defending our rightful position. Or perhaps that was just wishful thinking.

The usher made his usual demand of 'All rise,' and the new judge entered rapidly from the door behind the raised dais of the bench and took his seat without looking at anyone, or acknowledging the existence of the players in front of him.

Everything about His Honour Lord Justice Harrap was narrow. His face was narrow, and a pair of steel spectacles were perched on his narrow nose. His eyes seemed to be too close together, emphasised by an oversized wig, which reached below his jawline. He had narrow hunched shoulders, and his robes hung off them as though they were two sizes too big. His narrow frame only seemed to occupy one corner of the judicial throne on which he was perched. I took a bet that his feet were in narrow little shoes, and that they did not reach the ground. I hoped that his mind was not as narrow as his appearance. He shuffled the papers in front of him, and then looked up, his eyes piercing.

'I have been instructed by the Lord Chancellor to take over responsibility for this hearing, following the sad illness and subsequent death of Dame Isobel Nicholson.' He cleared his throat harshly. 'I am sure that all of us here, whichever side we are on in the case, would like to pay tribute to her, both as an individual and as a very fine judge, and to offer our condolences to her husband and family. She was a credit to her profession, and will be sadly missed.'

My heart warmed to him a little. He need not have made those comments, and it was good that he did.

He went on. 'Dame Isobel, as one would expect of a judge of her ability, made comprehensive notes of the hearing thus far, and of her impressions of the only witness heard. I have had the opportunity to read these notes, and also to peruse the verbatim court record of the proceedings. In view of this, I have concluded that it is not necessary to re-start the hearing, but that it is safe in law to continue it from the point when it was so tragically interrupted. I will give each party a moment to consider my ruling, and to consult with their client about the advisability or not to challenge it.'

I caught Brooks' eye, and shook my head. There was nothing to be gained by having another go at the professor with the eyebrows, and a lot to be lost. He would have learnt the hard way from his first experience, and would not fall into the same traps so easily. The plaintiff might not even call him again, given his miserable performance. I looked along the bench towards the other end. Gwen Richardson and Henry Doggart were having a whispered discussion, and were obviously disagreeing. Finally, Doggart shook his head vigorously, and turned to Harrison, who was sitting just behind him. By straining my ears, I could just catch what he said.

'Mr Harrison, I feel strongly that we should accept the judge's ruling, but Mrs Richardson wants to re-run the first witness. She thinks he might do better this time. Ultimately, it's up to you; we act on your instructions. What do you think?'

The thin shoulders shrugged, and the face remained impassive.

'Don't know. Don't really mind, as long as we win.'

Doggert was irritated. 'So you'll accept my advice on this?'

Another shrug. 'OK.'

Doggert turned to the judge. 'We are happy to accept your ruling, My Lord.'

'And so are we, My Lord.' from Brooks.

'Excellent.' Lord Justice Harrap rubbed his narrow hands together. 'Let's get on with it then. Mr Doggart, you were about to call your next witness.'

'Thank you, my Lord. I call Dr Marcus Brain.'

Once again, all the heads did their Wimbledon turn towards the door, and, after a moment, the smooth man we had glimpsed a month before walked to the witness box. He declined to take the oath, but affirmed that he would 'tell the whole truth, and nothing but the truth', and turned to face the Court.

As before, Doggart took the new witness through his name, qualifications, training and work. He had almost as many letters after his name as the professor of gastroenterology, and was also a consultant at a teaching hospital, this time a London one. He did not mention something that I knew, that he had a flourishing private practice amongst the rich and famous, the glitterati and Hello magazine denizens, and spent a lot of his time at the Priory Private Hospital. Perhaps that was why he looked so thoroughly smooth, almost suave.

'Why do you think that this doctor,' indicating Nick, 'failed this patient?', pointing to the Harrison. Doggart cut straight to the chase. He had obviously learnt from the first witness not to give his experts too much time to think.

'Well,' Dr Brain drew a breath, and thought for a moment. 'For three principle reasons.

First, he failed to consider whether the huge psychological stress which Mr Harrison had been under for the month of his hospital admission had distorted his judgement. Second, he failed to consider and to check whether Mr Harrison was suffering from a toxic confusional state. And third, he failed, in the face of Mr Harrison's reluctance to be readmitted, to get a second opinion to try and persuade him to change his mind.'

Brooks scribbled away furiously. To my way of thinking, each of those reasons could be countered fairly comprehensively.

Doggert clearly felt far more confident in Dr Brain as a witness than he had done with the professor. He carefully took him through each of his reasons at length, allowing him to expound on the anxiety caused by unsuccessful hospital treatment and how it could muddy logical thinking. He enlarged extensively on the causes and management of toxic confusional states, stating that 'non-psychiatrists often missed it', to the patient's cost. And he was very clear that if one doctor could not persuade a patient to do what was best for him, it was mandatory to get another doctor to have another go.

After eliciting just over an hour of evidence, Doggart sat down, satisfied. His witness had given a good account of himself, and made a good impression. Brooks stood up slowly, adjusted his glasses, positioned his legal notebook in the little lectern in front of him, grasped his lapels, and turned to Dr Brain.

'How much general practice have you done, Doctor?'

Brain was caught off guard. 'Er, a little.'

'Please be precise, Doctor. How much general practice have you, a consultant psychiatrist, done?'

'Not much. I did a short locum soon after I qualified.'

'When, and for how long?'

'Well, I qualified in 1981, so it must have been in about 1983. It was for a week.'

'A week!' Brooks let the word sink in before he spoke again. 'So you think that your experience of doing a general practice locum for one week, over thirty years ago, allows you to judge whether a general practitioner today is managing a patient properly?'

'Well, yes. It is not my experience as a general practitioner that I am making my judgement on, but my experience as a psychiatrist.' Brain was not going to be brow-beaten. His whole attitude exuded confidence and authority. 'It is me, and people like me, who often have to deal with the fall out after others, especially GPs, make mistakes.'

'But in order to make an objective judgement about a GP, you would agree, would you not, that you must know at least something about general practice?'

'Yes, but that is not the point.'

'Well, what is the point, Dr Brain?'

The psychiatrist paused to collect his thoughts. He was on the back foot, and knew it. But he was a far more intelligent man than the professor who had been such a hopeless first witness.

'Look at it like this,' he said. 'all doctors, whatever their specialism, start from the same point, that the interests of the patient in front of them are paramount, and that your whole function is to do the very best for them. So, if you have a patient who has a symptom you don't understand, or who behaves in a way that is abnormal, then you can, indeed should, consider all options. And one of those options is to call for specialist help. In this case, this patient exhibited unusual behaviour – he refused to take medical advice when he was ill. So his responsible physician could and should have asked for help, or at least excluded some of the common causes of aberrant behaviour'.

He sat back in the witness chair, pleased with this reply.

'And you, as a specialist in aberrant behaviour would have been able to help him?' Brooks sounded almost bored.

'Of course.'

'And diagnose the cause of a toxic confusional state, one of the possible causes of his aberrant behaviour?'

'Well, not the cause, necessarily. But make an informed guess that his behaviour was due to a confusional state. As a psychiatrist, I deal with diseases of the mind, not the body. Although the two can sometimes overlap.'

'An informed guess, doctor?'

'Well, yes. You cannot prove such things straight away.'

'So if my client', said Brooks, indicating Nick, 'had called you, you would have been able to say what was wrong, perhaps, but not what to do about it. Assuming that is, that you would have been immediately available?'

'Well, if it was confusional state, then I would have encouraged both the doctor and the patient to get it properly diagnosed.'

'And where would he go to get that done?' Silkily.

'Hospital, of course'. The psychiatrist suddenly realised what he had said, and looked crestfallen.

'And if he refused to go, Doctor?'

'I'd persuade him, or try to.'

'So you are a specialist in persuasion now, Doctor, are you?'

'Well perhaps better at communication than other doctors. It goes with the job.' Brain sounded smug.

'And when did you last have training on communication, Doctor?'

A pause. 'I haven't had specific training. But it is definitely part of the job.'

'So you've never had any specific training, doctor, but regard yourself as better at it than most doctors?'

No reply.

'Just one last little question, Doctor'. Brooks was always at his most dangerous when he looked benign. 'When did you last go to a patient's home in response to a request for help from a GP in the sort of circumstances which this doctor found himself in?'

A long pause. 'Never.'

'Thank you, Doctor. No further questions.' Brooks sat down quietly.

I looked at Harrap. He finished writing and looked up, his glasses perched on the end of his narrow nose. His eyes were hard, shrewd.

CHAPTER 15

'This next chap' said Brooks, tipping back in his chair dangerously, 'is likely to be difficult'.

We were sitting in the seedy little café across the road from the Royal Courts, and it was raining. Not proper rain, but that tedious all-enveloping drizzle that gets through macs and under umbrellas, and dampens spirits as much as it dampens clothes. I had a cup of instant coffee in an attempt to wake myself up after a sleepless night, but the others, perhaps wisely, had stuck to builder's tea. The coffee was unpleasant, but at least it was hot. I felt as though I needed a stiff drink as well to get my mind working. Nick and his 'carer' from the Local Medical Committee sat opposite me. She had contributed nothing to our case so far, and as far as I could tell, nothing to my doctor. My irritation at her presence flared. She just sat there in court, solid and stolid, her tweed suit betraying her personality and her lack of imagination. I wondered what Nick thought of her, and looked across at him. He must have been watching me, and, to my surprise, he winked. Ah ha. Observant man. He must have worked out what I was thinking and sympathised with it. The wink created a bond between us, and I felt cheered.

Brooks was speaking again. 'This chap comes with a formidable reputation as a witness. I've looked him up, and he isn't nearly as benign as he looks.'

'Who is he?' My doctor's alleged 'friend' Joan Withers spoke for the first time. She had a surprisingly low and melodious voice which betrayed her dowdy appearance. Perhaps there was more to her than I had thought.

'He,' Brooks spoke carefully 'is the GP's GP. He is recognised as one of the national authorities on primary care and its evolution. In fact, he's written one of the standard text books on the subject. He was a founder member of the Royal College of General Practitioners, became its president, got a knighthood, advises the Government, and so on and so on. You name it, he's done it. And surprisingly, you may think, despite all these honours and plaudits, he's said to be a wise and genuine man, with the common touch despite his eminence. Unlike,' and he grimaced theatrically, 'many other leaders of the medical profession. Some senior Royal College apparatchiks I have met have been so far up their own backsides as to be entirely intolerable. 'Inebriated with the pomposity of their own verbosity', as Benjamin Disraeli so aptly put it. Like senior military men who nobody ever says 'no' to, they have forgotten that they, too, are human. And are very often far removed from the reality of the coal face. But this chap, apparently, is not like that at all, so will be much less easy to undermine. We must watch him very carefully.'

'I've heard of him' Nick said, 'and read one of his books. It was called 'The Art of the Consultation'. I was an examiner for the RCGP for a while – the Royal College - years ago, and he was the vice president, and generally considered a wise man. I didn't know that he had become a hired gun.'

Brooks and I exchanged glances. Once again Nick Malenkov had surprised us with his knowledge of the legal jargons. 'Hired gun' is the derogatory phrase often used by lawyers to describe the regiment of expert witnesses who tour the courts of the country, tailoring their expert opinions to fit the set of circumstances which their instructing solicitor wants. There is a good living to be made, but there are quite stringent qualifications before you can become an expert witness.

First of all, you must be competent, somewhere near the top of your particular clinical tree. You must have a career that is, if not glittering, definitely well above average. You will probably have done some research, and published many papers. You will be regarded as an authority by your peers. Secondly, you must be able to perform, to be entirely plausible, in court. It is no good being a world authority on in-growing toenails if you mumble and look defensive when giving evidence about the best way to treat them. And you must be able to defend your position under cross examination which may range from sneering to aggressive. You must remain calm, not take offence at being severely criticised, and at having your expertise questioned.

But the real confusion about expert witnesses concerns their impartiality. They have a legal duty to the court, to give evidence that they believe to be true, but they have also been retained – and are paid by – one side in an argument about fact. So each side finds an expert whose views coincide with those of the person they are representing, and inevitably, human nature being what it is, such experts tend to be at the extreme ends of a debate. They are rarely people who understand compromise, or see both sides. Most solicitors like me keep lists of useful experts; people who we know can perform well, who impress juries and judges, and who will not be too easily swayed by the opinion of the expert on the other side. This is how they have come to have the name of 'hired guns'. They do and say what the person who pays them wants, just like the hired gunmen in the Wild West. And if they don't, the prosecutor will find another expert who will.

Brooks tipped his chair forward. Just in time, I thought. The vision of a barrister in his robes flat on his back on the floor of a greasy spoon made me smile.

'I have a feeling that this chap is one of the rare experts who is genuinely not a hired gun. I have searched for any weakness in his professional life or personality, and read some of the testimony he has given in the past. So far, I haven't come up with anything that hints at bias or weakness.' He smiled at my doctor. 'But don't despair. If he's as good as he is said to be, he'll be fair. And often, even the best expert gives one an opening. So – once more unto the breach, dear friends…!'

And we collected ourselves, put on our damp macs, picked up our bags, and trudged across the road into the Royal Courts. I took the opportunity to have another quick word with my doctor about my mum. I had rung the ward every day, but had the usual response that 'the doctors waiting for all the results before deciding what to do'. She was a bit better in herself, they said, after a blood transfusion.

He promised to ring the consultant who was in charge of her and let me know what he said. 'Don't get your hopes up too much,' he said, smiling down at me as we skirted behind a taxi. 'My instincts tell me that she has something significant going on. But whatever it is, we'll cope with it'. By 'we', I thought, he possibly meant 'you and I'.

*

Professor Sir Jim Cameron appeared to be a thoroughly nice man. Everything about him smacked of a friendly, homespun and trustworthy person. He wore his eminence and experience lightly; you could see him having a pint in his local with a farmer just as easily as he could discuss policy with a minister. He was one of those men who generated an aura of calm about them, one whom you instinctively liked and trusted. I could see exactly what Brooks meant when he had said that he would be dangerous.

He walked to the witness stand slowly, and took the oath in a deep and gentle voice, the sort of voice that would calm a panic attack or break bad news gently. He glanced at the judge, and his eyes smiled very slightly. I could see that he had already got him near, if not in, his pocket. He took in the whole court in a sweeping glance, ignoring my doctor, and then focussed his attention on the plaintiff's bench and Henry Doggart.

'Why do you think that this doctor failed in his duty of care to this patient, Professor?'

Once again Doggart cut straight to the chase, ignoring the usual process of building up his witness by taking him through his career and achievements. Cameron was in a class by himself, and he knew it, and he knew that the whole court knew it.

Professor Cameron paused for a long moment to gather his thoughts. 'A clever move', I thought. 'A true professional.' It added gravitas and thoughtfulness to what he would say, and focussed everyone's attention on him. I waited for the next trick in the book, the quiet voice, which would make the room become silent and ensure that everyone had to concentrate to hear him. A technique as old as public speaking itself, and always effective. Sure enough, the professor spoke with quiet authority, and the courtroom fell quiet in response.

'I have thought long and hard about the difficult situation that this doctor found himself in,' said Cameron. 'Although not exactly the same, I have had to deal with comparable circumstances myself. When a patient decides to reject the medical advice he has been given by a doctor, whoever that doctor is, and whether it is in hospital or at home, there is a duty of care that a doctor must continue to undertake.'

He paused to let his words sink in. He was saying, in effect, that even if a patient rejected advice, that a doctor of any kind, could not wash his hands of him. He still had to do his best for him in the altered circumstances of the patient's refusal.

'Take, for example, the obvious case of a severely mentally ill patient, a schizophrenic, for instance, who refuses to have his regular monthly antipsychotic injection. I think we can all agree that no doctor could or should take that refusal to be the end of his responsibility for the patient. The doctor knows, with some certainty, that the patient is likely to become severely ill without the treatment, so he should use every tool in his armoury to make sure that, either the patient is persuaded to change his mind, or, if that fails, that the patient comes to no harm. Agreed?'

Doggart nodded. So did nearly everyone else in the Court. I checked all the watching faces in the gallery. All eyes were on Cameron. He had us all in thrall.

'But', you may say, 'the schizophrenic has a mental illness that stops him thinking or behaving rationally, and we owe it to him to protect him from himself'. The Professor helped us along his line of argument. 'And you would be quite right. 'But what about the patient who does not have a mental illness, but who is just confused, or drunk, or stupid, or angry, or misinformed? What about the diabetic who declines to have his insulin injection, even though all conventional wisdom tells him that this, too, will make him very ill? Do we not owe him just as great a duty of care? Is it not up to us to use every, and I mean every, means we can think of to persuade him that he is at risk, at just as much risk as the schizophrenic, or the drunk in control of a car, or the mother who refuses to have her child vaccinated against meningitis? Each of those is putting themselves or someone else at risk, often at serious risk. A doctor who is contracted to care for such patients, as a GP is for a patient on his list, remains obligated to do his very best to reduce or remove that patient from the risk he can see, just as a man walking along a pavement is obligated to push someone out of the way if a brick is falling from a rooftop. I contend that this doctor, although he tried a bit, did not do nearly enough, not everything that he could have done for this patient.'

'And if the patient still refuses?' Doggart was trying to ask the questions which he knew would be asked by the defence.

'One of the greatest traps any doctor can fall into is to think that he and he alone is the only source of wisdom.' The professor had a clever way of answering questions by painting pictures of human or professional frailty. 'No doctor, however eminent or highly qualified, is perfect. No doctor should ever fail to call for a second opinion, to ask for advice, to request help, when his treatment or management is not successful. And that is exactly where this doctor failed. We only have his word for it that he spent an hour trying to persuade the patient to go back into hospital. The patient says he did not. The patient says that he was dismissive and disinterested. The patient denies absolutely the doctor's story that he offered to find a different hospital or a different consultant. Normally we would have some idea of what went on from the notes, but these', the Professor paused and looked directly at my doctor 'are, for some reason, missing. Perhaps conveniently'.

You could almost hear the communal intake of breath from the courtroom. That was below the belt, and Brooks was on his feet immediately.

'My Lord, I must protest most strongly. The witness is implying that somehow my client has a hand in the absence of the notes, when the exact opposite is true. My team and I have searched diligently for the notes, as we contend that they would vindicate my doctor. They are lost because of the failure of the NHS, and nothing else, and to suggest otherwise is malicious.'

He had underestimated the powerfulness of the professor's personality, and the great effect it had had on the court.

'That is for the Court to decide'. Mr Justice Harrap was dismissive. He had taken the bait.

I felt my heart sink. This was the great unfairness of the civil justice system. It was not just about what was true or false, what was right or wrong, what was good or bad. It was about who could make the best case, who was the most convincing in court, who could persuade and manipulate a judge most effectively. I cursed the inequity of it all, aware that all other systems of justice had just as many defects.

Brooks sat down reluctantly, obviously angered. He glanced at me and shrugged slightly.

'Putting the absence of the notes on one side,' Doggart knew when not to overplay a hand. 'What would you have done in these circumstances? What would be best practice?'

'As I was about to say,' - Cameron was smooth, aware that he had scored already - 'the most common weakness amongst doctors is their opinion of themselves. They tend to think that, where they have failed, no one else will succeed. The obvious thing for this doctor to do in this situation would be to get help. To ask another member of his practice to talk to the patient, or get a consultant to do a domiciliary, or to see if he could get another patient with Crohn's disease to talk to Mr Harrison. But to allow him to embark on a long car journey without notifying anyone, let alone arranging for a doctor to be alerted at the other end, that is far below the standard of care expected from a competent doctor. I would call it negligent.'

The dangerous word hung in the quiet air of the courtroom. 'Negligent'. The ultimate insult that a doctor can receive. I saw Nick flinch under the impact of the word, as though his face had been slapped.

Doggart knew how to quit when he was ahead, and sat down. He also knew that, by not spinning out his examination of his star witness, he was making sure that Brooks had to start his cross-examination straight away, without a lunchtime pause to gather his thoughts and prepare his arguments. Games-playing; another weakness inherent in all legal systems.

Brooks took as long as he could, but Mr Justice Harrap was not a very patient man.

'Mr Brooks; are you ready yet? Or do you have no questions you wish to ask this witness?' The unspoken implication was obvious. Harrap thought that that the professor's evidence was conclusive.

'Yes, My Lord. I do have some questions.'

'Well, get on with it then'. Harrap sounded Testy. My heart sank even further.

Brooks stood up, and addressed the professor across the courtroom. 'Professor, you stated that my client could and should have asked someone else, another doctor in his practice, perhaps, to try to persuade the patient to be readmitted. What if my client was a single-handed practitioner? He would not have a partner to ask, would he? '

'But he did have a partner, didn't he' said the professor. 'In fact he had several. And even if he was single handed, he could have got an urgent domiciliary from a consultant.'

No point in pursuing that.

'Why have you chosen to believe the patient about the commitment and interest of my doctor in his case, and not my doctor, who says he spent an hour trying to change Mr Harrison's mind, and when he couldn't, wrote a letter to the next doctor likely to see him, and later rang him up?'

'Well, he would say that, wouldn't he?' The professor sounded entirely reasonable. 'He's hardly likely to say he left after five minutes and did nothing.' It sounded obvious when put like that. I began to dislike the professor. 'And,' he added, unasked, 'I believe you have been unable to find the letter he alleges he wrote. It was said to have been given to the patient to hand on to his doctor in Newcastle, but no trace of it can be found, nor any record of the so-called phone call that is described. Telephone logs, both outgoing and incoming, are not difficult things to keep.'

Brooks tried one last time. 'But his unblemished record? His background as a senior doctor, accepted by the Royal College of which you were president, to be one of its examiners? Does all that count for nothing? Does that not make it clear to you that this is a competent doctor, and that to doubt his word, as you obviously do, is a slur without foundation?'

The Professor was unperturbed. 'In the Navy, a long service medal is often described as evidence that the recipient has got away with forty years of undiscovered crime. Just because no one has complained about a doctor does not mean that he is good or caring or competent. It just means that no one has complained.'

He paused before delivering the coup de grace. 'And I would remind you that the most dangerous doctor in the last hundred years, the most notorious mass murderer of modern times, Dr Harold Shipman, who probably killed two hundred and fifty of his patients deliberately, was a hugely popular doctor, venerated by patients, and respected by other doctors and by the police. Being nice, or clever, or popular does not exempt you from being incompetent.'

It was as vicious as it was unfair, but there was no answer to it. My heart sunk.

CHAPTER 16

My soon-to-be-ex-husband Richard rang the following day, the morning after the bad day for us, just after I got home after taking the children to nursery and school.

'I hear the mother-in-law has taken a tumble.' He had never liked my mother, and had not taken much trouble to conceal it. His mother, he had always implied, was in a different league. 'How is the old bat?'

'The old bat is not very well, Richard. She's in hospital having tests.'

'Oh well, it was bound to happen to her sooner or later after the sedentary life she's led in front of the telly.'

'Thank you for your sympathy. I'll tell her how concerned you are about her.'

He laughed nastily. 'She never liked me, either.'

'No, apparently with good reason.' He really was a shit.

This was getting us nowhere.

'So to what do I owe the honour of this call?' I tried to keep my tone civil.

'I wondered how far you'd got in thinking through my offer. And whether we can manage this entre-nous, so to speak, without washing our dirty linen in public. '

With the avalanche of pressures on me at the moment, I had put his brief mention of an offer, made on the doorstep some days ago, out of my mind. And I hadn't spoken to my solicitor about it. As usual, he had put me on the back foot.

'Richard, I'm afraid that I haven't put my mind to it all. Sorry.' Why did I need to apologise? Never explain, never apologise – the golden rule of the games player. 'And I haven't heard from my solicitor either, so I'm afraid I've nothing constructive to say at the moment. I'll chase the solicitor, and see what your offer is, and get back to you.'

'It's quite straight forward, really. A fifty-fifty split, with you buying me out of the house. As we are both good earners, there is no need to bargain about income.'

I suppose that I should have felt relieved that he wasn't trying to claim the house for himself, but something about his casual tone rang warning bells.

'And the children?'

'I thought a fixed sum monthly to cover their costs would be reasonable.'

So I would be saddled with a vastly increased mortgage, bringing up the children, balancing them with work, and all in return for an unspecified fixed sum for an unspecified length of time. It sounded a typical Richard ploy, plausible at first sight, but murky and ill-defined below the water. My mind started to think like a solicitor, running through the options and arguments for and against, and I had to pull myself up short with a jerk. I was a wife and mother in this situation, not a lawyer, and I must not, must not, confuse the two.

'Well, I suppose that is a starting point, but I'll need to look at the detail carefully, of course, and talk it through with my solicitor. As you know very well, Richard, the devil is always in the detail. And we haven't touched on the whole business of responsibility for the children. But I'll get on with it as soon as I can, I promise. And the most important thing is that we remain friends, or at least civil to each other, if only for the sake of the children. We both know how catastrophic the consequences are if the end of a marriage descends into open warfare.'

What on earth had made me say that? I was aware that there had been a slightly pleading tone in my voice, almost a supplication. Was I pleading for something else, in fact? Was I still searching for times past, for the relationship with the man I had married fifteen years ago? I must have loved him. In fact, I knew that I had loved him very much, admired his brain, worshipped his charisma and success, and adored his body and things that it did to mine. We had been so happy, exuberantly happy. Was I trying subliminally to recreate that relationship, that trust? So much love lost, so much happiness, joy, laughter, trust, intimacy, all sacrificed on the altar of a hard demanding inflexible world, and two characters who, for whatever reason, fell out of love with each other. So sad.

'Of course.' Richard's voice was sarcastic, and brought me back to reality, 'but don't forget that it was you that rejected me and my family. Get back to me as soon as you can be bothered.'

He put the phone down without waiting for a reply, preventing me from pointing out that it had been a mutual decision that he should move out, and that 'rejecting his family' had nothing at all to do with it, any more than his dislike of my mother had.

I thought for a long time after I put the phone down, sitting on the floor in the hall of the house in Islington with my back against the wall, trying to hide the fact that I was crying. The cat strolled coiling himself around my leg with his tail in the air, in faux affection. It wasn't really love, I thought, from the cat. Had it really been love from the husband, either? Or a combination of release from teenage constraint, lust, enjoyment, trophy hunting, escapism, and the exuberance of youth? It had not been all that long, just a few short years, before it became very apparent to me that his standards and behaviour, what I thought of as his ethos, were very different to mine, and that it was expected that I should change, not him. I suppose it was inevitable, therefore, that when I wouldn't change, or couldn't change, or couldn't change enough, that our lives would slowly separate, and that love would be lost. So sad; so very sad.

Eventually I creaked to my feet and pottered into the kitchen. I left a message with my solicitor about fixing a meeting to discuss Richard's offer, and another with the ward my mother was in sending her my love. Then I pulled myself together, figuratively straightening the seams of my stockings, as my mother would have said, collected my papers for the day, and, shoulders back, walked to the tube, to get on with the business of being a successful solicitor. The personal bit of me lay in a heap of muddle and misery behind the smart front door of the house in Islington.

CHAPTER 17

His Honour Mr Justice Stephen Harrap was not a malicious man by nature. He sat in the drawing room of his rather unattractive flat south of the River Thames, thinking about the woman who had preceded him as judge in his current case, and wondering what he ought to do about her. He had respected Dame Isobel Nicholson, and admired her gravitas, fairness and impartiality as a judge. He thought her judgements logically argued and cleverly written, and had secretly noted down some of her better phrases for future use in his own reports. So he wondered, as he sat in his chilly and rather anonymous drawing room, whether he ought to mark her passing in some way, or at least pay tribute to those who were close to her.

He was vaguely aware of his reputation as a cynic and a bully, and rather relished it. It set him apart from the usual run-of-the mill judges, the clever but occasionally complacent few who had climbed the steep steps of the legal profession and been deemed by Her Majesty's Lord Chancellor to be fit to deliver justice, not just argue for it on behalf of clients. When he had been in the ranks, working his way up, first as a jobbing barrister and then as a silk, specialising in family law, he had distanced himself from the friendships and social life of his chambers. It was partly because he was not very good at the desultory chatter of the coffee room, which he considered trivial, and partly because he simply was not very good at friendship. He knew, with some certainty, that he was not what others called 'clubbable'. Indeed, he considered the term rather derogatory. So from the start, he concentrated his mind and his skills on being a very competent lawyer rather than a friendly one. In his own mind, he justified this by reminding himself that friendliness did not win cases, while being a competent lawyer did. He forgot that lack of friends, or at least the inability to form friendships, could give the impression of haughtiness or disdain or arrogance. And also that it led to loneliness.

He occasionally, very rarely, allowed himself the luxury of self-analysis, and wondered, in a forensic sort of way, what it was that isolated him from the vast majority of his fellow humans, who seemed to get such pleasure from spending time in each other's company, and indulging in the meaningless chatter that he labelled gossip. He learnt mechanically that there were protocols and courtesies which society, or at least the society in which he moved, demanded be followed. When he attended Bencher's dinners in his Chambers, he struggled to obey these, aware that he categorised this behaviour under 'good manners' and 'being polite', things that his Edwardian father had held dear. He never realised that there is a world of difference between appearing self-contained and appearing rude.

His father, whom he had hated, had been an anachronism.

He was that most bizarre of English phenomena, a senior cleric who actually believed in and lived out the socialism of the Christian faith. He was very fond of quoting verbatim from the Sermon on the Mount, and using as an exemplar the phrase 'sell all that you have and give to the poor'. As a result, His Honour Mr Justice Harrap's childhood had been plain and joyless to the point of deprivation. All the simple things that other children got so much fun from were removed from him and passed on to the deserving poor. It did not take a highly intelligent child to realise that he was just as poor as most of the deserving poor, and in many ways, much poorer. The deserving poor, living in the noisy scruffy environment of their large and chaotic families and communities, made friends and had fun in a way that he could only imagine. He watched from a distance at Sunday School outings as the children of the deserving poor rushed into the sea at Bognor with screams of joy, while he sat, lonely and embarrassed in his corduroy shorts, at the top of the beach, a lonely child, constrained by his father's dog collar from joining in. But the socialism in which he had been brought up had left its mark, and he remained an active – devout was a word he avoided – supporter of the left wing and its principles.

*

After carefully considering all the options, as was his habit, he had written a carefully worded letter to Dame Isobel Nicholson's husband, the deputy leader of Newham Council, expressing his deep regrets and profound sympathies about her loss. He was surprised when, a few days later, he received a reply which did not just acknowledge his letter, but asked if Nicholson could meet for a few words and perhaps a drink to mark their mutual respect for his wife. He was surprised and a little touched by this. He knew something of Nicholson's background and activities in Newham, and recognised a fellow socialist, as well as someone who was outside the standard social circle of lawyers. It would be interesting to meet him, and, for the life of him, he could not think of a good reason to refuse the request.

So, a couple of weeks later, they sat opposite each other one evening, on each side of the 1950s' mock marble fireplace in the drawing room of the flat south of the River, each nursing a whiskey. Neither was much of a drinker, but each recognised that this was an occasion of some significance for both.

'Thank you for coming. It can't have been easy for you.'

Neither was particularly skilled at the niceties of social chit-chat and Harrap twisted the glass that he was holding in his hand as he spoke. He had lived alone for so many years that he had lost the art of entertaining. The cloak of the lonely man had settled on him, encasing him in the isolation and rigidity of his own routine. He had had to search for glasses before Nicholson arrived, eventually finding a set of cut glass whiskey tumblers that had been a present to his father by his parishioners on his retirement. The whiskey was from a bottle of Johnny Walker's that had been sitting unopened in his rather ugly nineteen eighty's sideboard for years.

Harrap let the silence settle for a few moments, searching for conventional words of sympathy.

'She was a remarkable woman. Greatly admired.'

Nicholson looked up at him. 'I know. I could never quite understand how we managed to be so happy together, with such different lives.'

There was no answer to that, so they sat again for a few moments, looking at their glasses.

Nicholson stirred. 'You are probably aware that I come from a very different world to the one that my wife and you inhabit – in her case, inhabited.' He paused. 'But she and I had a common goal, and I suspect we share it with you. The greater good, fairness and justice for everyone were the things that drove her. And they drive me too. Especially now.'

Harrap looked up and met the man's gaze. 'You know, I think we have a common theme there. I was brought up in a family that put service above everything, even, perhaps, above the needs of its individual members.' He smiled rather whimsically. 'But you and I both believe in striving for equality in how people are treated, you for the people you represent, I for the people I judge. So perhaps we are doing the same thing from different angles.'

'So what are you doing about my wife's case?' Nicholson asked. 'Her last case?'

'She left me excellent notes.' Harrap was aware that it would be improper to let on too much, but this man was the widower of a colleague, a mature senior Councillor, and he was entitled to know what she had left behind her. 'She was dealing with a litigant, a young man who had been let down by his GP. Or so he claims. She left a detailed account of the opening of the case and her impression of the first – and only - witness she heard. I have to take it on from there.'

'Keith Harrison, you mean? A young man with bad abdominal problems?'

Harrap looked up, surprised. He vaguely remembered from his papers that the litigant Harrison worked at Newham Council. Did Nicholson know him? Was it possible that Nicholson had some ulterior motive in coming to see him? He realised that he was on dangerous ground.

'Could be. Sounds as though it might be the same chap. If it is, of course, it goes without saying that we shouldn't discuss the case.'

'Of course. But if it is him, I know him. He is my right hand man, what you might call my PA. And a fine socialist and honest man, despite the traumas he has been through.'

Another pause. Harrap's sharp eyes appraised the man sitting opposite him. He knew a little of his reputation as a shrewd and crafty political operator, and of his ability to manipulate a situation for what he perceived to be a beneficial end. Harrap wondered if he was being quietly manipulated. He knew very well that Lady Isobel would have refused to be drawn on any case before her, even by her husband. But the litigant was another matter. Of course he would have told his boss about the court case. He sighed. Had he made a silly mistake in asking Nicholson here, however reasonable his motives?

He moved the discussion onto other matters, and they

chatted about a series of uncontentious and superficial issues until they could both safely feel that duty had been done, and they could put an end to this rather uncongenial meeting. But, as Nicholson was putting on his coat in the little entrance hall of the flat, the subject came up again.

'I'm sure you'll do the right thing by poor Harrison', Nicholson said. 'He's a sound colleague, and has been put through hell by what sounds like an unfeeling and very incompetent doctor. I'm sure that my wife would have known where the blame lies, not that we ever discussed it'.

'Of course,' Harrap murmured.

'The thing is, I feel duty bound to make sure that the case goes the right way. Isobel always fought the good fight, and she believed in taking care of the underdog. I would hate Harrison's life ruined by its outcome. I'm sure I can count on you as a man of the same principles as my wife and I to do the right thing.'

They shook hands, and Harrap watched as Nicholson walked down the stairs to the front entrance. The crease between his narrow eyes deepened as he walked slowly back into his flat. He didn't like being manipulated, didn't like it at all, but on the other hand, there was some truth in what Nicholson had said. Doctors were very good at covering their backs, just as all the professions were, he thought, and it was his job – in fact, his duty – to protect the underdog from their vested interests. It did not occur to him that he was a member of a profession as well, perhaps the second oldest one, and the one whose tentacles were perhaps most deeply entangled with power.

CHAPTER 18

"I'm afraid you mother has taken a bit of a turn for the worse.'
Nick's voice was calm and sympathetic when I took the call at
my desk. 'They rang me from the ward, as they knew I had
admitted her and would like to be kept informed. I nipped in
to see her before surgery this morning. I think it might be a
good idea if you could get down here sometime soon. There
are a few options to discuss and decisions to be made.'

'What do you mean?' I said, more sharply than I intended.

"Well, when someone of her age has something that threatens
her life as well as her independence, the people who care for her
need to know what she and those she loves feel to be in her best
interests.' He laughed, a bit cynically, I thought. 'Doctors are
always being accused of playing god and making DNR decisions
without asking anyone.' He paused. 'Sorry Antonia. That stands
for Do Not Resuscitate. So we need a guide from you about what
she might want. Taking instructions, in your language.'

There was a knock on my door, but I ignored it, and after a
few moments I heard footsteps walk away.

'Are you still there, Antonia?'

'I am. Are you telling me that she is dying?'

"No, but she is very ill, iller than she was when she came in, and we need to recognise that, and act accordingly."

I supressed my immediate emotional response and thought rapidly. I could get rid of most of the clients, but I'd have to get someone to stay with the children tonight and do the school run tomorrow. Richard was in New York at a conference. 'I'll be at the hospital by 7.00ish this evening. Will you be there?'

'I'll do my best. Depends on how many turn up at the afternoon surgery.'

'I'll see you then. And thank you for ringing.'

Why had I sounded so prickly? He had gone out of his way to help me, and all I had done was sound like one of his stroppy patients. And poor Mum. It had all been so sudden, and was now such a huge thing that was happening to her. She couldn't just die like that, without something being done. Or could she? Think about it rationally, woman. Of course she could. People died all the time. So it was up to me to make sure the best thing was done for her, the right thing. None of this feeble being sorry for myself as well as for her. Show some character.

I figuratively straightened my seams again, and began to reorganise my day so that I could leave early.

*

Nick was right. My mother was obviously much worse. She seemed to have shrunk and aged in the forty eight hours since I had last seen her. Her hair seemed much thinner, and her skin more translucent. She lay in the complicated hospital bed, surrounded by the paraphernalia of modern medicine, drips, machines that bleeped, electrodes on her chest, wires, oxygen masks, tubes disappearing under the sheets. Her eyes were shut and her breathing was shallow and irregular.

I sat down beside her and took her hand. She opened her eyes and gave me a tiny tired smile, and then closed them again, and seemed to be asleep. So, as there seemed to be nothing to do, I did nothing, but sat and watched her for a long time. A flood of memories jumbled into my mind; the soft, sepia-tinted memories of childhood; the mixed memories of the time when, as a teenager, I had realised that she was not the fount of all goodness, but was, like the rest of the world, capable of human frailty; the adult memories of a nice but ineffectual woman, soft as a marsh mallow, but always there for me, even in the bad times. And now, when a very bad time seemed to be looming, she suddenly, unaccountably, was not there for me. Or, at least, only a fragile shadow of the original person was still there. Bloody tears; catching me out again.

Nick walked into the ward. I saw the nurses at the nursing station smile at him and wave, and thought that they liked him. I wondered how often he came onto this ward to see his patients when they were dying.

'Hello.' The vivid eyes crinkled at me. 'You OK?'

'Yes, thank you.' I began to stand up, but he motioned me to stay seated. 'I'm sorry I sounded so – officious – on the phone this morning.'

'Not a problem. I just thought you were busy.' The eyes smiled again.

We both turned to look at the silent figure in the bed. She appeared to be sleeping.

'Is she unconscious?'

He was watching me. 'Do you mean 'is she so ill that she isn't able to wake up'?'

'I'm not sure what I mean. She seemed very dopey, and then just drifted off and didn't respond to me. But that could be painkillers, I suppose. Has something else gone wrong?'

'Probably not. But I think that the problem in her stomach may have turned into a bit of an avalanche, though.'

'So what can the doctors do?'

'Look…..' He started to reply, but as he did so, a new doctor I had not seen before walked up to the end of Mum's bed. She as a small Indian lady, so small, in fact, that she barely came up to my shoulders, and she was very beautiful. Her face had that benign gentleness about it that seemed to permeate the air around her, creating an island of calmness in the centre of the busy ward. Her skin was perfect, with a faintly coffee-coloured creaminess that was set off by her coal black eyes. So black were they that I could not see the irises from the pupils, and the kohl on her eyelids emphasised them. In startling contrast, the scarlet dot between her eyes indicated her Hindu background. A bit of my mind recalled that it was the bindi, which represented the third eye, the seat of concealed wisdom. Where on earth had I dredged that up from? Underneath her white coat she wore a vivid dark blue sari.

She was followed by a small retinue of what I supposed were junior doctors or students, and the ward sister marshalled them round the bed.

'Hello'. Her voice was low and the accent musical, almost sing-song. She held out a hand to shake mine, and I took it cautiously. It was so small that I feared I might break it.

'You are the daughter?'

'Yes. Her only daughter.'

She nodded and smiled at my doctor, who nodded back. They obviously knew each other.

'I am Dr Kahn. I am the oncologist who is in charge of managing your mother's cancer. Would you like to hear my plan for her treatment?'

'Cancer? I didn't know she had cancer? The doctor two days ago mentioned something going on in her tummy, but I had no idea it was cancer!' My mind whirled, and I looked helplessly at my doctor. He intervened.

'I expect that this has come as a big shock to Antonia, and there seems to have been a bit of a breakdown in communication about what is going on. Perhaps we could talk it through in private.'

'Of course.' Dr Kahn smiled gently again, and led us to a small office behind the nurse's station. There were piles of notes in it, and a couple of worn chairs. I perched on one, while Dr Kahn sat on the other. My doctor leant against the window ledge, his arms folded, and the retinue of junior doctors shuffled their feet outside the door. The Sister closed it gently, excluding them.

Dr Kahn smiled at me. Her eyes were very kind. I was struck by how many of these busy professionals seemed to have the ability to be nice to people, even though it was obvious that they were run off their feet. The words of the large lady in the

A&E department came back to me - 'the staff are lovely; they do their best.'

'I am afraid that it is often my unhappy task to be the bearer of bad news.' The slightly archaic phraseology and the accent reminded me of the Dr Aziz in 'A Passage to India'. One of my favourite films. 'You know that your mother came into hospital without a clear diagnosis, but once we had stabilised her, we could feel a mass in her abdomen, and an enlarged liver. She told us she has been losing weight for several months, she thinks, as her clothes had become lose.'

Why the hell hadn't she told me? And why the hell had I been such an uncaring pre-occupied daughter that I hadn't noticed? Guilt. Always guilt.

Dr Kahn went on. 'A scan showed what we suspected, that she has what is almost certainly cancer. It is possible, in fact probable, that it has come from her ovary, but I very much regret to tell you that it is very widespread, much too widespread to be removed by surgery.'

She spread her hands in a gesture of sympathy and support. My doctor shifted as he leant against the window. Behind him, in the alley outside the window, I caught a glimpse of a tired-looking middle aged man settling a rather racy looking bicycle helmet on his head. I noticed that the sign on the side of the helmet said 'Flash' in reflective letters. Then he took a pair of old fashioned bicycle clips out of his pocket, folded his trouser legs into them, and wheeled his bike, which had drop handlebars, out of sight round the corner. What was his function in this huge organism of a hospital, I wondered. What did he do?

I became aware of a silence in the room, and brought myself back to the present, embarrassed.

'Sorry. It's just that it's rather a shock. Are you telling me that my mother is dying?'

'Well', Dr Kahn lent forward. Our knees were nearly touching, and she placed her tiny hand on mine. 'Well, we are all dying, although at different rates. But the honest answer is, yes, your mother has a disease that is going to end her life sooner rather than later. The question we have to look at now is how much we should try to extend what life she has left. In other words, how intensively we should treat her. And that is something we need your help in deciding, although of course the final decision is up to her, if she is well enough to make it.'

And she sat back, the sari rustling as she moved.

'And you're sure that surgery isn't possible? Or radiotherapy or whatever it's called?'

'I'm afraid not.' The sing-song accent was very apparent now, and she moved her head sideways slightly. 'Her best chance is to get fit enough for chemotherapy. That may delay things, and improve her chances of survival by thirty per cent or so.'

My doctor cleared his throat and uncrossed his arms. He clearly wanted to say something, but could not decide whether to interrupt or not. We both looked at him.

'Er, yes,' I said. 'If that is the best treatment, of course she must have it.'

'Could we have a few minutes to think this through?' Nick couldn't contain himself any longer. 'These are big decisions, and my friend', he looked at me 'needs to know all the options.'

'Of course.' Dr Kahn's pager went off, and she glanced at it before silencing it. 'But please do not take too long. Your mother is very ill, and needs the chemotherapy soon if we are to help her live'. And she smiled again, a tired smile, and left us alone.

'Thank God they are able to give Mum some proper treatment after all.' I said, 'at least we can do something.'

My doctor took a big breath before answering.

'I wonder if it might be helpful to consider all the implications of treatment before you give the go-ahead. And of course, her view on what she wants is the most important thing.'

'OK. The specialist said that.'

'The only thing that modern medicine can do is extend her life a little. So we need to think about the quality of that life, and what she would have to go through in order to possibly get a few extra weeks or months, the thirty per cent Dr Kahn mentioned. OK so far?'

'Yes, I think so, but....?'

'We need to be clear what oncologist mean by 'delay things'. There is quite a lot if hidden meaning in that phrase, and you – and your mum - need to understand it.'

'Do I detect a hidden agenda here?' I had read about this in a Law Journal; the desire of doctors to treat people for reasons that were not necessarily for the benefit of the individual, but more to gather data and include as many people as possible in clinical trials. I had been reluctant to believe that it happened, but it seemed it might be happening to my mum.

'Not hidden,' Nick smiled tiredly, 'just very poorly communicated by us doctors. I believe, fairly passionately, that every patient has the absolute right to be fully informed about the benefits and also the disadvantages of any suggested treatment. I'm afraid that doctors still haven't grown out of the paternalism of medicine a generation ago – the 'doctor knows best' attitude. And what motivates doctors is not necessarily the same as what motivates patients. 'The treatment was a success but the patient died' is still an all too common consequence of enthusiasm for treatment.'

'Hang on'. My mind was whirling again. 'Give me a break. I just can't take all this in at once; you are talking about medical principles and I am worrying about my mum needing treatment.' I felt almost angry with him, raising all this now. Surely it was right that she had the best?

He smiled again. 'Sorry. Perhaps it's none of my business and I'm interfering too much.' And he looked at me apologetically. Perhaps he saw the confusion I was feeling, because he stood abruptly.

'Let's go and get some fresh air or a coffee, or something, and you can either tell me to get lost, or pick my brains about what to do for her best.' And he took my arm and steered me out of the horrid little room and down the ward.

The oncologist was at the foot of another bed with her retinue. I wondered if she was having to break more bad news. It must be a wearing job.

Nick nodded to her and smiled, and we walked out of the hospital in silence. He led me across a road to a little park that ran down to the edge of an inlet at the top of Chichester harbour, and we sat side by side on a bench watching a serene pair of swans drift effortlessly past, followed by a gaggle of slightly scruffy cygnets. A peaceful scene. My mind calmed down a bit.

He turned towards me. 'Recovering?'

'Yes, thanks. Better. It's all such a muddle. I thought that being ill was straightforward; you just did what the doctor said and got better. Or not, as the case may be.'

He laughed. 'Like the law. You just do what your solicitor tells you.' I smiled ruefully as I remembered how he had come to the first meeting with Brooks with his own ideas on how the case might be managed. 'But life is never as simple as that, is it? Or as clear. We are always faced with decisions, many of which we don't feel qualified to take. You are guiding me through your professional minefield with your skills, and I am there to help you through my mine. If you want me to.'

'I do. I can't think of anyone I'd rather have,' I said, and then, for the first time for many years, I blushed, a schoolgirl blush.

'Right.' He went into professional mode, just a slight change in tone and expression that I recognised in myself. 'There are significant things we need to be clear about before we let the full force of modern medicine loose on your mother. 'Let's look at them in order.' He ticked off his points on the fingers of his left hand. I noted – irrelevantly - that the wedding ring had gone but the white skin where it had been was still discernible.

'First of all, I want you to be clear in your mind what 'a good outcome' means. In hospital terms, it means getting your mother fit enough to go home, fit enough for chemotherapy, and perhaps prolonging her life by a few weeks or months. But there are several aspects of that which need thinking through. As Dr Kahn, who is a lovely person, said as gently as she could, she has a terminal disease, something that is going to end her life sooner rather than later. The only thing that modern medicine can do is extend her life a little. But in doing so, it may – will – reduce that quality of life very significantly. Chemotherapy is a poison, which kills normal cells as well as cancer cells, and often – usually – makes people miserably ill during treatment. We all know about losing one's hair, having less immunity, and so on.'

'OK.'

'So we need to be clear about the quality of the extra life we might be giving her, and balance that against the misery of the treatment.'

'Yes, I can appreciate that.'

'Secondly, we need to understand the figures you were quoted, the thirty per cent increase in survival. That can mean several things. It may mean that she will live thirty percent longer than she otherwise would. But it usually means that thirty per cent of people respond to chemo, and get some extra time, but that, of course, means that seventy per cent get little or no extra life, yet still have all the misery of the treatment. Their final days, in fact, are made worse by the treatment, with no gain at all. '

'Wow. I'd never thought of it like that.' The thought of my mum enduring the misery of chemo brought tears to my eyes.

How would she cope? How would I cope with her?

'Nor do most people. Or doctors.' He smiled. 'Just the same debate applies to lots of medical treatment, such as raised blood pressure, for instance. You have to treat a hundred people to help one or two not have a stroke or a heart attack. It's called the NNT, the number of people you need to treat for one person to get a benefit.'

'Please don't confuse me with statistics. I was hopeless at maths at school. But I can understand that some people – lots of people – aren't helped by treatment, and are made worse by it. But surely you must treat everyone in case they get benefit?'

'Of course, if they want it, and properly understand the down side.'

We sat in silence for a minute or two. I thought of mum, lying in bed, so vulnerable.

'So you are telling me, if I understand it, that if we agree for her to have intensive and possibly unpleasant treatment, there is only a one in three chance of it benefiting it at all, and it may disadvantage her without any benefit. True?'

He held my gaze. 'True.'

'And the benefit may only be for a short time?'

'Also true. Back to the thirty per cent figure again. If she has three months to live, treatment might only give her an extra month. If she only has a month to live, you would be putting her through fierce treatment for just an extra ten days.'

'What would you do?'

'Everyone asks that'. He laughed gently. 'You will have gathered that I am deeply ambivalent about some of what we do in the name of prolonging life. Of course there are marvellous treatments – heart and kidney transplants, repairing leaking aortas, and so on. When I was a junior doctor, all children with leukaemia died within two years; now nearly all of them have a normal life span and live to a ripe old age. An amazing technical achievement – a modern medical miracle, as the Press would say. But it is very different talking about someone who is thirty, or even sixty, who has cancer, and someone in your mother's situation, in the last stage of life. This is how people have died in the past, of an overwhelming disease at the end of their lives. We used to accept this, but now we have developed techniques that defer that end, often at huge cost to the dignity and quality of life of the individual. The law of diminishing returns applies. We do more and more for less and less benefit, and risk forgetting that quality of life, in old age, is at least as important as quantity.'

I sighed. 'I understand all that. It just seems so hard to let her go without doing anything. She's still Mum. She knows who I am and where she is.'

He waited in silence while two mums with toddlers strolled by chatting, pushing baby buggies. So carefree and happy, I thought. At the start of life. One of the toddlers ran towards the cygnets, which had settled on the shore. The mother swan hissed vigorously and raised her wings defensively, and the child sat down with a bump and burst into tears. A mother ran to the rescue.

'Put yourself in her shoes. Try to imagine what she would be feeling in this situation. After all, it is her life, her illness', he said very quietly. 'Most of us say we want the very best for our nearest and dearest, but sometimes the very best might be accepting with her or for her that she has an illness that is bringing her life to an end, and coming to terms with that. Now, because of the wonders of medicine, we can defer the time we die for a while, length undetermined, but that comes at a cost. Although we might stop her dying soon, we can only put off the day when it will surely happen. We cannot give her back her health or her independence.'

He paused, and sighed again. I wondered if he had been through the same debate with someone he loved.

'There is an aphorism in medicine that "in some cases, modern medicine does not so much prolong life as prolong death." That is what I am encouraging you to think about. If she is the sort of person who wants to battle on bravely, to take every opportunity to live longer whatever the odds, fine, go for it. Have the chemo, encourage her to confront what she will have to face, and help her through it. But if she is someone who has had a long and good life, and who will be upset by indignity and dependence and loss of control, think hard about allowing us doctors to extend her life, a life that would be much less pleasant and meaningful.'

He stopped, and we sat silently looking at the dappled water in front of us, while the enormity of what he had said sank in. The sun came out from behind the clouds. The swans took to the water again and glided out into a patch of sunshine.

'Sorry to confront you with this,' he said. 'I've probably interfered far too much. It is her life, and you owe it to her to help her reach the decision that suits her best.'

I watched the toddlers run about aimlessly, and thought of my mother. Fussy, prim, lonely. Her husband, her *raison d'etre*, long gone. Her world had closed in over the last few years, as her mobility and interests had waned. She had lost her joie de vivre. Apart from the grandchildren, there was little that interested her, and she saw them only rarely. She existed now, rather than lived. The last time I had seen her well, several months ago, she had raised the subject herself in a roundabout way.

'I think I'm just waiting to join your father now, dear', she had said, as I brought her a cup of tea. The TV was on with the sound turned down, one of those interminable afternoon programmes about escaping to an ideal house somewhere. The carriage clocked ticked away on the mantelpiece, and I took in the piles of magazines that seemed to be the only interest she had now. She had never wanted to move nearer to me, away from the home she had shared with Dad. 'I'm in God's waiting room. Never put me in one of those ghastly homes. You know, like the ones like Auntie Maggy was in. Rows and rows of gaga old people being kept alive by pills and waiting to die. Don't you ever let me go to one of those.' And she had laughed , a little shrilly. I thought then that I knew what she meant. The loss of independence, of control, of continence, of coherent thought, were things that I would dread just as much as she did. But unlike her, though, I didn't have the warm blanket of a religious faith to act as a comforter, and in some ways I thought that this must make things easier for her, having the confidence that she would go on to something better. I was frightened of dying, both the process, which could not be much fun, but more of the fact of not being there, of ceasing to exist. I had always reassured myself that it could not be any worse than the lack of existences before one was born, but that still didn't make the idea any easier. But for Mum, the concept definitely wasn't one to be frightened of, and if that was the case, I was obligated to try to work out what she would want in these circumstances.

I looked at Nick, at the vivid blue eyes. They were watching me curiously.

'I think – in fact I'm sure that I know what she would have wanted if she had been able to decide for herself.'

'Which was?'

'She would have hated having to be cared for. She dreaded incapacity, loss of independence, nursing homes. She told me so firmly only a few months ago. She said that she was ready to join my father.'

'Did she ever write that down? Make a living will?'

'She saw her solicitor last month, but she didn't say why. She may have thought it would have upset me if she was making a living will, especially in view of what I've been going through.'

His eyebrows went up in an unspoken question, and I realised with a little shock that he actually did not know anything about my miserable husband and my miserable marriage and my miserable impending divorce. I had been so careful to hide behind my professional persona that I had forgotten that this was my secret. I felt an overwhelming desire to tell him all about it, to let him reassure me and protect me from the slings and arrows of outrageous fortune that seemed to coming at me from all sides. I felt small and alone and a bit frightened.

I must have shown something of this, as he put his hand gently on my arm and left it there, without saying anything. After what seemed a long time, I put my own hand on top of his. We sat like that for several minutes, my mind whirling from subject to subject – my mother; her wishes; what to do for the best; the children; and the hand on my arm beneath my hand.

*

I bumped into Dr Kahn and her retinue as I went back to the ward to see if I could talk to Mum. Nick had gone back to his busy surgery, and anyway, he said, it was none of his business to discuss this with her, or even to listen to the conversation. I knew that this was true, but still wished he was there.

Dr Kahn paused in the corridor, smiled her gentle smile at me.

'So?'

'So.' I took a deep breath. 'I've thought very hard about what you said, and what I think my mother would want, and I was just going back to see her to confirm that I am right.'

The smile remained unchanged, and the black eyes looked into mine.

'I think,' the small melodious voice said, 'that you are telling me that she will not want treatment from me.'

'Yes, I think that is what she will decide.'

'It must be her decision, not yours. But you know that. I

think that you are a good daughter, and are trying to do what you think is best for your mother, but the law is clear on this – it has to be her decision, if she can still make it.'

'I understand that.'

'Unless, of course, she has written down her instructions for what she wants, what some people call a living will.'

'I understand that too. I'll find out if she made one. I know who her solicitor is.'

'Well then.' Dr Kahn nodded, and began to move away. Then she paused and turned back, and her face was very kind.

'You only lose what you cling to. The Buddha said that. If she wants to go, you must let her go.' She touched my arm, then turned and walked away, tiny steps, the sari rustling.

I felt hot tears behind my eyes. Such kindness, such understanding. Perhaps it was true, medicine truly was a calling.

CHAPTER 19

I tried to ring my mother's solicitor as soon as I could, but of course his office was shut. I spent a long time at her little house, going through piles of paper, hoping against hope that I would find, in the heaps of letters from old friends and old bank statements, something that would satisfy the demand for a clear instruction, a statement of intent about how she wished to a major illness to be managed. But as I searched, I knew the chances of finding such a directive were slim. My mother was of a generation that trusted to the collective wisdom of the professionals, and regarded the words of her doctor or bank manager with awe. 'Of course we'll do what the vicar thinks is best, dear' is the kind of remark that she would have made. So the possibility of finding that she had thought for herself about how to deal with moral dilemmas was remote, and, even more remote, that she had formally written it down.

After several fruitless hours of sifting through piles of old photographs, mementos of my father, and the other detritus of a long life, I gave up. I wandered round her small garden, and noticed that it was very un-kept. There were weeds between the paving slabs on her back patio, and lots of the pot plants hadn't been watered for many weeks. Her problem had obviously been coming on for ages, but I, obsessed with my own worries, had been too self-absorbed to notice. Her bed was still unmade from the day she was admitted to hospital, and her dressing gown still hung on the back of the bedroom door. I pulled the chintzy bed-cover up over the sheets with a sense of almost overwhelming guilt. What a failure of a daughter I had been. The black and white photo of my father, smoking his pipe, sat in its silver frame by the bedside table. I noticed that she had stuck a small photo into one corner of the frame. It was of me.

I drove back to London much later that evening in the pouring rain, my mind a mass of confused thoughts. It was late, and the traffic was light, so it was before midnight when I parked outside the house in Islington, and got out and stretched my back, stiff from driving. It was still bucketing down, and I pulled my mac more closely around me. It was an old one of my mother's that I had picked up from her house, as it had been fine when I left London, and my own smart raincoat was safe on its hanger in the cloakroom at home. The mac smelt of gardens and of her. There was a piece of garden twine in one pocket. I parked the car opposite the house and got out, reaching into the passenger foot well for my handbag. As I reached across for it, I noticed that the little gate to our tiny front garden – 'the dog patch' as my almost ex-husband called it – was open. And there was a figure standing on the path, the face hidden by a hoody. He was standing stock still, looking at the front door.

Suddenly, I was alert. And frightened. Burglars. I felt in

my bag for the rape alarm I always kept there, struggling to find it underneath purse, keys, phone, make-up bag, and all the other rubbish that I, like most woman, found it necessary to cart around with me. There it was. But how old was it? Was the battery flat?

What to do? Call for help? Run away? Confront him? The police advice about avoiding confrontation came to my mind, and how it was taking a stupid risk, and asking for a knife wound. But the street was quiet, no one about. Should I just let the dark figure get away? And get away with it? All my instincts told me not to be a weak woman, but to do what my career had trained me for, confront injustice. I took a step towards the gate, unsure what to do.

But the decision was taken away from me. The dark figure turned, caught sight of me, and hurried through the gate towards me, brushing past me as I walked from the car, almost knocking me off my feet. I felt a hand push hard at me, and the thought 'my god, I'm going to be stabbed' flashed through my mind. But there was no pain, no blow, nothing. Not even a grab at my handbag. As the figure rushed by me, I caught a glimpse of a face half-hidden under the hood, a lock of long hair concealing most of it in the dim light from the street lights. A woman. I was sure, almost sure, that it was a woman. A druggie, after a quick burglary? A rough sleeper, looking for an empty house to sleep in out of the rain? I looked after the running figure as her footsteps echoed down the street away from me, in and out of the lights of the streetlamps. She had knocked the rape alarm out of my hand, and I bent to pick it up, my hand shaking as it scrabbled for it in the gravel of the front path.

I struggled with the front door key, and, once inside, slammed it shut behind me, and leant against it. Fear produces such a big physical reaction, and I waited, panting, until my breathing calmed down. Should I ring the police? A waste of time; nothing had actually happened, and they would put me as another anxious woman. The children were at Richard's, so at least they were safe. Probably just a drug addict, out for a quick break in to satisfy a habit.

I made myself a cup of tea and went to bed. I made sure to set the burglar alarm, but sleep took a long time to come.

CHAPTER 20

It is interesting to try to analyse the tendency we have to like or dislike someone instinctively at the first moment of meeting them. It is a curious phenomenon, and deep rooted. It is not obviously based on any single attribute or characteristic or behaviour pattern, although there are a few notable exceptions to that rule. You may, for instance, have an aversion to very fat people, or feel automatically intimidated by someone who is very tall, or who is very saturnine. You may feel comfortable with someone who is shorter than you, or the same ethnic group. But these are generalisations, and take no account of the way a person may look or walk or behave or speak. But simple things, such as bearing, gaze, expression, attitude often seem enough to tip one into an almost instant like, dislike, or wary watchfulness. Circumstances obviously play a part in this opinion forming; you are unlikely to instinctively like someone you find in your bedroom with a knife in his hand, and you may well want to hug the doctor who tells you that you haven't got cancer. But these situations do not really explain the instinctive feeling we are aware of when we first clap eyes on an individual.

It was undoubtedly circumstances which made me instinctively dislike Mr Keith Harrison, although there was something about him that made me fairly sure that I would not have liked him even if I had met him in entirely neutral circumstances – at a party, for instance, or standing next to him in a bus queue. I watched him come into Court two days later, and was struck how disinterested he looked, how distant. His pale eyes looked round, taking in all the runners and riders, and caught my eye. He seemed to look through me rather than at me, and his expression did not change one iota. He was one of those individuals who it was impossible to sum up from their expression, as he simply did not have one. He walked slowly to the witness stand with just the hint of a limp. Gwen had coached him well. I could just hear her: 'Don't over act; just make everyone aware that you have suffered.' He affirmed that he would tell the whole truth, rather than taking the religious oath. Given what I had learnt about his politics, I would have surprised me if he had done otherwise. His voice was thin and high-pitched, with a hint of east end about the glottal stops. That did not surprise me either. Political correctness in those of his persuasion often requires a degree in working class assimilation. Received BBC or Oxford English would have been a betrayal.

He looked at his interlocutor, the pale eyes expressionless. I could not fathom what he was feeling. Most people are scared witless when giving evidence of any kind, let alone in the High Court, especially when, as in his case, a great deal hung on the outcome. It wasn't just financial gain or reward for what he had suffered that he was after, but justification for all the prejudices that drove him and his views. He betrayed none of the stress that usually came with all this, and stood, a pale tall figure, ready to give his version of what had happened all those years ago, and who was to blame. I noticed Mr Justice Harrap watching him closely, the narrow eyes penetrating.

Henry Doggert QC took his time. He carefully arranged his notes in front of him, took a sip of water, adjusted his references files, and cleared his throat. Finally, just as I was getting really impatient with his performance, he tucked his hands into the lapels of his gown, and looked at Harrison.

'Mr Harrison, I want you to take your time in answering the questions I shall put to you. You know that a lot hangs on what you say, and I want you to be absolutely certain that your answers are accurate and clear. If you don't know the answer to a question, don't be afraid to say so.'

The sandy head nodded, the face expressionless. Doggert, I knew, was laying the ground for his client to be considered as absolutely truthful.

'You have been through, and are still going through, a very traumatic period of ill health, are you not?' More groundwork being done, to ensure that everyone knew how much the poor man was suffering because of my doctor's failure.

'Yes'. The voice was quiet, weak, reedy. He had been well coached in how to demonstrate suffering, I thought. Even Harrap might fall for it. He did.

'In view of your ill health, Mr Harrison, would you like to sit to give your evidence?', the judge said.

'You're very kind, Your Lordship. That would be a great help'.

I ground my teeth in fury. This was games playing of a high order. I had seen Harrison walk briskly away from the Court a couple of days before, his girlfriend by his side, her long hair swinging. His girlfriend.... A train of thought started at the back of my mind, but got nowhere, and was interrupted anyway by Doggert.

'Now, Mr Harrison, would you take us through your early life, before all this started, so that the Court can get a picture of who you are and what your life was like.'

Keith Harrison drew a slow breath, and, with only a little prompting from Doggert, took us all through his profoundly ordinary childhood and adolescence. I could see where he got his antipathy to the world from. His parents sounded a nightmare. Conventional was far too weak a word to describe their behaviour. They sounded like the ultimate working class pillars of society. You could just see his father tipping his cloth cap to any passing squire, and his mother's interests were focussed on royal infants to the exclusion of her own child. They had been born into the pre-war class system, apparently, and felt safe and secure remaining in it. They were deeply upset by their only son's rejection of their standards, and his desire to change, even overthrow, the present system. For them, a regular job, however menial or boring, meant safety, security, and a hierarchy that they understood and trusted to last. They lacked, apparently, even the slightest traces of ambition.

So when Keith went first to the grammar school and

then into a red brick university, their pride was mixed with a sort of fearfulness that he was lifting the lid of a Pandora's Box of uncertainty and insecurity. The industrial mayhem of the nineteen sixties and seventies had just taken place, with mass closures and redundancies, and the new world of the Wilsonian technological revolution was the future. They found Keith's brand of mildly revolutionary socialism difficult to comprehend, and he, in turn, resented and rejected their solid unexciting conservative lives. The regularity with which he changed jobs, and the ridicule in which he held figures that they revered built a widening gulf between them.

All this Doggert extracted from him with smooth skill, making us aware of the pressures and conflicts which had formed his character and opinions. I almost felt sorry for the man, caught as he was between his background and the new world he had entered by dint of being cleverer than his parents. But then I pulled myself up with a start, and realised that I had fallen into the trap that Doggert had laid, of providing a rationale, an excuse for any perceived malice in his subsequent behaviour. Crafty sod.

We moved onto the events of the week before he was admitted to hospital.

'Did you feel satisfied with the way the doctor managed your first consultation' Doggert asked innocently.

'Well, of course, I had to fight to get an appointment'. I felt my doctor shift restlessly beside me. 'And he was brusque and disinterested' Again my doctor shifted.

'What do you mean by that?'

'Well, he just prodded me about a bit and ordered some tests. He didn't make any attempt to explain what it might be. I don't think he cared very much, but doctors don't, do they?'

Brook, our barrister, half rose to his feet, but then sat down again, and scribbled in his legal notebook. 'Sensible', I thought. 'No point in objecting now. Take him to pieces in cross examination'.

'And then what happened?'

'I had the blood tests – obviously. The doctor didn't bother to ring me with the results, of course. I got really bad during the week, and after another fight, I saw him again on Friday, and he arranged for me to go into hospital.'

'We'll pause there, if we may', Doggert said smoothly. 'My Lord, you may be aware that the performance of the hospital in caring for my client is the subject of another hearing, alleging incompetence and lack of duty of care by the Hospital Trust and its employee doctors. May I suggest that we move, therefore, to the next occasion when my client was under the care of this doctor.'

This time, Brook rose smartly to his feet. 'Not so easily done, My Lord. The alleged failure of the hospital has a direct bearing on this hearing in several ways. My learned friend is aware of this, and in glossing it over, is at risk of misleading the Court.'

This is nearly the most insulting thing one barrister can say in public about another. Barristers have two obligations. The first, obviously, is to do the best for their client. But the second obligation is to the Court, to do the right thing in the eyes of the law. All barristers are so-called officers of the Court, and to say that a colleague is deliberately misleading a judge is tantamount to pistols at dawn.

Doggert bristled.

'It is no such thing.'

'My Lord, may I be allowed to explain why I submit that it is?' Crafty chap. By asking if he could explain, he opened the door to Harrap declining to hear him, and therefore laying himself open to the accusation of not hearing all the relevant details. This would be a strong argument for an appeal if the case went against us. Brooks knew this, and Doggert knew it as well. So did Mr Justice Harrap. It only took him a moment to make up his mind.

'If it bears directly on this hearing, we must, of course, hear it. Unless, Mr Doggert, you have cogent reasons to argue that it has no such bearing.' He looked at Doggert enquiringly, who fumed quietly, but remained seated.

'In that case, Mr Brooks......'

'My Lord, to put it in a nutshell, the plaintiff Mr Harrison discharged himself from hospital against medical advice after an admission of nearly four weeks, and returned home. He then summoned my client to visit him, and declined to follow his strong advice to be readmitted, either to the same hospital or indeed to any other hospital. The central plank of his complaint against my client is that he, the doctor, did not make it clear to him how ill he was, or try hard enough to persuade him to be readmitted. So the details of the hospital admission, and the physical and psychological effects it had on Mr Harrison, are of crucial, one might say central, importance to this hearing.

Furthermore, the hospital staff, in trying to persuade him not to discharge himself against their advice, will inevitably made him aware of the risks and consequences. So to say that the plaintiff lacked explanation is simply untrue.'

He sat down.

'Mr Doggert?'

Doggert hauled himself to his feet. 'The duty of a doctor, and the actions he takes, My Lord, depend on the clinical situation in front of him, not on what has gone before. A doctor presented with a stab wound treats the wound, he does not agonise about what led up to it'.

'Hardly a relevant analogy, Mr Doggert'. Harrap was fierce when he wished to be. 'In fact, of no relevance at all in the light of what I have heard from Mr Brooks. We will hear evidence on the hospital admission. But not today, I fear. In view of the rapidity with which I was – ah – parachuted,' a thin smile 'into this hearing, it was inevitable that I had unavoidable commitments in other Courts. One of those has to take precedence over this one, and we will therefore adjourn for seven days. I know this is inconvenient, but I am afraid it is not avoidable, or, indeed, open to debate'.

Doggert busied himself with his papers, and Gwen Richardson, solicitor to the stars, harrumphed audibly, earning a direct look from the judge. Nick caught my eye, and I smiled at him to encourage him. His eyes crinkled a little at the edges in return. He knew better than I how significant this was. It helped us in two ways: by giving us time to work out how to demonstrate that Harrison's frame of mind and behaviour was influenced by his experience in hospital, and by putting the whole story before the judge, showing how the hospital's cock-ups had influenced him. If only we had the clinical notes, the key to the whole situation. Bloody NHS, incapable of keeping track of its own records.

Little did I know how much the adjournment would affect me personally as well.

CHAPTER 21

My mother's solicitor was that rare and threatened creature, the old-fashioned family lawyer. The sort of solicitor who we all need to help us through the jungle of making a will, winding up an estate, becoming a family trustee, or getting a divorce. He might not be the sharpest knife in the box, but if asked, he would probably know where to find a sharp knife, and how to access him. Or her. He was a sort of legal version of that other dying breed, the family doctor. Both were professionals who knew you and probably your family as well, and understood the dynamics of your life and your needs. They are – or were – sensible, wise, and above all, available. Both have been superseded by a new breed of professional; younger, technically more proficient, more mobile, more impersonal. I knew with some sadness that I fell into the latter category, even though my heart yearned in a vague sort of way to be the former. But life-style and career and success and ambition simply didn't allow for that. You couldn't be an old fashioned solicitor in a London practice.

I had rung him that morning after digging out his details from Mum's address book. He had offered to see me, but there didn't seem much point in dragging all the way down to Sussex just to find out if she had made a living will. He would be able to tell me that over the phone. He was understandably reluctant to talk about it at first; 'data protection, and all that', he said. But as soon as he had established that I was who I said that I was, and that I was Mum's next of kin, he was helpful.

'I'll dig out her file. I'm almost certain that it was a living will that she came to see me some time ago, not her ordinary will. But I'll have to see it to be absolutely sure. It will be in my storage room. I'll get it out and ring you back. Would you mind if it was this evening? I've got to work late for once.'

'Not at all. I don't usually get home myself till late, and I'm in the middle of a court case that needs a load of research, so ring whenever is convenient for you.'

I heard him laugh down the phone, a nice laugh. 'You bright young London solicitors all work far too hard. I couldn't keep pace with you – far too old.'

So as I walked home from the tube station that evening, my mobile rang.

'Yes, your mother has definitely made an advance directive. She executed one last year, after your father died. I think she was becoming aware that *anno domini* was catching up with her. I know the feeling.' I heard him chuckle again down the phone. 'She was very particular about covering issues that she felt were important, things like not wanting treatment just to keep her alive in the event of a disease that would inevitably be fatal, and not being resuscitated if that would lead to a life in a nursing home.'

'She had always dreaded going into a home,' I said. 'In fact, she made me promise that it would never happen.' I thought of Mum lying in her hospital bed. 'A promise easily made and difficult to keep.'

'We must always remember that anyone has the right to change their mind when confronted with the reality of the last phase of their life,' he said thoughtfully. 'Not that you'll need reminding of that. The point of the directive is to give an indication, a broad-brush outline if you like, of what she would want to happen if she couldn't make the decisions herself.'

'Thank you. That's really helpful, and it sounds as though her directive answers a lot of questions. I wonder if you could fax or email it to me, so I can show it to the hospital doctors, and I gave him my office number.

'I'm very sorry to hear that she's so ill,' he said finally. 'She and your father have been clients of mine for many years, and it has always been a pleasure to see her. Like lots of longstanding clients, we became friends. Let me know if there is anything else I can do.' And he rang off.

*

I walked on through the dark streets to the house in Islington. My footsteps echoed on the pavements. It was raining, that slow insistent London rain that soaks your feet and drips down your collar. I was still wearing my mother's tatty old mac, and it hadn't been reproofed in years, so that it absorbed the rain like a sponge. I felt cold and miserable. My mind had been a blur of facts and unanswerable questions: how to undermine the plaintiff's convincing story; how to demonstrate his bias against my doctor; how to explain to Rupert, a toddler, that Richard and I were probably parting for good; and how to do what was best for Mum.

Suddenly I had an eerie feeling that I was being followed. My footsteps echoed just a little too late as I walked, and I was aware of the hairs on the back of my neck rising. Someone was behind me, keeping pace with me, stalking me.

It is curious what fear does to people. Some people freeze. Some people run. Many people scream. It tends to make me angry, just as it had when the rough sleeper had been in the garden last week. Why should anyone, whoever they are, have the right, the sheer effrontery, to make me frightened? To interfere with my peace of mind, my equanimity? Bastard. How dare they?

I whirled round, ready to confront whoever it was, to deal with the mugger or the rapist, or the man with the balaclava and the knife. The street stared back at me silent and empty. A dark cat ran across the pavement fifty yards away, its belly almost touching the paving stones. I turned and walked on slowly, listening. After a few paces, I whirled round again. Just at the corner of my vision, in the darkened patch of road in between two street lights, I glimpsed a movement, the hint of a figure receding into an unlit doorway. So there was someone there. And if they were there, and did not want me to see them, they must be up to no good. Only logical.

What to do? My house and its safety were a hundred yards

further up the street. Someone could easily catch up with me before I reached it, especially as I couldn't run in these blasted heels. Bang on the nearest door? He could get to me and be long gone before anyone came to the door. Confront him?

Down the street, a figure emerged from the shadows and started to walk hesitantly towards me. I braced myself, but some of the fear receded; surely, if he was going to kill me, he would have at least hurried towards me, not taken small hesitant steps, as this figure was doing? And, come to think of it, it wasn't a very big figure; tall, but slim; almost skinny. Unless he had a knife, I would be able to give at least as good as I got. I tightened my grip on my bag, ready to swing it at him with all my force.

As the figure came into the cone of light cast by a street lamp, I could see that it wasn't a him at all. It was a girl, a tall skinny girl, her face hidden by a hood with a fur rim round it. There was something in the way that she moved that seemed familiar, that struck some chord at the back of my mind. Was it the same figure who had been in my front garden a few days before? It was! I was sure of it.

Her progress became more hesitant as she came closer to me, and the palpitating fear that I had felt at first receded. It was replaced with resentment. Who the hell was this, scaring the shit out of me late in the evening, after the day I'd had? Bitch! I started to form a scathing sentence in my mind, with just the right touch of vitriol. I'd tell her!

Suddenly, when she was about ten yards away, she started to run towards me. I backed away, all my new found bravery dissipated by the quickness of her movement. She came straight at me, and I ducked my head away from the expected punch or stab. I was about to be mugged, I thought. This can't be happening.

But the blow did not come, and as she came close I saw her face for the first time. Pale, sallow, a fringe of hair almost concealing her features. At the same instant that I realised this, she banged into me, seeming to grab my shoulder, and I flinched, expecting a blow. Then she was gone, feet pattering rapidly down my street. The figure momentarily reappeared as it ran beneath the street lamps, until it disappeared round the corner, and I was left, breathless and shaken. Then I turned and ran; ran to my home, as though the devil himself was after me. There was a pattern to this. It was the second time some girl had lunged at me. What the hell was going on?

The front door slammed behind me, and I leant against it, breathless. Then the phone rang, shattering the silence.

Insistent, urgent. It was the hospital again. Mum was fully conscious now, but failing. I was needed straight away. If I didn't go now, I might miss my last chance to talk to her. I glanced into the mirror in the hall, and was shocked how tired I looked. I threw a few clothes into a bag, grabbed the car keys from where they hung on their hook, and, still wearing the damp raincoat, closed the front door carefully behind me, and ran to the car. There was no sign of the girl. It was still raining.

CHAPTER 22

I was just getting to the hospital when my phone rang yet again. I expected it to be Mum's solicitor with some more details, and was relieved that I had found him such an ally. At least I knew now that I could tell the hospital what she wanted. But the voice on the other end of the phone brought me back to reality with a nasty bump.

'Antonia, what the hell do you think you're up to? You haven't answered my solicitor's phone calls or letters. I had hoped we could behave like adults over this, but it seems that you are determined to be childish about it. Thinking about it, I'd have expected nothing else.'

Richard paused for breath, and I waited for the tirade to run its course. When he was on a roll, my sodding husband tended to morph into barrister mode the longer he went on, and the insults were delivered in the dictatorial tone of a judge delivering a sentence. Just as he started to head-bang again, I used the well-known back hand lob down the line technique, guaranteed to put anyone off their stroke.

'If only you'd........' he started again.

'Sorry; who is that? I can hardly hear you; it's a very bad line....'

'It's Richard.' Very loudly. 'Who did you think it was?'

'Oh hello, Richard. Thanks for ringing. I was just about to ring you, in fact, to update you on Mum.'

He snorted.

'She's very ill, probably dying.' I said, slowly and clearly, 'I knew you'd want to know. I'm in the hospital now.'

Another snort. Even he couldn't bring himself to be rude about someone in Mum's situation, or to me who was having to cope with it. I could visualise how irritating he found that, and it made me smile. Whatever had I seen in him? Such a bastard.

'How long will she last?' And, grudgingly, 'I'm sorry to hear she's on her way out.'

'So I'm afraid I'm rather tied up with her at the moment, and haven't had the chance to deal with our little problem. It seems a lower priority just at the moment.'

'Yes, well, I can see that.....'

'So I'll get back to you or your solicitor when I can.' And I rang off. It was always good to finish a conversation without him by being in control. One of his more unpleasant talents was always to insist on having the last word.

I walked down the ward, and sat beside my mother and took her hand. She was awake now, and smiled at me and squeezed my hand in reply. She still looked very old and very ill, but I could see a little bit of the old Mum looking up at me. It made me want to cry. I dug my fingernails into my palm. She had always been strong for me. Now it was my turn.

'Hello darling. It's lovely to see you.' Her voice was thin and weak, but it was her again, and I felt calmer about what I needed to say.

'Yes, Mum, it's me. You've been in a right pickle.'

'She smiled wanly. 'Sorry.'

'Don't worry. It's not as if you chose to be here in hospital. And think how often you looked after me all those years ago.'

'Yes dear. You were such a pretty girl.'

'And a naughty one, too,' I said briskly, trying to keep it upbeat so that I had the courage to be honest. I didn't want this conversation to become maudlin.

'Mum, don't go back to sleep. I need to tell you something, and ask you something.'

'What, dear?'

'Do you remember that conversation we had a few months ago? About feeling that you had had enough of the world, and felt almost ready to meet Dad again?'

She smiled at the mention of him, and I stroked her sparse grey hair, fighting back tears.

'Yes. I've been very tired recently.'

I took a deep breath and waited until I had my voice under control again.

'And do you remember talking to that nice Mr Lacey, your solicitor, about not having too much nasty treatment if you became very ill, and just letting things take their course?'

She gave me a quick look that told me she knew exactly what was coming. 'Yes, dear. I remember that very well. I signed something. I don't want them to mess me about. I just want to be peaceful when my time's up.'

'Well, Mum, it looks as though you were able to see the future. The situation you talked about with Mr Lacey has happened.'

'Has it, dear?' She looked at me sharply now. Definitely no flies on her.

'Yes I'm afraid it has.' I looked away until my chin stopped its stupid wobble. 'You've got something very nasty in your tummy that the doctors can't remove, and we – you – are faced with two options. You could have a very strong treatment that will make you feel very rotten, but will keep you going a few months longer, perhaps even a year. But it's very unlikely that you'll be able to live independently at home again, so it might mean going into a nursing home. Without the treatment, though, you will not keep going for very long. It's up to you to decide, of course, although the thing you signed for Mr Lacey says that he and I can do the deciding for you if you are too poorly to do it yourself. Do you understand all that?'

I broke off and looked round the room. Its neutral colours and anonymity was in stark contrast to the intensity of the conversation I was having.

She pulled herself up on her elbows, although the effort made her grimace, and looked me in the eye. Her gaze was clear and direct.

'Darling, how long have I got?'

'Perhaps only a few weeks, if you opt not to have the treatment'

'And will the treatment work?'

'Not necessarily. It helps some people for a while, perhaps about a third of people who have it. But it makes them really grotty, and the ones that aren't helped by it suffer the grottiness without any benefit.'

'No messing about,' she said clearly, and brought my hand to her cheek. ' I'd hate that. Much better to let things happen. God's will.' And then 'Well done, darling. That can't have been an easy thing to ask.' And she smiled at me. 'So there you are. I've made my decision.' And she sank back on the pillows.

We sat in silence for a while, her old hand holding mine, and occasionally squeezing it gently. Then her hand relaxed, and I saw that she was asleep.

I felt a huge sense of relief. My doctor had been quite right; this was about quality of life rather than quantity, about accepting death as a normal thing in old age, not something to be fought off and deferred at all costs, about accepting that technology was a means to an end, not an end in itself. And above all, it was about caring for someone as an individual, not as a statistic on a graph of survival times. To acknowledge that there was such a thing as a good death, and that medical care need not, should not, be a frantic fight for longevity.

'Well done, Mum.' I stroked the thin hair back from her face. 'I knew you were a wise old bird, but you have just proved that you are a brave one too. I'll make sure they don't mess you about.'

She smiled a little in her sleep, and I wondered if she had heard me.

*

I spent the night in Mum's house, sleeping in her bed. It smelt of lavender. To my surprise, I slept well, and woke up to a bright sunny morning. I sat at her little dressing table to brush my hair, and noticed with affection the scattering of talc on the floor next to it. How things change from one generation to another. I had never used talc.

I saw the oncologist the next morning, in the crowded little office behind the nurse's station. .

'Thank you very much for finding the time to see me, Doctor Kahn. I know how busy you all are. And thank you as well for all the care you are giving my mother. I know you have her best interests at heart.'

'Of course.'

I paused, partly for emphasis, partly so that I phrased my words carefully. 'As you may have guessed, I have had some worries about whether chemotherapy is the very best course of action for her, given the circumstances.'

'Yes.' The gentle smile again.

'And I've talked to her about it, and discussed it with those near her.'

'Yes.'

'And she is very clear in her own mind that she does not want active intervention or unpleasant treatment just to prolong her life for a few months. She would rather let nature take its course. And after all, it is her right to decide.'

'I understand.'

'And she has written an advanced directive that covers this situation.'

The black eyes looked up at me. I noticed that she was wearing a different sari today, this one a rich dark green.

'You are a good daughter to your mother. I wish that more

of my patients were as calm and sensible as you are being. We all have to die at some time. My job is to defer that happening when it can be deferred. But,' and the Indian accent was very pronounced, 'but I wonder, as you did, whether it is always for the very best. I respect your mother for her decision, and you for supporting her.'

She smiled her gentle smile once more, and I shook her tiny hand, and she turned and walked off down the ward, the sari rustling, her retinue following her.

*

I spent some time with the ward sister, a wise and practical lady, arranging that my mother should be referred to the palliative care team, and transferred to the hospice for their assessment. Then I made my way out into the sunshine.

The effect of the last few days hit me suddenly, and irritatingly hard. I felt exhausted. Everything had changed; the wheels had turned, and now I was the one caring for Mum, not she for me. The presence of a parent, whatever the relationship and history between us, gives a sense of permanence and continuity. The realisation that this was to end brought a new wave of emotion over me. I wandered through the narrow Chichester streets, and found that I was near the cathedral, that wonder of mediaeval craftsmanship. How on earth had the mediaeval masons produced such a masterpiece, with their simple tools, no cranes, not much in the way of plans. Mum's impending death brought out a memory of all the funeral services I had been to over the years, and a vague familiarity with things religious. As a devout agnostic, I had little time for the church, but had a deep subliminal memory of the rituals and rites of passage that the Church provided. Despite not living by its precepts, the beautiful words and cadences of the King James Bible and the poetry of Cranmer's English was deep in my emotional bones.

I sat on a bench in the Close, in a patch of sunlight, and let my mind relax back into something near calm. Quite suddenly, I was overwhelmed with a deep sadness, and felt myself crying silently. It seemed natural to do this, almost normal, and realising that helped. A man – presumably a priest of some sort, as he was wearing a long black cassock – was walking down the stone-flagged pathway towards the West Door, and he paused as he came by and looked at me.

'Can I do anything to help?'

No. I shook my head, unable to speak. This was a private moment, not one that he could ameliorate with his milk-sop words about his God's greater purpose. I shook my head again, and he moved reluctantly away.

A butterfly settled on the bench near me, and fanned its wings to pick up the warmth of the sun.

CHAPTER 23

It was nearly four weeks later when we all reassembled in Number 3 Court after Mr Justice Harrap had dealt with his other pressing engagements. There was a much more spring-like feel to the air, and the blossom in Covent Garden was falling like confetti onto the pavements when I left my office for the Court, struggling under a pile of papers. But things weren't nearly so spring-like when Mr Keith Harrison resumed give his evidence.

He had finished giving the main part, the so-called evidence-in-chief, which was his version of events, before the adjournment. He had made it very clear that he felt that Nick, my doctor, had failed him at every turn, and had no interest in him or sympathy for him at all. In fact, without attempting to conceal his contempt for doctors in general, he made clear his animosity towards Nick. He implied that he had deliberately put him in harm's way. I had watched Nick flinch under this assault. It had attacked him at the very centre of his ethos, the ethos that any doctor has to care for and do his best for his patient. It implied a callous disregard for his standards, his behaviour and his commitment. It was unfair, it was vicious, and I knew from his reaction that it hurt deeply.

So now it was our term to cross-examine Keith Harrison, to put our side of the story, and to test his version. This process of cross-examination is where barristers really earn their money. They must have a clear idea in their minds of what actually happened in a given event, and separate that from the gloss or interpretation that the witness is putting on them. That is not as easy as it sounds. We all know how emotion can colour a situation, and distort our recollection of it. Just the simple fact of being frightened or threatened can make us view a normal event in an entirely different way. And if that wasn't enough, we all have differing ways of remembering events. There are lots of examples of how, when three or four people view a piece of film, and are asked to describe it, they produce three or four different versions of what happened. Almost as though it has become an internal game of Chinese whispers, we interpret events in different ways, and the interpretation becomes the fact. On top of that, time plays a part. The longer after an event is remembered, the more fixed the distortion becomes in one's mind. What 'might have been' evolves into 'it probably was', and eventually into 'it definitely was', and finally 'I am absolutely certain, beyond any doubt at all' that this is what happened. This is the sequence that has led to the so-called 'received memory' syndrome, where a suggestion by a third party that something might have happened can, if not counteracted, segue into a perception of truth. Many child abuse accusations have foundered on the realisation that they were entirely received memory.

But James Brooks made no progress at all with Mr Keith Harrison.

He spent most of the first day picking away at the detail of Harrison's story. He tried to get behind his pathological dislike of doctors in general and my doctor in particular. It was difficult to work out where it had started. Perhaps the rigid 'doctor knows best' attitude of previous generations of doctors had abraded his feelings about class and equality. Or perhaps he had just come across an unpleasant doctor, who upset or offended him in some way. Whatever it was, his views about doctors were seemingly set in stone, and nothing Brooks could say would move him from his conviction that they did not act in his best interests. And to give him his due, when we came on to the details of his long admission to hospital, it sounded as though they really hadn't done so. Perhaps not deliberately, but by default. And it just so happened that of all the doctors who dealt with him, Nick was first in the firing line.

Brooks took him through his stay in hospital in detail. We heard how he had felt abandoned, how the impression that no one was in charge had slowly developed, and how that had been reinforced by injudicious comments from junior doctors and nurses. We also learnt that he had been frightened of doctors as a child, had been warned by his mother about how painful vaccinations were on the way to the surgery to have his boosters at the age of five. Predictably, they were 'agony'. I marvelled at the sheer stupidity of a parent who would create an expectation of pain in a child before the event, guaranteeing a lifetime's problem with needles. Inevitably, therefore, he was tense when Nick took blood from him at the first consultation, and flinched away, so that Nick had to have a second go at finding a vein.

We heard, in his dry flat voice, how he felt that the noble motives of the NHS had been deliberately subverted by an arrogant and greedy profession and equally arrogant and greedy politicians, who just wanted to 'privatise it for their own ends'. There was rigidity about his views that made discussing them with him, let alone debating them or trying to change them, a near impossible task. Brooks did his best, repeatedly demonstrating that the consultants who looked after him had no private practice, so that his concept of an ulterior motive did not hold water, but he was unmoveable. Even when Brooks told him that my doctor had inherited private patients at the start of his career, but had insisted as a matter of principle that they all become NHS patients, he stuck to his guns, that doctors were rich and arrogant, and that my doctor in particular did not look after him or care for him. I ground my teeth in frustration that we did not have the notes to demonstrate otherwise. If only....... but hoping wasn't going to help.

Doggart watched with a sly smile as Brooks wearily persevered. He knew that his client was winning on points, and winning well. The certainty with which he gave his evidence would carry a lot of weight with a judge, and demonstrating that he disliked doctors as a group would make not one jot of difference in determining whether the actions of an individual doctor were negligent or not. When, finally, Brooks sat down after a long and fruitless cross-examination, and Doggart was asked by the Judge whether he wished to re-examine, as was his right, he shook his head with confidence. He knew that his client had passed the test, had won the sparring match of the cross-examination. Once again, I wondered at the vagaries of the law and the way it worked. How being good or clever at being questioned was more important to winning a case than the truth. The distance between truth, justice and the law in our system seemed increasingly elastic at times. Winning was all.

Harrison left the stand with the same distant blank expression with which he had taken it, aware, no doubt, that he had held his ground. I watched with despair as His Honour Mr Justice Harrap wrote busily,

*

Then it was our turn. The case for the defence.

This was what my job was all about. It was up to me to plan how we could best defend my doctor, to discuss and refine this with the barrister I had chosen, and come up with a water-tight defence to the accusations against him.

We only planned to have two witnesses. The first was our expert on Human Rights, the chap we hoped would demonstrate clearly that, as the patient was in his right mind, his refusal to be re-admitted was down to him and him alone, and that any attempt by my doctor to coerce or manipulate him was infringing the absolute rights of anyone to decline treatment if they so choose.

We had settled on a Professor of International Law at

the LSE. He had come over well when we talked to him, expressing the nuances of the law clearly and accurately. He was a senior academic with a list of publications as long as your arm, and a significant international reputation. Sadly, he was not a charismatic personality, but you can't have everything, and the field was limited anyway.

'Professor Windruff, tell us, if you would, why you feel that my client's actions in caring for Mr Harrison were in accord with the law of land.'

Brooks had taken the Professor through his background and career, and encouraged him to describe the way in which international and European law had been absorbed into English common law. He had moved on to the way in which the law defined the rights of an individual, and explored the situation in which someone might not be capable of making an informed decision. He touched on the area of competence, when an individual is not capable of making a decision because of mental illness or dementia, and pointed out to His Lordship that this situation did not apply in this case, as the plaintiff had not argued that his illness had clouded his judgement.

Mr Justice Harrap sniffed dismissively. 'If competence is not part of the Plaintiff's case, why are you raising it, Mr Brooks? Please stick to the point.'

Brooks took that on the chin. There was no point in arguing with a judge about a minor point. He was merely making sure that Doggart didn't slip in a sub-plot of lack of competence during his closing statement, and he moved quickly on to the main issue. He had to work hard to get Woodruff to demonstrate that he was at the top of his professional tree, and there was a slight feeling of pulling teeth in the way the answers had to be extracted from him. My heart sank a bit as I watched the exchanges. This chap might have been the expert's expert, but he wasn't going to set the Thames on fire, let alone Court Number 3 of the Royal Courts of Justice.

Woodruff took a long time to formulate his answer to Brooks' questions; one could almost hear the cogs turning. When the answer came, it was delivered in a voice that did not carry the weight and conviction I had hoped for.

'I think', he said, and paused. 'I think that it might be better to put the question the other way round. You perhaps should ask 'Was there any other action your doctor could have taken that did not infringe Mr Harrison's human rights?'. And I would answer – 'No, there was not.' If he forced Mr Harrison to be readmitted, or coerced him in any way that was beyond the normal medical advice that a doctor may give, then he would be exceeding his remit, and would undoubtedly be breaching his human rights.'

'So,' Brooks encouraged him, 'you are saying that a doctor should not bring pressure to bear on a patient who does not want to be admitted to hospital?'

'As long as the patient is in his right mind, and is in the full possession of the facts, no.'

'And if he still refuses, does the doctor's responsibility stop there?'

The expert on law prevaricated. 'That's not really for me to say. That is something that a practicing doctor is better qualified to answer. My expertise is in the principle of the law, not its application in complicated circumstances such as these.'

There was a sharp intake of breath on the lawyer's benches. This expert had done the unforgiveable, had declared that his view, his expertise, only applied in principle, and that practicalities might over-ruled principles, and were more important. 'Idiot,' I thought. 'Why did you not just tell me that you weren't prepared to put your head above the parapet, argue our case? Call yourself an expert. The only expertise you have is in chickening out.' I was furious. This was the expert I had found, who was going to make the case for us that a doctor shouldn't bully a patient to accept a treatment, and all he had done was pass the responsibility back to the doctors, and say, in effect, that the plaintiff's expert doctor was better able to make a judgement about this situation than he was. Brooks glanced at me, and gave the faintest of shrugs. He knew, just as Doggart knew, and every lawyer in the Court knew, that the sooner we got this man out of the witness box the better.

Brooks asked a few more anodyne questions, but the damage had been done, and we both knew it. When he sat down, Doggart was on his feet in a moment.

'Just two simple questions, Professor. If I understand you rightly, you say that the opinion of the doctor on the ground, who is faced with the practicalities of the situation, is a better judge of the degree of pressure to be brought on a patient than the abstract interpretation of the law of human rights?'

The professor half closed his eyes in indecision. 'Er, yes. I think that is what I said.'

'And therefore, Professor, that our medical expert was right when he said that a doctor is obligated to ask for help when he has tried unsuccessfully to persuade his patient to follow a course of action?'

'Well, I'm not sure that that is exactly what I said, but I suppose that the implication must be just that. The law on human rights is a guide, not a mandatory set of rules, and its interpretation must depend on the circumstances.'

'Doggart smiled. I could have gladly kicked him. 'Thank you, Professor. No further questions.'

I looked at the judge. Mr Justice Harrap's thin face was expressionless, but his narrow eyes were looking hard at my doctor. 'Time for lunch, I think.' he said. 'Adjourned until two o'clock.'

*

'Has he screwed us completely?' Nick asked, as we walked across the road to our grotty café. I thought I had managed to conceal my fury and frustration at being let down so catastrophically by the LSE professor, but perhaps not.

'That largely depends on you.' Brooks answered for me, as he opened the door, and we trooped in. He was much more in control of his irritation than I was, and was better at putting a professional gloss on failure as well. 'You are our last and most important witness, and it is up to you to cut through the fog of sanctimonious opinion that we have been listening to, and persuade the judge that you really had the patient's interests at heart, and did your best for him. You are a highly intelligent man,' Brooks took a seat at our usual table, and looked straight into my doctor's eyes, 'and it is not just the outcome of this case, but your future lies in your own hands. Make the best of it, and you will clear your name, and lay down a standard that others will look to in the years ahead. I have complete faith that you will be able to do that.'

He was giving a back-stiffening pep-talk, and we all knew it, but it was appropriate, and it worked. I could see my doctor visibly pull himself together. He smiled at Brooks, and then turned to me and smiled again. I was suddenly lost again in the blue eyes.

'I'll do my best.'

CHAPTER 24

'Why did you become a GP, Doctor?'

Brooks set about painting a picture of a highly motivated caring individual. I watched from the lawyer's bench, trying to assess the impression my doctor was making to someone who did not know him. I had been surprised to see that the public gallery was nearly full; there were several people scribbling away in notebooks. Was it his local Press, I wondered, there to get a juicy story? On the witness stand, my doctor looked strained. He stood straight and calm, but I could see that his fingers, resting on the lip of the stand, were gripping it tightly. He swallowed nervously.

'Well, I did stint as a junior hospital doctor in the high-tech end of medicine, and although it was fascinating and challenging and skilled, it did not allow me to fulfil something that I felt quite strongly about, the holistic and long term care of a patient through all of life's medical tribulations.'

Mr Justice Harrap leant forward, his spectacles perched on his narrow nose.

'Do I understand you to be saying, Doctor, that you are not interested in what you call high-tech medicine?'

'No, My Lord, not at all. The two branches of medicine, specialist and generalist, are complementary. Neither can survive without the other, or at least survive in our present health care system. The specialist has unique skills and expertise in specific areas that the generalists like me cannot aspire to, but the generalist has skills as well, different skills, that allow him to manage different conditions and circumstances. So the two can and should work together and respect each other's role.'

'But you do not like specialist medicine?'

'With respect, my Lord, that is not what I said.' The doctor leant forward to emphasise what he meant. 'It is not about liking or disliking specialism. It is about finding the niche in the whole range of medical careers that I thought would suit me best, and where I could contribute most.'

'Are you not just saying that specialists are cleverer than generalists, and that you did not have the ability to achieve in a specialist field?'

Brooks was on his feet, but the judge waved him away imperiously.

'Once again, my Lord, no. That is not what I said, nor is it true.' Nick was very direct in his contradiction. I felt nervous. Rule number one in any court – do not fight with the judge. 'I said that the skills are separate and distinct: I most definitely did not say that one was better than the other, or cleverer. Their functions are different.'

Harrap sniffed, a world of condescension in his face.

'I'm not sure that many Harley Street specialists would agree with you, Doctor.'

'No, my Lord, they might not, but that is a reflection on the limits of their perspective, not on reality.'

Brooks intervened definitely. It was one thing to contradict a judge, but to imply that he had limited perspective was definitely pushing it.

'If I may be permitted to continue my examination-in-chief, my Lord? I am grateful to you for raising issues that I had hoped to explore later.' If in doubt, be emollient.

Harrap made a harrumphing noise that could have been displeasure, or could have been permission to continue. Wisely, Brooks took it to be the latter.

'You were telling us, Doctor, about your decision to leave hospital medicine and become a GP.......?'

'Yes, ...well... after I decided on that career, I had to find an appropriate training course. And as most GPs, like most consultants, finish up working long-term in the area they train in, I looked for a Registrar post in the south, where I hoped to find a permanent job.'

Once again, Harrap intervened. 'You have to be trained to be a GP, do you, Doctor? I thought that you learnt that in medical school.'

'Once again, not so, I am afraid My Lord.' I could see that my doctor was getting as irritated as Brooks and I with the judge's obvious ignorance. I tried desperately to catch his eye to send calming signals, without success. 'That is about as accurate as saying that getting a degree in Law makes you a competent barrister. Even the cleverest of us only gain the background knowledge during the qualification process. As the Dean of my medical school said to us when we qualified; "you have shown that you have the basic knowledge to enable you to become a doctor. Now you have to learn how to apply it in the real world of patients." Each speciality, be it heart surgery or psychiatry or general practice, has its own post-graduate training, and final examination to demonstrate that an approved level of skill has been reached in that speciality.'

Once again, Harrap harrumphed. He was not used to being put down so deftly. 'Go on, then, Doctor.'

There was a pause, and my doctor finally caught my eye; I raised an eyebrow, which I hoped he would interpret as 'go easy', and he nodded slightly.

'So I found a training course for general practice in the Wessex Region, based in Winchester, and applied for it, and got appointed.'

'And what did the course consist of, Doctor?' Brooks prompted.

'It was a three year course, the first two in hospital posts as a junior doctor, and the third full time in training practice as a registrar. The hospital jobs were selected to be useful to someone doing general practice, but like many aspiring GPs, I found them fairly useless. So I arranged a further year of attachments myself which I thought would be more relevant. These included dermatology, psychiatry, ophthalmology, and a few others.'

'Gastro-enterology, Doctor?'   Harrap again, with an antagonistic note in his voice. He was becoming difficult.

'No, My Lord. I had already done six months of that as a

pre-registration houseman in my teaching hospital.'

'Six months, eh? ' The judge's mouth had settled into a hard line. 'Not long to learn all about it?'

'Enough, my Lord. When you remember that barristers are expected to learn the entirety of legal practice in just twelve months of pupillage before they embark on independent practice.'

The Judge and my doctor glared at one another for a long moment. This wasn't just rash, it was dangerous. And it played into the plaintiff's hands. I looked desperately at Brooks, and he reluctantly got to his feet.

'My Lord, with respect I must protest. You could be interpreted as demeaning this witness's answers.'

Harrap gave him a long hard look. It was a clever interruption, as it implied that others, such as an Appeal Court, might interpret Harrap's comments in this way, should his decision go against us and we appealed. Counsel for either side can bully a witness, but not a judge. He is meant to be an independent unbiased arbitrator, and any hint of bias is gold-dust for an appeal.

'Get on with it, then, Mr Brooks.'

'Thank you, My Lord', and Brooks continued to take my doctor through his career, highlighting the things that made him stand out from his fellow GPs. He had been elected by his colleagues to represent them on the Local Medical Committee, which was the interface between GPs and their managers. He had qualified as a GP trainer, one of those responsible for the one-to-one training of junior doctors on their way to becoming independent GPs. Perhaps most important, he represented all GPs in his county on a body called the Ethics Committee, which had to approve all new research and treatments proposed. And he had become an examiner for the Royal College of General Practice, the standard setter for that branch of medicine. So quite apart from his clinical skills, he was someone whom his peers respected, and whose judgement they valued. I was rather touched by the diffidence with which he admitted to these various roles, almost as though he wished to be reticent about his achievements. Very different to many of the senior doctors I had had to deal with, whose own trumpet-blowing skills had to be seen to be believed.

'All very interesting, Mr Brooks, but what has it got to do with how competent and caring your client was?' Harrap was in a profoundly waspish mood today, which did not bode well.

'If you would permit me, My Lord, I am painting a picture of a doctor who was held in high esteem, not just by his patients but by his colleagues as well. And that, of course, is highly relevant to his performance and the probability or otherwise of him falling below good standards. It is, if you like, a demonstration of not just a good but an exceptional professional character.'

'Very well. But keep to the point. We haven't got all day.'

I watched Brooks preparing to give a broadside in response to this inappropriate remark, and then decide against it.

'Thank you, my Lord. I am sure you will allow us as much time as you allowed the plaintiff, and enough time to see that justice is done.' That was about as pointed a reaction as he could safely get away with. But it told me that he felt that the judge was already against us, and was laying the grounds for an appeal.

*

We paused soon after that for the lunch break, and sat glumly in the café across the road. We all knew that things hadn't gone well, and there was nothing useful I could say to break the atmosphere or encourage Nick. He knew as well as I did how finely balanced the situation was. I watched him across the grubby formica table, picking at his sandwich, and thought how lonely he looked. The blue eyes were troubled, and his shoulders, usually so square and upright, were slumped. It was all so bloody unfair, I thought. He had been doing his best, doing what he thought was reasonable in the circumstances.

It was a long horrible afternoon. Before the case, Brooks and I had discussed whether to try to explain the difference between general practice and hospital medicine to the Court, and had decided, on balance, that it was worth doing. But it went wrong, almost from the start.

'Could you explain to us, doctor, how general practice management of patients differs to hospital management?' Brooks asked.

'Well, putting on one side the obvious differences that arise from patients being static in a hospital bed, with access to all the hospital facilities, there is an inevitable difference in approach. We GPs are the first point of contact, and our role is twofold. First, to manage chronic disease, and secondly, as in this situation, to act as a filter, to make sure that hospitals are not overwhelmed with self-limiting or minor illness.'

'Give me an example of what you mean by that, doctor.'

'Perhaps the simplest example is headache. Everyone in the world gets a headache, every single one of us. Most of us get one or two a year; some get many more, perhaps one a week, or a cluster of one every day for several days. But only a very small number of headaches are caused by significant disease that needs urgent or specialist intervention; the vast majority are, for want of a better description, normal headaches. Yet people want help with them. They either want them cured, or they want to make sure that they are not due to something sinister, such as a brain tumour. It is the role of the GP to act as a sieve, to separate out the headaches that need specialist care, and to manage the other 99 percent in the community. Without this sieve process, secondary care, the hospitals, would be overwhelmed.'

'I understand that, doctor,' Brooks was encouraging, 'but could you explain to us how you do it, how you sort the sheep from the goats?'

Nick Malekov smiled a little. 'That is the thousand dollar question. That is the skill that it takes a lifetime to learn. And it involves understanding two things.' He turned to the judge. 'Is it OK if I go into this more fully, My Lord?'

'Harrap shrugged. 'That is up to your barrister, if he thinks it will help your case.' Hardly an encouragement.

Nick turned back to Brooks, who nodded his permission.

'The first thing is simple. It is the red flag signs. If a condition meets a generally agreed set of criteria, then it qualifies for referral. In headaches, it may be one of several things. It may be the history, the way the headaches have evolved over a few days. It may be an algorithm, that they are following a recognised pattern. Or it may be a clinical sign, something you find on examination, such as papilloedema in headaches, evidence of increased pressure at the back of the eye. One of these so-called red flag signs mandates referral.'

'I'm with you so far.'

'The second criterion is far harder to define. Or explain. It involves that difficult concept of the seat of the pants.'

'There were some sniggers in the Court. 'What on earth do you mean by that?' Harrap said.

'I mean, My Lord, that we all develop a sixth sense. Sometimes you see a patient, and although there are no signs of anything untoward, no red flag symptoms exist, and all the tests are normal, you have a worrying sense that all is not right. It is a sense, a skill that comes with experience. It is an early warning sign. And you have to decide whether to trust it or not.'

'So?' Harrap was at his most weasel-like.

'Then', Nick paused, 'you have to decide whether to take a risk.'

There was an indrawing of breath in the Court. Risk. The word hung in the air.

'Do you mean, doctor', Harrap's voice was low and sinister, 'that you are prepared to take a risk with a patient's life?'

Nick realised what he had done, and struggled to put it

right. 'No, My Lord, not at all. That is definitely not what I meant. The word I perhaps should have used is judgement. A huge part of medicine is about making judgements, deciding on which course of action to take, whether to investigate or not, whether to intervene or not. Often these judgements are finely balanced – whether to operate, whether to resuscitate, whether to take the X Ray, whether to refer or not. All these are judgements. And like all judgements, they carry a degree of risk, the risk of being wrong. And since they haven't yet made the doctor – or the lawyer - who has perfect judgement, it is inevitable that some of these judgements will be wrong. That is what I meant by risk.'

Harrap and Brooks spoke at once. 'I see.' And I think we all saw what he was trying to explain. But we saw it through different eyes. Brooks and I saw it as someone trying to be open and honest about the way he made decisions. Harrison and Doggert saw it as a vindication of their opinion that he had taken a risk with his patient's life. And Harrap? How did Harrap see it? We would only find that out later.

*

After Brooks had finished his examination in chief, and got my doctor to confirm several times that he had done all that he thought was right, and that it would have been as morally incorrect as it was impractical to manipulate a patient to do something he was determined not to do, Henry Doggart showed why he was such a successful barrister for the world of complainers. He didn't bully; he didn't hector; in fact he did very little except return over and over again to the central point: that the patient said one thing, and the doctor said another, and that there was no evidence to support the doctors' version of events. Furthermore, of the two experts, one for each side of the argument, the medical one was far clearer in his opinion that the doctor should have called for help or a second opinion, while our so-called expert had proved a damp squib, and had failed to confirm that it was the right of an individual to determine his own actions, whatever the circumstances. Over and over again, Doggart put it to Nick that all he had had to do on that day several years ago was to ring one of his partners, or the hospital, or a consultant, and ask them to confirm to the patient that he should do what he didn't want to do, go back into hospital.

I watched my doctor becoming wearier and wearier under this repetitive barrage, and saw that Doggart was playing the well-known technique of trying to break self-belief. Every time Nick explained the way in which any doctor made a decision, reached a judgement on a course of action, that he was balancing many factors, both clinical and practical. And that judgements, by definition could be wrong only in hindsight, but if made in good faith and in accordance with commonly accepted practice, could not be deemed negligent. And over and over again, Doggart chipped away at his confidence, questioned his judgement, and asked him if he would do the same thing again. It was a good technique, and played on the tendency that most honest men have to question themselves and begin to doubt that, at the time, they really did do what was best.

As soon as he saw a chink, he changed tack and questioned Nick about the lack of a referral letter, the lack of a phone call about a patient who he acknowledged was very ill. Try as he might, my doctor could only reiterate that he had written, had phoned, and that the lack of any record of the letter was the fault of an incompetent system, not him. And then Doggart would jump back to questioning why my doctor had such confidence in his own judgement alone. Was that not just arrogance?

Finally, the inevitable happened, as it does with anyone who is intellectually honest. Doggart had asked, for the umpteenth time, why the doctor felt that he alone had the right to make a judgement to risk a patient's life in circumstances like this. I saw Nick's shoulders slump, and his eyes, those vivid eyes, drop.

'Perhaps you are right, Mr Doggart,' he said. 'Perhaps, like all doctors do at some point in their careers, I made a decision that turned out to be wrong, and the patient survived this despite me rather than because of me. But as I have tried to explain to the court' and he raised his eyes and looked at me, 'one can only do what is practical, given the circumstances, and that in the cold light of day, looked at by academics or lawyers in isolation, there might have been other or better ways to manage the situation. But that is the nature of medical practice. Idealism and academic perfection comes hard up against the practicalities and constraints of the real world of delivering care with limited resource and time.'

'Thank you, Doctor.' Doggart was at his most bland. 'At

long last you have accepted that what you did could have been wrong, and in the event, turned out to be wrong. I have no further questions.'

The closing summaries from Brooks and Doggart were brief. We left the Court in silence. Mr Justice Harrap had been brief and to the point in closing the case.

'Having heard all the evidence in this hearing, and reviewed the notes made by the late and much lamented Dame Isobel Nicholson, I shall now consider my verdict. As Counsel on both sides will be aware, this is a lengthy process, and there are many other calls on my time. This Court is adjourned, therefore, for' and he consulted the Court diary in front of him ' one month. We shall reassemble on May 19th, when I shall deliver my judgement'.

CHAPTER 25

The hospice was a lovely place. Not lovely in the sense of being beautiful architecturally, or having wonderful grounds or views, but lovely in the sense of the extraordinary calm that seemed to pervade it. The sensation of intensity, of rush and bustle, that overwhelms you when you walk into an acute hospital was noticeably absent. In the hospital, everyone seemed to be walking about briskly doing something important. There was noise everywhere, and activity, and stress, and people. I suppose that this kind of atmosphere is inevitable, given that activity and stress and people are what acute hospitals are all about. While Mum was still in there, I yearned for a sense of quiet and peace, and I'm sure many of the patients did as well. If only the nurses didn't chatter so loudly at the nursing station, or the doctor's bleeps have such a penetrating tone, or the lunch trolley crash against the doors of the ward as it came in. Mum told me that it was almost as noisy at night, with the machines beeping and buzzing, and patients snoring or crying out, and nurse's shoes clacking up and down the ward. I wondered vaguely where the old principle of a hospital being a place of refuge had gone, and then banished the criticism as unrealistic.

The hospice was different. The calmness seemed to come as much from the staff as the place itself. You know that sense of warm calm security you used to feel as a child, when everything seemed safe, and you were curled up in front of the fire, figuratively speaking. Well, the hospice generated the same sense of safety. It opened its arms, welcomed its patients, and wrapped them in a cocoon of pain control and peace and symptom management. It wasn't that they knocked people out with strong pain-killers; it was that they seemed to realise that pain, or even discomfort, was something that needed managing, and managing properly. And that anxiety, which is an inevitable companion of pain, needed managing too.

I thought long and hard about what the staff were doing during the days I sat with my mum, holding her hand in the light and airy room with a distant view of Chichester Harbour. I came to the conclusion that the real difference, the key to producing the peace that pervaded the place, was honesty. Every patient who came through the doors knew, or must have sensed, that they were reaching the end of the road, that they were dying. I watched, fascinated, as the doctors and nurses – who seemed to be on equal terms here, not trapped in a hierarchy – asked open questions of the new patients, developing what I believe is known as 'the difficult conversation', the conversation that tells a patient that he or she is dying, and helps them come to terms with it. Often, the conversation evolved very slowly and gently, over many episodes and several days. How wonderfully different, I thought, than the rushed and blunt message so often given in an outpatient clinic, that 'nothing more can be done'. I realised that the skill in managing a soft landing for this most important message of all was an art, and one that was rarely practiced. It was not something that could be easily taught. You either had the empathetic skills or you did not. I was hugely impressed by the way that the whole family was involved in these conversations. Husbands, wives, children, friends, were all gently included in the sharing of anxieties, of fears about the actual process of dying, about the normality of emotion and grief, and about how to deal with it. I watched as the little community of the four bedded ward developed a caring process all of its own, the patients sharing their experiences, and supporting each other through them. I was surprised – amazed – at the amount of laughter I heard in the hospice. It was a credit, not just to all who worked there, but to the indomitable strength of the human spirit.

Mum didn't need to have the difficult conversation. She knew exactly what the implications of not having chemo were, and accepted, almost welcomed it. I felt shamefaced at the realisation that I had ignored her isolation, the consequences of long widowhood and children far away. Her last few days were calm and almost happy, as though she was welcoming death, looking forward to it. I could understand that the tedious process, the loss of dignity and control, however skilled the nursing, was something that she would like to get over and done with. In her words, she was ready to move on. I admired her for it, and it made me proud of her, and tearful.

Over the next few days, I watched as she slowly receded from me and from her surroundings. She became focused inwards, and her periods of lucidity became fewer and shorter. The speed at which she moved away from life was rapid, almost bewilderingly so. The doctors had said a few weeks, but in the event, it turned out to be only a few days. The doctor in charge of the hospice, a gentle and kind woman, explained to me that her organs were being compromised by the growth in her stomach, and were failing. 'But', she said, 'no one really understands how and why people die. Sometimes people just turn their faces to the wall, as though they have decided that enough is enough, and they just want to get on with it. I think that is what is happening to your mother now. She has decided that her time is up, and her mind is willing her body to die'.

I nodded. That made sense to me. Her periods of sleep became longer and longer, and her periods of being rousable shorter and shorter. The figure in the bed receded, drifting in and out of consciousness, seemed to be completely peaceful. But as I watched, she made an effort to open her eyes. I leant over and spoke to her.

'Mum.'

Her eyelids fluttered.

'Mum, it's all OK.'

She turned her head a little to look at me, and smiled.

'Just lie still and be calm, Mum. Everything's OK.'

Her eyes shut again.

*

A day later, I sat and watched as, when the end came, it was calm and peaceful, and almost good. My mother became sleepier and sleepier. Once, when she seemed nearly unconscious, she turned to me and seemed to recognise me, and made a little inarticulate sound. Then she just closed her eyes and relaxed again, and her sleep became deeper and deeper, so that finally she did not wake up. I sat besides her, watching as her breaths became shallower and fewer over an hour or two, and then, for half an hour, she breathed just every few minutes. I could feel the muscles of her hand relax as it lay in mine, and the faint tick of her pulse become less and less apparent. Every now and then, a nurse would come quietly in, as much to make sure that I was OK as to do anything for Mum. I was moved to notice that they seemed to care for me as much as for her, and that the touch of a hand on my shoulder carried an implied understanding of what I was going through. Finally, after a particularly long pause between breaths, one that seemed to go on for ever, she took a deep shuddering breath, and very briefly opened her eyes. I have no idea whether she could see me or hear me, but I needed to say something.

'It's OK, Mum,' I whispered. 'You can go now. There's no reason to hang on. Everything's fine.'

There was the tiniest faintest flicker of a smile at the corner of her mouth, and then nothing more. I felt her pulse slow, fade, and then stop. There were no more breaths. Her time was over. She had gone.

I don't know how long I sat holding her hand after that. There seemed to be no hurry. Nobody came in to disturb me, although

I knew they were aware that she had died. A long line of images passed before my inner eye, images of her life and my life with her. Good pictures. Happy pictures. Pictures of love. So that when I finally detached her old hand from mine and stood up, I didn't feel sad at all. I felt that I had just been a part of something amazing, something deeply moving and something that humankind could be proud of. For the first time, I understood what my doctor really meant by 'a good death'.

*

There are lots of different kinds of funerals. The majestic funeral of a crowned monarch or a Churchill; the big funeral of an individual in the prime of life, struck down by accident or illness; the outpouring of vicarious emotion at a Diana funeral. Many, the vast majority, are much smaller and less ostentatious, marking as they do the end of ordinary lives. Sometimes there are just a few family members at a short, almost perfunctory service in a municipal crematorium, conducted by a priest who never knew the star player. This often reminded me, rather cynically, of the similarity with a patient seeing a locum doctor, someone with none of the sense of continuity and personal knowledge of a family doctor.

My mother's funeral was something between the two ends of the spectrum. Because she had lived in the same village for donkey's years, lots of local people knew her, and a surprising number came to pay their respects. Because she was a regular churchgoer, the C of E was there in force, choir, churchwardens, vicar and all. My brother came from Canada, where he had lived for over twenty years, separating himself deliberately from his roots. I hardly recognised him at first so much had he changed, and felt almost as though we should shake hands when we met, rather than kiss as brother and sister.

Richard came, and behaved well, to my relief. He was in charge of the children, and looked after them with a tenderness that I had not seen for years. I recognised something of the man who I had fallen for so completely all those years ago in the way he held them as they cried, and talked to them quietly. 'How sad', I thought, 'how desperately, miserably, sad it was that we had failed to build on what we had had, and gone our separate ways'. He had kissed me on the cheek outside the church, and said, apparently genuinely, how sorry he was about Mum, and could he do anything to help, and had looked at me with that old attractive look. Despite all the hurt and anger and distress he had caused me over the years, and all that I knew was to come with the divorce, I could not help feeling a stab of fondness for the old bastard. He had been such a big part of my life. I wondered if we would ever manage to become friends again, or at least manage to rekindle some of the friendship we used to have.

Nick Malenkov came as well. He stood at the back of the church, and I only knew he was there when we all filed out behind the coffin. I caught his eye, and he smiled, and then he was gone.

I saw him again one month after the funeral, when we assembled at the Royal Courts to hear Mr Justice Harrap's verdict. It was a bitter cold day, with a cutting wind and occasional flurries of sleet. I could see that he was desperately nervous, as anyone would be when they came to find out whether their professional competence and reputation had been found wanting. For some reason, doctors seemed to take this much harder than other professionals. Solicitors sue each other with monotonous regularity, and win or lose, and put it down to experience with a shrug. But, perhaps because the ethos of practicing medicine is to care for people, and to make everything all right for them, doctors find the process of being sued particularly hard to deal with, and it leaves deep emotional scars on them.

Mr Justice Harrap swept into the Court and took his seat. His expression was just as calculating, his eyes just as shrewd and hard, and his demeanour gave nothing, absolutely nothing, away. He adjusted his narrow glasses on his narrow nose, shuffled the papers in front of him, waited till the rustling in Court number 3 had died away, and began to read.

'I have carefully considered all the evidence that was presented to me in this hearing, and also that which was presented to my predecessor in the hearing, the late Lady Isobel Richardson. I have read all the expert witness statements, and considered the extensive evidence presented before me in this Court. Furthermore, I have taken account of the testimony of the character witnesses called on behalf of the defendant, and the account of the events that led to this hearing from the individual most intimately concerned, the plaintiff. My findings, and the decision of this Court, are as follows…….'

*

Afterwards, we stood in a huddle outside the Court, while the wind whipped our coats round our legs. I shook Nick's hand rather formally as we said goodbye.

'I can't thank you enough for all you have done.' he said.

'It's was nothing. I only wish that it had had a better outcome…….. I know you are a good doctor, even if that horrible judge doesn't.'

He smiled at me again, a sad smile that barely reached the blue eyes, and I realised that I was still holding his hand. Reluctantly, very reluctantly, I let it go, and he turned and walked away. I watched as he reached the corner and, without looking back, disappeared.

CHAPTER 26

Three weeks later, I managed to find the time to get down to Sussex to start the job of clearing out my mother's house. My brother wanted to have nothing to do with it. 'You deal with it, Antonia, and have the house,' he said. 'I moved on years ago,' and he disappeared back to Canada. There had been so much to do after the funeral, letters to write, bills to settle, probate to organise. The house was still full of her; the mementos of a lifetime, clothes, books, old photograph albums with pictures of a younger Mum, smiling at the camera in her 1950s clothes, or sitting on the beach in Cornwall with my father laughing behind her. Drawers full of things she hadn't worn for years, smelling faintly of mothballs, dated, faded, full of memories. I sat on her bedroom floor, slowly running through my hand a blouse that she could not have worn since the '80s. All that was left of a life.

Downstairs, her little desk was orderly and tidy, bills that had been paid neatly clipped together in a pigeon hole on the right, and the ones waiting to be paid in its pair on the left, with a cheque book beside them. It had always surprised me how well she had coped after my father's death. The years, and my own problems, had blurred my memories of how distressed she had been after he died, how the rock on which she had anchored her life had gone, leaving her bereft and forlorn. She had slowly emerged from the fog of grief over a year or two, and had set about her new life with a determination and pragmatism that I had rather admired. But I had been busy myself at the time, learning to be an adult, and as I sat there, I felt another wave of remorse at how little I had helped then, and how few demands she, in turn, had made on me.

I wandered round the little house, picking up objects and ornaments, allowing the memories that they invoked waft over me, and putting them down again. Pictures in silver frames, a vase of withered flowers that no one had thought to throw out, a book laid face down half read on a table beside the reclining chair in which she habitually sat, her reading glasses beside it. I felt a wave of nostalgia sweep over me, and noticed, almost distantly, that tears were running down my cheeks once more. Stupid emotional woman. Just because my life was a mess at the moment. Just because my divorce was going through. Just because a man with blue eyes who I had felt something for, and who I had thought had felt something for me, had walked away….. .

I pulled myself together and got on with the job of clearing out the house. I had to be back in Islington that evening to let the baby sitter get home, and tomorrow I was in Court again, defending another doctor, although this one wasn't worth defending.

The last place that needed clearing was the rather pokey back porch, the place my mother had always called the boot room. She had kept her wellies in there, and her secateurs, and a few old coats and macs, which were hanging up on pegs on the back wall. 'There you are', I thought as I spotted her old mac, the one I had borrowed when she had been admitted to hospital, and had returned to its place when I first visited her. I took it down and shook it; it was still slightly damp, and I remembered how hard it had been raining that night in London. The mac was old and scruffy, and I wondered if Oxfam would want it, or whether I should add it to the pile that I was taking to the tip. Probably the latter. I folded it in half, but it resisted a bit, and I felt in the pockets to see what was bulking it out. This was the coat I had been wearing when I had got back late to London after my mother was taken ill and went into hospital. I had been wearing it as I walked back to the house in Islington, when that odd person had seemed to be stalking me, and had bashed against me. I remembered the spasm of fear.

I checked all the pockets. Stuffed into the one on the left was an envelope, a small envelope crumpled into a ball. A tiny alarm bell rang insistently, shockingly, at the back of my mind. I took it out cautiously, and smoothed out the crumples. In it was a letter. Folded twice, creased and crumpled, as though thrust into a pocket. On the front of the envelope, handwritten, was the name of a doctor I did not recognise. I unfolded the contents slowly, and carefully, a growing realisation coming over me at what it might be. At the top was a printed address, the address of Nick's General Practice. Underneath, in hurried handwriting that I recognised as Nick's was a long letter. It started with a name in capitals – Mr Keith Harrison – and street name and number. It was addressed to 'Dear Doctor', and started… 'This patient will very shortly be arriving in your area to stay with his parents, who, I gather, are patients of yours. I am giving him this letter to hand to you. He has been under my care for…..', and it went on to describe in detail the sequence of events that had happened to Mr Keith Harrison, and how my doctor had tried 'for over an hour' to persuade him to have further treatment and to be readmitted, and how he had refused the offer of a second opinion.

I sank to the floor, a horrible thought coming over me. The face, the pale, blank, expressionless face with a curtain of dark hair, suddenly came into focus. It was the girlfriend; the girl who had sat silent and still in court behind Mr bloody Keith Harrison, while he told the judge something that I had been sure was untrue, that my doctor, *my doctor*, with the amazing blue eyes and the social conscience and the gentle smile, had not cared, had not bothered, had not done the right thing. It was she who must have been aware of the existence of the letter, and knew that it would exonerate Nick. She must have been trying to give it to me when I found her in front of the house that first time, but she took fright. The second time, when I thought she was a stalker, she must have pushed it into the mac pocket as she ran at me. And I never thought, never knew. .

I read on down the page, breathless, and turned over to the second sheet. It listed the investigations that had been done, the hospital treatment that had failed to help him, and then, a crucial sentence:

'I have offered him second opinions from different hospitals and other doctors, or a domiciliary visit by a different consultant, but he is adamant that he does not trust the NHS down here, and is determined to return to Newcastle, despite my warnings that this will put him in serious danger. His girlfriend heard me give these warnings, but supported his decision.'

Finally, it ended by saying 'I will try to contact you by phone before he arrives .'

I stood, stunned. This was it. So that was why she had hung about my house, frightening the living daylights out of me. She had become aware that an injustice was being done, that the truth was being deliberately hidden. It didn't matter whether the letter had been given to the doctor in Newcastle or not. It was here, in my hand. This was the key to the case, the crucial bit of evidence. And I had committed the cardinal sin of missing crucial evidence. It had been there all along, if I had only thought to find it.

CHAPTER 27

A couple of years before I met my doctor, I represented a journalist who was being sued by someone. I can't remember all the details of the case now, but it was something to do with a scientist feeling aggrieved that his work had been misrepresented in a newspaper article that my client had written, and that statistics had been abused to distort the truth of what he was saying. I seem to remember that the outcome of the case was a sort of score draw – the scientist won, but only received derisory damages, which meant that the judge didn't think anyone had suffered very much. The newspaper – one of the tabloids – coughed up the costs of the defence, so no one did suffer much except the scientist, whose reputation was trashed, and whose work was demeaned, and who, because of a rather harsh and arbitrary decision by the judge on costs, had to bear most of the very considerable expense of trying to clear his name. The truth, and the accuracy of his hypothesis, was of course completely lost in the messy detail of claim and counter-claim. The law, as so often, became the referee in a tussle between individuals, rather than an arbiter of truth.

I disliked the journalist from the moment I met him. He

was tall, self-confident to the point of arrogance, and his face was ruggedly good-looking. He had that sort of louche charm which implies that every woman will fall at his feet, and if they did not, they were the losers. He had worked for the Beeb – predictably using a personal services limited company to reduce tax – and wrote for any newspaper that paid well. His programmes, usually detailing the 'appalling' failings of some government-controlled health or social organisation, were slick, well produced, and invariably anecdotal, using a few outraged citizens whose rights had been infringed to demean an entire service. His newspaper articles were similar; beautifully written accounts using one example or one individual failure to castigate the whole system, and going on to question why one allegedly failing social worker or doctor or care home had not been blamed, held to account, and banished into outer darkness. I had to do a lot of research into journalistic standards and behaviour to decide whether my client the cocky journalist was defensible, and if so, how to defend him, and I spent a lot of time discussing his standards and thought processes with him, all the while fending off his rather blatant attempts to get me into bed.

According to him, the story was king, and selling the story was the object of the exercise. Truth, accuracy, objectivity, fairness, the common good, all came a long way second in his world, and getting the headline, the scoop, ratcheting up the ratings and selling the tabloid were far greater priorities. The individuals whose careers happened to be damaged, sometimes irreparably, along the way were just collateral damage. Those on the receiving end would have to live with it, sacrificed on the altar of journalistic independence and the rights of a free press.

I learnt other interesting things as well. Very few, if any, journalists have any understanding of scientific method. I wasn't very clear on it myself, but at least I understood the principles – that a hypothesis is the starting point, and then evidence is collected to support, or contradict, it. And that evidence has to be independent, verifiable, and repeatable. And that, only when it passes those tests, can something begin to be regarded as fact. Starting from the other end – trying to prove an opinion by cherry picking evidence that fits the theory, as was done, for instance, in the MMR scandal, is a sure way of getting the cart before the horse, and of getting it wrong. Yet it is just this method that is standard practice in the world of journalism. Your editor feels that the EU is a bad thing, and you set out to find a story, or facts, or anecdote, that corroborates this. Objectivity and balance are lost before you start. It is always possible to find figures to support your position, even if you have no understanding of statistics at all.

Another thing I learnt from him, as I removed his hand from my knee, was his understanding of the principle of the Radical Centre. Any politician who proposes any policy change is subjected to what the journalist calls a probing interview, or 'being held to account', which is in fact a dissection ad absurdum of the detail, with scant regard for the principle. It tends to concentrate on the consequences for the individual, so that any potential greater good is disregarded.

As a result, politicians have resorted to talking in the vague and anodyne language so detested by the public, which makes everything they say sound defensive and self-serving. They are so anxious never to say anything that might be pounced on as contentious that they very rarely say – or do – anything original at all. Catch-phrases such as 'postcode lottery' are used to denigrate any local initiative or improvement, so that everything has to go at the pace of the slowest. So journalism has itself become a brake on progress, although journalists and newspaper editors would never, ever, consider that this might be so.

I thought of all this when Nick rang me in some distress the day after I found my mother's raincoat and the envelope. He wasn't in tears – 'strong men don't do tears', he said to me with a smile some years later – but there was a catch in his voice that made my heart go out to him.

'This is awful,' he said. 'First the court, and now the papers. The local rag is having a go at me, telling all my patients that I'm incompetent and shouldn't be working. I've had three patients leave my list this morning. This is what they've written; I'll email it over.'

'This' was an article in a prominent position on the front page his local paper which had a banner headline 'Local Doctor Ruined My Life', followed by a dramatic description of the allegedly grotesque incompetence of my doctor which led to Keith Harrison's persistent health issues. The remarks of Mr Justice Harrap in his conclusions were misquoted and taken out of context, making my doctor sound like a cross between Crippen and Shipman. It was a quiet news week, so the article had been picked up by the national tabloids in their never-ending search for lurid copy to fill in the gaps between the adverts, so now he was not just the recipient of local opprobrium and gossip, but the national press was using his name in one of its sanctimonious blame-game sermons about quality of medical care. 'If only', one of the more facile of the tabloid editorials trilled, 'our doctors lived up to the standards set by their predecessors in the early days of the NHS, and thought less about their pockets and their pensions, medical disasters like this would happen less often.' I felt my blood pressure rising. My doctor had done all he could for Harrison, but now he was the one being scapegoated.

I sat in my smart swivel chair in my office, listening to him talk, and staring at the envelope on the desk in front of me. How could I break the news to him that we had lost his case because of my carelessness? We would appeal, of course, but the damage was done. It was open season on his professional reputation.

'And that's not all,' he said. 'The bastard has reported me to the GMC as well. So I'll have that to go through. I'm not sure that I can face another hearing.'

The GMC – the General Medical Council – is the body that regulates doctors. Set up in the late nineteenth century to stop anyone claiming to be a doctor, it oversees medical training and post-graduate education, and most important of all, their fitness to practice. Any doctor who makes – or is alleged to have made – a mistake can be reported to the GMC, who investigate him, and refer him to a tribunal to decide if he is still competent to continue work. The complaints department deals with thousands of complaints a year, many of which are spurious ('I couldn't get an appointment to have my ears syringed on Sunday', or 'I didn't like the way my doctor spoke to me'). Some, however, are serious. Doctors who are dangerous, or incompetent, or grossly rude, all need identifying and dealing with. Ultimately, they can be 'struck off', have their name erased from the Medical Register and no longer be doctors.

So being reported to the GMC opens a whole new can of worms for a doctor, and means he or she may have to defend himself for a second time in a different Court. It is a curious fact that for a single mistake or 'crime', a doctor can be tried in three separate courts – the civil courts for damages, the criminal courts for criminal negligence, and by the GMC for incompetence. This is the so-called triple jeopardy trap facing a doctor who makes a mistake.

So another sword of Damocles was hanging over my doctor.

When he paused to gather his thoughts, I spent twenty minutes talking him through how to cope with this unwelcome attention, while I tried to think of the best way forward. He was deeply hurt, and I could hear that his faith in the system was badly shaken. As he said, it wasn't so much that it was unfair – you can't expect life to be fair, but it was untrue, a gross and apparently deliberate distortion and exaggeration of the facts of the case, as well as of findings of the court. 'What can we do about it?' he said. 'Surely they can't libel me like this and get away with it?'

The horrible fact is, I told him, that they can, and that any attempt to set the record straight is a sure way to pour petrol on the flames. Remember, I said, that today's headlines are tomorrow's fish and chip paper, and that people have very short memories. Try as much as you can not to let it get to you. Remember that the failure in this situation is of the journalist that wrote the piece, and that he (or she) is a mere nothing compared to you. You know that you are a good doctor, and although the court found that you might have, in this one instance, done things a bit differently, that is a judgement call it made with hindsight, and without the pressure of the situation. Also, I said to him, I've got some exciting news. I've found your letter, the one we really needed.

That brought him up short.

'Which letter? How? Where?'

'I can't tell you just yet,' I said, hating myself. 'What is important is that I've got it, the letter you hand-wrote to the doctor in Newcastle. And, it gives us strong grounds for an appeal.'

How on was I going to tell him that it was my fault that it had been missing? That if only I hadn't been distracted by my mum, by my bloody soon-to-be ex-husband, by being stalked, by the case, and by – yes – by him, I would have noticed that an envelope had been thrust into my pocket, and spared him this whole misery. He would hate me for ever.

'Wow.' A long intake of breath. 'That's encouraging. What do we do now? And where on earth did you find it?'

Once again, I went into professional mode. The default mode for any professional under pressure. And I could feel that pressure weighing down on my shoulders like a mountain of despair. I had fucked up. I had failed him.

'Leave it with me. I'll get a transcript of the letter done, and send you a copy, and get another independent expert to look at it, and discuss it with Brooks. Then we'll all get together and decide whether there are grounds for an appeal. At first glance, it looks as though there are, but don't go getting your hopes up yet.'

'Thank you'. I could hear his smile down the phone. 'I don't know what I'd do without you, Antonia. So thank you.'

And he rang off. The sound of his voice, and the smile in it, echoed in my ears. One day soon he would hate me.

My humourless secretary came into my room. As always, no knock. She looked at me keenly.

'How was the doctor, then?' She knew who it was as she had put the call through to me.

'Upset at first. The bloody newspapers have been having a go at him, worse than usual. Creating a huge drama out of Harrap's conclusions, and saying he is a dangerous incompetent. And the GMC. Enough to upset anyone. But he cheered up when I told him some good news. I've got hold of the referral letter he wrote.'

'How?' She looked at me again. She had been involved in the original protracted search for the notes, and knew that we had moved heaven and earth to find them, without success. 'Where was it?'

I paused. 'It was….' I began, and then I stopped. Infuriatingly, I felt my chin wobble. She might as well know, I thought. She would find out sooner or later, and the more I tried to prevaricate, the worse it would look. Better to come clean.

'I found it.' I looked at her defiantly. 'It was given to me, in fact – anonymously, although I didn't know I'd got it at the time. I think I recognise now who gave it to me.' And a tear rolled down my cheek.

To my surprise, my secretary closed the door and came and sat down beside me on my side of the desk, and took my hand. She said nothing, just held it. It was, of course, the last straw, and I cried buckets. She gave me her hankie, and waited patiently until I had finished, gently massaging the hand when I didn't need it to mop my eyes.

'I'm so sorry.' I managed to say at length. 'I don't know what came over me.'

'You may not, but I think that I probably do.'

I looked at her properly for the first time. She returned my look, calm and direct, and I saw none of the hostility that I thought that I had seen before. She suddenly looked – and felt - immensely reassuring. I realised that I had committed another cardinal sin, of assuming that, because she was part of the background, one of the people who provided a service for me, that she wasn't a personality in her own right. Her face was kind now, and her whole posture was supportive.

'Would you mind if I said something rather personal?'

I nodded. 'Of course not.'

'Antonia, we are all very fond of you here. And proud of you. You are our rising star, our High Court Judge in the making. You are diligent, caring, and very, very good at your job. If I needed a solicitor, I would insist on you above all others.

And I've seen lots of them.' She smiled at my ill-concealed astonishment. 'But we've all been worried about you and for you. For the last few months, and particularly over this case, you have been worrying yourself sleepless. You've lost weight, you are snapping at people, and you look awful.' She smiled again, and the sting went out of her words. 'You've just lost your mother. You're losing your husband. And you've definitely lost your peace of mind. So for once, just for once, let us take care of you. We need you fit and well and happy and on top of your game, not miserable and droopy. So – if there are things that need unloading, unload them. Don't bottle them up. Share them, even if it means sharing them with an old maid like me.'

There was complete silence for a moment in the smart room in the office with its book-lined shelves, its big desk, and its comfortable chairs. The distant noises of the office at work, the chatter, the footsteps, the doors slamming, receded, and even the background noise of London disappeared. My whole world coned down onto the kind, lined, middle-aged face in front of me, and the hand holding mine. The face, which I had always thought cynical and humourless, smiled again, and I felt my last defences fall away. I leant my head against her shoulder, and let myself relax for the first time for weeks. And of course, I cried again. I cried and cried and cried.

When the worst was over, she took her hankie – which I noticed was a surprisingly pretty Liberty's one from that shop in Regent Street – because it was saturated with tears, and replaced it with a handful of tissues. Then she patted me hand and went to get us both a cup of tea. By the time she came back,

I had regained enough control of myself to smile back at her and say thank you, and mop my mascara. I must have looked a terrible mess, but she didn't say anything, just sat there being a calm presence. Years later, when she finally retired, I gave a little speech at her leaving party in the office. Afterwards, as she was leaving, I took her on one side and reminded of her that day, the day when I wept on her shoulder.

'You saved me, you know,' I said. 'Without you that day, I might have gone under. You gave me the strength to go on. I shall always be grateful.'

She didn't say anything, but smiled, and patted my shoulder, and kissed my cheek, and then turned and went down the stairs into the busy street outside. Despite my best intentions, I never saw her again.

*

I felt hugely better after telling her everything. She had guessed of course, that I felt much more for Nick than was proper for a solicitor to feel for a client, more, even, that I was prepared to acknowledge to myself. And she understood, far better than I, how much the saga with my mother had drained my emotional reserves. I didn't discuss my divorce with her, but I'm sure she also understood the internal turmoil that it had generated, the sense of failure, of rejection. In the course of one afternoon, she changed from being an employee, and became an ally, a supporter, a confidante, and almost a surrogate mother. I told her about the hearing, and how disappointed I had been at my defence experts, and how I felt that, in choosing them, I had failed my doctor. I told her about how it had been when my mother was dying, and how my doctor had helped me. And finally I told her about the letter, and how it came into my possession.

'He'll never forgive me. He'll hate me for ever.'

She was far to street wise to offer platitudes and make soothing noises. 'Well, either he will of he won't. My guess is that he feels just as much for you as you feel for him, even if neither of you can acknowledge it. If he doesn't forgive you, so be it. At least you'll have been honest with him, and maintained your self-respect. If you hide behind a lie, or a prevarication, and he does forgive you, that will always come between you. Honesty is always best.'

So that made the decision easy.

*

I went back into efficient solicitor mode with a spring in my step the next day. I went through the letter with a forensic tooth comb. I discussed it with Brooks. I arranged for another, different expert GP to evaluate my doctor's performance in the light of the contemporaneous evidence that the letter gave us. It was handwritten, obviously hurriedly, on Practice headed notepaper. It used the sort of short hand that I had seen before in medical notes, but it was legible, and made it very clear that my doctor had offered a second opinion at Harrison's home. He had asked Harrison if he would wait while he arranged a home visit by a consultant, or, failing that, if he would like to see a different GP. The letter concluded '1 hr persuasion no avail. Letter to GP in Newcastle written and given to pt.' So my doctor's version of events was true, and Harrison's description of an uncaring and disinterested professional, anxious only to cover his back, was the axe-grinding of a man with a deep-rooted aversion to doctors. The letter to the GP in Newcastle confirmed all this. It included the telling sentence 'Tried best and at length to persuade him to be readmitted. Offered him a Dom or second GP opinion, but he determined to go to parents in Newcastle, even though warned him and girlfriend that health/life could be at risk.'

CHAPTER 28

'Antonia.' The voice on the ansaphone was my husband. It was unusually friendly. 'I need to talk to you. Can I come round? Ring me.' Nothing else. No hint of what it was all about, but his voice sounded less self-assured than usual. So much else had been filling my mind for the last few days that he and everything to do with that bit of my life had receded into the distance. I honestly had not thought about him at all, and the children, too, had taken second place. I had forgotten that I was meant to be a mother, as well as a lawyer and a confidant to distressed clients. I had definitely forgotten that I had a divorce to go through, and had put off going through the offer that Richard's solicitor had sent to mine. Another load of guilt dumped itself on my shoulders. It had been Richard's turn to have the children for the last couple of weeks, and I had regularly failed to make the goodnight phone calls to them that I had promised. Poor kids. Hopeless mum.

I had just got in, but the thought of the children made me call him straight away. He picked up the phone at the second ring.

'Hello Richard. Sorry I've been so hopeless at keeping in

touch with the kids. You know what it's like – work, a case coming to a head, and all that.'

My excuses sounded hollow, even to me.

'Thanks for calling so quickly, Antonia. The kids are fine – they've really settled in here. It's not that which I want to talk to you about it. It's about us. What we're doing.'

There was something in his voice that made me pause. His whole ethos was always of control, of being in command. He had always been the leader, the winner, the victor ludorum. His voice, however, was less confident, more pleading. A couple of months ago, all my hackles would have gone up and I would have searched for an ulterior motive. Now, however, he genuinely sounded – and it took me some time to find the word – contrite.

'OK. Of course we can talk.' I adopted the same conciliatory tone. 'You're due to bring the kids back on Friday evening. Why don't you stay to supper, and we can talk after the kids are in bed.'

'That would be brilliant. Thanks. I'll look forward to seeing then. Lots of love.' And the phone went dead.

What was that all about? 'Take care,' I thought. And 'lots of love?' We hadn't thought in terms of love for many months, not since – whenever. A wave of suspicion crept over me, but his tone…. So like the old Richard that I had once been so smitten by. He had been such a lovely man, and we had been so good together. Had it been me, and my obsession with work, that had come between us? Or was it the children, the divided loyalties and priorities? Now that they were through the most demanding part of infancy, would that distraction lessen, and the old feelings return? Was it me that needed to change, not him?

Friday came. I made a real effort, mostly for the children, but partly, I had to admit to myself, for Richard. I was very curious to see what he wanted, and, true to form, neglected to ask my own solicitor for her advice. We lawyers are as bad as doctors in treating ourselves. I knew that both Richard and the kids loved slow-roast pork, so I put a big leg in the oven when I left for work, and left it simmering slowly all day. The smell filled the house when I got home early on Friday evening, making it seem like a friendly home once more, not just a dormitory where I had been crashing out, lonely and exhausted. I plonked some flowers in a vase, which added to the feeling of a proper home again. Even the cat seemed to recognise the mood, and stopped being a slinking alley-cat for the time being, and twined itself round my legs in faux affection. All I needed was an open fire to make the domestic scene complete, but that was a step too far for Islington's smokeless zone rules.

When he arrived, Richard had the tact to ring the bell and wait for me to open it, rather than just letting himself in. I knew he still had a key – it was, after all, still his house as well as mine. The children threw themselves at me in a chaos of coats and shoes being thrown off, and hugs and squeals of delight. They rushed round the house in that zooming-about mode that children adopt when they have been away for a while, as if making sure that it was still there, and that nothing much had changed. Then they settled down in front of the telly, as though nothing had changed, and the Simpsons were still their first priority. At the age of six, I don't think Sophie understood many of the jokes and references, but the characters still entranced them. I sometimes wondered if they saw me as Marge. I looked up and caught Richard's eye across their heads, and we smiled at each other, a smile that acknowledged pride in the children we had produced together. He had kissed me chastely on the cheek, and thrust a bunch of flowers into my hand and put a bottle of wine on the table in the TV room. As usual, the flowers were overdone – a huge bouquet that must have cost him a fortune, and I saw that the wine was Chateauneuf-du-Pape, an equally extravagant present. Never one for the small gesture, my Richard. I felt my suspicions subside a little, and relaxed.

It was a lovely evening, the first truly happy evening I had had with him for several years. The children behaved surprisingly well – surprising because they had many reasons to be angry with me, their absent mother. The supper was a success, and was greeted with oohs and aahs of appreciation. When bedtime came, the children were obedient and well-behaved, and Sophie only needed a couple of reminders to get into her pyjamas and clean her teeth. Richard, to my surprise, volunteered to read them a bedtime story, and we both tucked them in and kissed them goodnight like any happy family without a cloud on its horizon. When the two of us came downstairs, I made coffee and he poured himself a large scotch, and we sat in the armchairs on either side of the fireplace, me with my legs curled under me in a position that always made me feel relaxed.

'Well, sweetheart,' he said, looking at me, using an endearment from the past. 'Here we are again. Just like old times.'

I smiled back at him. I wasn't really thinking about anything at that moment except the shape of the flames in the mock electric fire, and the taste of my coffee. It was just so good to sit and do nothing for a change. 'Yes,' I said, 'You know, it's such a novelty to have you back here to help with bedtime routine.' And I repeated 'just like old times.'

'Mmm', he said, and leant forward. 'So, Antonia. Where do you think we should go from here?'

'Go on,' I said. A tiny prickle of warning ran through my mind. What was he up to? I hadn't looked at his offer yet. Was he planning to move the goalposts? What if he wanted to sell the house to get the equity from it? But this was the Richard of years ago, charming, friendly, the ideal husband. What had changed? Was there an ulterior motive? Or was I just being a nasty cynical hurt wife, looking at us through the prism of an impending divorce.

'I've been thinking,' he said, 'and talking to people. Do you think we might be rushing at this a bit? Might we give it another go?'

Another go....? I looked at Richard, sitting on the edge of his chair, and realised with a start just how much of an effort he had made tonight. He was wearing the shirt I had bought him for Christmas two years ago, and his hair had been recently cut.

'You mean..... you want us to try again?, I said slowly.

He smiled. 'I think we might be rushing into a course of action that both of us might regret in the future,' he said. 'Would you let me explain?'

I didn't know what to think. Part of me, the Antonia who wanted to re-live our happier past, was overjoyed. The other part, the part that had been hurt and angered, was completely flummoxed. We had come so far down the road towards permanent separation already.

So I nodded and waited while he took a long swig of scotch, and embarked on an account of how sad his mother thought it was to see him getting divorced, and how expensive a divorce would be for him, and how it would be a stain on his otherwise spotless life and career. He talked about how happy it would make her to see us back together, and how we had standards of behaviour to uphold, and examples to pass on to the children. He spoke at length about the house, and what a wonderful home it had been for him, and how difficult and expensive it would be to replace it with two separate establishments.

I listened silently, at first hopeful, and then with an increasing wave of angry resentment slowly building inside me. In fact, I felt so angry that I stopped listening after a while, and tried to let his words wash over me while I regained control of myself. Everything he said, every benefit that would accrue from us getting back together was about him, was to his advantage. Nothing he said had included how he felt about me; not a hint of how I might feel about his behaviour in the past or about to his infidelities before and after he left. Not a hint, not a single word, about love. I could hear his bloody mother's voice in the words he used. She, of course, knew that he was perfect, and that all he had to do was to crook his little finger and I would come running to support him again. It was probably all my fault anyway, she would have implied, putting my career before his. It came to me that I was listening to a closing speech for the defence, a skilled and emollient case being made to the jury – me – to let him off the hook, to find him not guilty. And to let him come home, where he could be looked after once more, in the manner to which he was accustomed.

When he finished speaking, there was silence. I tried to think logically, to consider whether I felt as I did because of my intense dislike of his mother, and whether he was genuinely holding out an olive branch. But then I glanced up, and caught a look in his eye that I knew from old, a sly look, a look that told me that he was making a calculated bid for a way of life again. This was a tactic, a move in the war that I felt sure would be inevitable if I gave in to his suggestion.

'Is that you or your mother talking, Richard?'

'Don't be like that, Antonia. I'm trying to make us friends again. And who knows, perhaps even lovers once more.' He stood up and walked across the room to stand behind me so that I couldn't see his face. I felt his hands on my shoulders, gently kneading the muscles in a way that I used to find infinitely sexy. Then the hands slid down over my chest and onto my breasts, and I could smell the whiskey on his breath. He nuzzled my neck.

'Can I stay tonight? Just once? To see if we can hit it off again, or perhaps just for old time's sake? ' I could hear the wheedling in his voice, charming and feline.

I thought of the long blonde hairs on the collar of his coat, and of the bachelor pad in Chambers with its notorious liaisons. I thought of his mother, and her controlling influence. I thought of his charm, and of his success, and of his ability to manipulate. But more than anything else, I thought of me, of what he wanted from me, and of what he was offering in return. Nothing. He hadn't mentioned a word about loving me, or wanting me, or needing me. It was all for him, nothing for me. And to my surprise, I felt a wave of fury such as I had never felt before rise slowly inside me. What right had he, what possible right, to play me like this, to expect me to fall on my back again so that he could have a good fuck? For old time's sake, for God's sake! I realised then, with an absolute certainty, that I could not and would not trust him, and that the original trust I had had when we were first married, blinded and confused by naïve love, was gone, gone for ever in a wave of resentment.

I lifted his hands gently from my breasts, stood up and turned to face him.

'Richard, I think you should know that the chances of us getting together again are vanishingly remote, and your attempt to get back into my bed again, even for 'old times sake', as you put it, are unappealing in the extreme. I, like all women, need to trust someone before I love them, and I need to love them before I sleep with them. And by now you should have worked out that I neither trust you nor love you. So I would be grateful if you would go, go before you say something you might regret.'

His face darkened, and he took a step towards me. For a fleeting moment I wondered if he was going to hit me.

'You bitch. You selfish bitch. I can't think why I bothered. All I wanted was to try and be nice to you, to be friends.'

'All you wanted, Richard, was to get into my knickers again, and to get back into the way of life you had before, with your reputation as a family man intact. To do what was best for you. You never once considered, or asked, what I wanted, or needed. But that was always a secondary consideration, wasn't it?'

He paced up and down the room once. The cat slunk out of the door, its belly on the ground. Then he turned to face me once more. His face was ugly with anger, and little flecks of spittle hit my cheek as he spoke.

'Right. If that's how you want to play it, so be it. You've asked for a fight, and you'll get one. You'll get one all right.'

And he swung round and stormed out of the room. I heard the front door crash shut with a bang that reverberated round the house, and I heard his car roar off down the Islington street. The cat slunk back in, and hid behind the sofa.

CHAPTER 29

It did not take long for my soon-to-be ex-husband to demonstrate his true colours and his anger. I learnt some time later that his attitude may have been coloured somewhat by a misfortune that happened to him on the same evening as our final denouement, soon after he drove away. He had drunk most of the bottle of Neuf-du-Pape that he had brought with him, and had had a stiff whiskey as well, so it was no surprise when he was pulled over by a roaming police car for speeding down Southampton Row, and breathalysed. Alcohol and the Bar had always been close partners – the Temple had some of the best cellars in London. He was well over the limit, of course, and spent and a demeaning night in the cells at Canon Row Police Station, cursing me and blaming me in equal part. The consequences were bad, and would involve public knowledge of his stupidity, a lot of laughter behind hands in several Chambers, and an appearance before the Bar Standards Board, where his wrist would be slapped hard for bringing the profession of barrister-at-law into disrepute. His driving insurance would escalate alarmingly when he got his licence back. He would have to take taxis for a year, as a ban was as inevitable as a fine. When I first heard about it, I almost felt sorry for him.

The evening had a more definitive consequence, though. I received a sheaf of papers from his solicitor, alleging that the only reason for our divorce was my unreasonable behaviour and my inability to behave as a proper mother to his children. Our ludicrously antiquated divorce laws still require one person to be 'at fault' unless both parties agree to a no fault divorce. If one party wishes to vent blame on the other, he or she can go for this particular jugular in order to demonstrate publicly that they are the innocent party in the break up, and that it is the other that is to blame.

Even if I agreed to the divorce, and I most definitely would, Richard could play the card of contesting it, leaving me to decide whether to let him blame it all on me, or to go to court to prove that that was not so. Accepting the blame would be easiest and quickest, but, knowing him as I did, it would almost certainly be used as a method of reducing his contribution to any settlement. And it would also be a big stick in the argument about child care. There was a possibility, a small but horrible possibility, that he might be using access to the children as a bargaining chip in the financial consequences of our break-up. That needed thinking about clearly, and I was in no position to think clearly at the moment. So I sent all the papers off to my own solicitor, with a request that she put her wisdom and experience to good use in advising me what to do.

*

We met again two weeks later, Brooks, my doctor and I, in Brooks' room in the Temple. I had emailed both of them a copy of the letter I had found, and the doctor had confirmed that it was the one that he had written for Harrison to give to his next doctor. Quite how and why he hadn't done so we didn't know, but it had remained in his possession, or at least in his girlfriend's possession until it reached me.

'Tell me about appeals,' Nick said. 'I've got a strong disinclination to get involved in any court case again unless I can be certain that I will win. My last experience was …. difficult.'

Brooks laughed. 'And you coped with it like a man,' he said. 'I can understand what you mean, but we are on very strong ground this time.'

The rules for submitting an Appeal to a higher court – to 'going up stairs', as it is called in the trade – are cleverly designed to stop litigants flogging a dead horse. Assuming, as my medical friends tell me, that about one per cent of the population are mad (and another one per cent bad), that means that there are a lot of people out there with fixed obsessions that they are right and the rest of the world is wrong. These people often become 'vexatious litigants', people who complain about anything and everything, and who are convinced, despite overwhelming evidence, that they are in the right. These people take up a huge amount of legal time, but are filtered out at the lower end of the ladder by the rules about who can or cannot appeal. Sadly, no such filters exist in the medical complaints world, and the same people can often make doctors' lives hell by complaining ad nauseam about a perceived error or failure. There is no such definition as a vexatious complainer in the medical world.

'In order to bring an appeal, we need to prove either that Harrap was wrong in his interpretation of the law – which he wasn't', Brooks went on, 'or that we have new evidence that materially changes the facts. And we have exactly that.' He glanced at me. 'I'm not quite clear how we came to have it, but that doesn't matter.'

I looked at my hands. I had put out of my mind the question of what I would say if a Lord of Appeal should ask how the new evidence had turned up. This was too big an issue to think of now when I was concerned with detail. It hung over me like a dark cloud; my reputation could be on the line.

'We've only got twenty one days after the original judgement to lodge an appeal,' Brooks reminded me, 'and so we've got five days left. Today is Friday, so it has to be in by next Wednesday. So get your skids on, Antonia!'

I scurried about like a demented beaver for the next few days, drafting and re-drafting, checking and re-checking, so that no loopholes were left. Everything was ready by late on Monday, and I took the completed application over to Brooks' chambers for him to check. He went through it word by word, line by line. He finally looked up and smiled.

'You're quite good at this, Antonia. I don't need to change a word. Well done.'

I preened myself a little. Words of praise are few and far between in my trade.

'Out of interest, where did you find the letter?'

My self-congratulation evaporated instantly. I felt my cheeks threatening to burn.

'It was left in my office last week. Pushed through the letter box one evening.' The lie tripped off my tongue far too easily.

'Any idea who did the pushing?'

'No.' I busied myself with my briefcase. 'But I've wondered about the girlfriend. You remember, the droopy girl who was with Harrison in court, the only one who was a real witness of what happened.'

'Yes.' Brooks looked at me thoughtfully. 'Yes, I suppose that's possible.' He looked away. I wondered if he guessed that there was more to it than I was letting on. He was a shrewd man, and a good one.

I locked my briefcase. I wasn't going to lose another document.

*

The taxi to the Court of Appeal office took an age. I handed the appeal in and saw that the time and date were recorded.

'Any idea when we'll hear whether permission has been given?' I asked the Senior Clerk in charge of the Appeals Office.

'Not really.' He indicated a pile of files in a basket behind him. 'We've got all these to get through before yours, and there is only one Lord of Appeal here today. But,' and he relented a little, 'don't worry. We always manage to keep up. You'll hear within your 21 days.' And he turned away.

I spent the next three days worrying. What if they didn't

give permission? What if they remitted it for another trial – sent it back to the lower court to start again? And more than anything, what could I tell my doctor? And when?

On Wednesday morning I sat in my office, trying to work, but in reality shuffling paper about ineffectually. At a quarter to twelve the phone rang. It was the Court of Appeal Clerk.

'You've got your appeal.' he said. 'But only just. Lord Grabbham wanted to remit it for a second hearing, but I nudged his elbow a bit, and he gave in. He's not so bad, but a bit of a stickler for process, and I had to remind him that the cost of a full hearing would be double that of an appeal. Or more.'

'Thank you,' I said, rather breathlessly. 'Thank you very much'. And put the phone down.

First hurdle crossed.

I rang Nick at home the next morning..

'It's good news. The Appeal Court has given us permission to appeal in the light of the new evidence.' A pause on the phone. 'Are you all right?'

He didn't reply for a moment, and I could picture his face. 'Yes. Plodding on. It's been rather a hard week, what with the Press fallout from the judgement and everything. And I spent most of yesterday with a family whose baby was dying.' Another pause. 'It can wear you down a bit.'

'That must have been hard.' I had forgotten that, for him, as for all my clients, their other lives go on, the lives that often have nothing to do with their cases. They still have to earn their living.

'Yes it was. It brought things back a bit. The baby was dying of an inoperable heart defect, the same one that my son had.

At least we had a few years with my son to remember him by. This baby was only a few months old. They had opted to let him die at home, with the support of the palliative care team. They were brilliant, as they always are, but it's a big thing to go through with a family.'

'Is there anything I can do?' My voice sounded inadequate in my ears. What the hell could I do to help someone dealing with something as awful as that?

'No. But thanks for offering.' There was a pause. 'Sometimes I feel like a sponge that is used to mop up other people's distress and emotion, and every now and then it feels as though the sponge is saturated, and can't absorb another drop.'

'I know what you mean.'

'But it is good to know that someone understands.'

And he rang off. Poor man. Poor lonely man.

The next morning, I emailed him the details of our new expert, and his opinion on the impact that the letter should have on a Court. I suggested that we meet up to go through the process of the appeal, but only if he had the time or wanted to. To my surprise, he emailed back almost straight away.

'Dear Antonia. I'm sitting in my consulting room after finishing a surgery, doing the usual boring paperwork. Getting your email rather crystallised something that has been in my mind since you rang. You asked if there is anything that you could do; and the answer is yes, there is. You could, if you really meant it, let me buy you lunch next weekend. If this breaches professional boundaries, or if you don't want to see a client 'out of hours', please say no. I shan't take offence, and you've already done more than enough for me. But it would be very good to see you.'

My secretary came into my room as I was reading this, as usual without knocking, although now I did not mind.

'What's got into you? You are grinning stupidly. Is it something I said, or didn't say?'

'No. It's nothing to do with work. Or only indirectly related anyway.'

She looked at me searchingly, but didn't say any more. She really did know me far too well. But then it struck me that I still hadn't told him the horrible truth, and my spirits, which had been doing leaps and summersaults on the ceiling, slumped to the floor. Courage, woman. You had got to do it sometime, and if he wanted to see you, it might as well be then. So I emailed him back straight away saying yes, of course I would like to see him next weekend. Let me know when and where. His reply was almost immediately. 'How about Box Hill on Sunday? It's about half way between us, and is a lovely place for a walk. We could have lunch in the pub in the village, if you like. Would 10.30 in the visitor centre car park be OK?'

'Yes', I emailed back. 'That sounds a lovely idea. See you then.'

The rest of the week went by in a blur of work. I checked and rechecked the draft of our submission to the Lords of Appeal, and searched for precedents when comparable new evidence that had overturned judgements. I found one or two, but none that were as definitive as our new evidence. I felt a growing sense of confidence. The Appeal Court did not hear new witnesses as a rule, so the report and opinion of my new expert had to be very watertight. I went through it with Brooks again, and tried to see what a prosecution brief might find in it to undermine its conclusions. We changed a few words, but the main message of his opinion was clear; that my doctor said had said and done everything that the prosecution expert had said he should have done, and which Harrison, in his anger, had denied.

*

Box Hill lies just north of Dorking, and looks over the gap that the River Mole has carved in the chalk of the North Downs. It is owned by the National Trust, and over the last hundred years, since the first bit of land was given to the Trust by a local philanthropist, more land has been bought, so that it now covers over a thousand acres. The Hill itself isn't much of a hill compared with lots of others, but it is the only high point for miles around, and there are wonderful views from the top in nearly all directions. Its unusual name comes from the curious scrubby growths of box shrubs which cover its chalky slopes. There are a couple of Bronze Age barrows on one side of the hill, and legend has it that it was the Bronze Age residents who brought box to the area. The whole area is criss-crossed with paths, with hidden places and private outdoor rooms to hide in, and with views for a visitor to stumble upon.

Sunday was another glorious day – cloudless and clear. I spent ages trying to decide what to wear. Casual but smart seemed obvious, but then, if we were going for a walk, smart might seem out of place. In the end, I plumped for jeans and a light sweater over a tee shirt, and carried an ancient Barbour that I used for gardening in the winter. I left before nine, and drove carefully the thirty or so miles to the car park below the hill. Of course, I got there miles too early, and read the paper, and then I wanted to pee, and by the time I got back to the car after that it was twenty five to eleven. I saw him before he saw me, leaning against his car, taking in the view. Not very tall; not particularly imposing, but with an aura of calm about him that drew restless souls like mine to shelter under the wing of his personality.

'Hello.'

He turned and smiled, and the blue eyes drew me in. It seemed entirely natural when he leant forward and kissed me on the cheek.

'Sorry to keep you waiting.'

'You haven't. And even if you had, it is a good place to be kept waiting in.'

We had a lovely day. We wandered along little-used paths, and drank in unexpected views, and sat on high points and looked south, imagining that we could almost see the sea. Of course we couldn't, but just thinking we might be able to elicited the sensation of beaches and sand, of the sound of halyards tapping against a mast, of holidays and escape. We didn't talk much, but we luxuriated in each other's company. Or at least, I did. I felt a sense of complete safety that I had never felt before, even when, at the beginning, Richard and I had been good together. I don't know what Nick was feeling or thinking, but he smiled at me every now and then, and held my hand for a long moment after he pulled me to my feet when we had been sitting on the grass.

We sat on a bench at lunchtime eating slightly stale ham rolls which he had made and brought with him in his rucksack, and drinking warm water out of plastic bottles. Hardly the stuff of heart-throbbing romance, but I found myself inexpressively touched that he had brought them with him, had remembered the little domestic things that a wife might normally have done. But all the time, nagging away at the back of my mind, was the thought that sooner or later I was going to have to tell him that it was all my fault, that it was me that had let him down and ruined his professional reputation. And then this wonderful peaceful bubble would burst, and I would be alone again, facing all the slings and arrows that Richard was preparing for me. I asked him how work was going, and whether his practice were looking after him, but he answered that he didn't want to think about work today, but yes, everything was OK, thank you, despite the chaos in the NHS. Fortunately, he then began talking about the NHS, and soon his words banished the worries from my mind. He seemed to have a natural intellectual curiosity, and was interested in recent social history in a way that Richard had never been.

'When we first met, you were telling me why the NHS isn't working' I said tentatively. I was aware that there was a risk of re-opening stresses that I knew had damaged his peace of mind, but I wanted to know, to understand, why this iconic organisation, set up with such high ideals, had gone so wrong.

He turned towards me. There was furrow of thought between his eyebrows, and his eyes, those vivid, compulsive blue eyes that still mesmerised me, were inward looking, reflective. He thought for a moment.

'It would be naïve beyond words to give you a single simplistic reason, or a single simplistic solution.' He said thoughtfully. 'Like all huge organisations – organisms, if you like – the NHS is the product of a set of imperfect parts and exists in an imperfect world, and is staffed by imperfect humans, and inevitably, like all big organisations, the propensity to fail is a direct multiple of its size. '

I gulped. 'That's a bit heavy. Stop generalising and talk English.'

He laughed.

'OK. That told me. Let's try and break it down into its component parts, then.

You may remember that I was describing how the evolution of the NHS led to different bits being run in different ways, and the key players being differently employed. Before the NHS, GPs had two kinds of patient, panel and private. Private patients were what the name implied; they were private, and paid the going rate for a medical service. Panel patients were those who had joined a sort of club, a mutual insurance scheme set up by Lloyd George before the First World War. They paid into a fund according to their means, often just a few pennies a week, and for that they received basic medical care from the panel doctor. He, in turn, could not make a living out of his panel patients, and subsidised them from his income from private patients. Hospitals were local organisations, run by counties or charities. They paid their junior doctors, but most of the specialists worked in them for free, once again subsidising them from income from private patients.'

I collected the remains of our lunch, and we got up from the bench and wandered along a path. We came to a little corner of the hill, surrounded by walls of box, so that it was almost like a room with one side open. We sat on the warm short grass, taking in the view.

He went on. 'When the NHS was created, the hospitals were, to put it simply, nationalised, and all doctors working in them became employed by the NHS. GPs, on the other hand, remained self-employed, and provided their own premises, staff and so on themselves. They were regulated by a byzantine set of regulations that have been constantly altered according to political whim.'

'Gosh', I said. 'That sounds like a recipe for confusion.' The view in front of us stretched to the South Downs, and it felt as though we were sitting on a terrace in front of a grand house. The sun was getting low, and the sky was beginning to show the first hints of the reds and purples of approaching evening.

''You're so right,' he said, and laughed. 'Inevitably, each bit of the NHS, both hospitals, or primary care, or whatever, protects its own territory and fights to maintain its own status and service. So a series of fiefdoms has emerged, each fiercely protective of its activities. Now these activities are all of value, each an essential component. GP's are useless without hospitals, and as we've all seen, hospitals are overwhelmed without GPs doing their job of filtering out things that don't shouldn't get to hospitals.

Over the years, our political masters have tinkered at the fringes. In my twenty-five years as a GP there have been five major reorganisations of the structures that run the NHS. None made any significant difference, and most of them have merely served to distract energy away from patients and towards the reorganisation itself. 'He paused. 'And they were bloody expensive, too.'

'OK. I'm with you so far.'

'All big structures have a life of their own that perpetuates them. The NHS is the third biggest employer in the world, after the Red Army and Indian State Railways. Like all such employers, there is a cut-off level in the hierarchy. Below the cut off level, the staff is primarily concerned with delivering the service; in the case of the NHS, treating patients as best they can. Above the cut off level, the primary concern of the senior staff is to keep their leaders and political masters happy and off their backs, and to deliver a political agenda. These are the bosses that have to balance the books, deliver targets, whatever they may be, respond to Departmental directives, and keep Ministers and the Press happy. Since Ministers have to bolster their policies by repeating, child-like, that the NHS is the envy of the world, there is an inevitable dynamic tension between those at the bottom, who deliver a service which is struggling, and those at the top, who have to maintain that it isn't. It is that tension that leads to distrust and distortion of priorities, as neither side really understand the priorities of the other. Doctors say they must do the best for their patients as individuals, while senior managers say that they must do what is practical for their populations within the financial constraints available. Inevitably, the two are different, and they clash.'

I lay back on the short grass and looked at the sky, still flawless blue, above me. After a moment, the doctor lay on his back beside me. There was a pause as we watched a skylark doing his vertical ascent and then descent, singing all the while. Then he went on with his history lesson.

'But the real issues aren't about structures or fiefdoms or money; those are merely the tools that deliver – or fail to deliver- the service. The real problem, as in all businesses, is supply and demand, and the expectations of the customers that drive these.'

'Explain.' This was like being at university again, listening to someone who really understood their subject.

'Well, if you succeed in making people better, they live longer. The average life expectancy has risen from the low seventies to the mid-eighties in just one generation. So now the vast majority of medical care takes place in the last few years of an individual's life, and as they are older, they have more problems as their bodies wear out and are repaired by cleverer and cleverer medical techniques. Twenty years ago, GPs saw each of their patients about 3 times a year on average. Now it is 7 times, and for much more complicated co-morbidities. The number of GPs has only risen by about twenty percent in that time, so, surprise surprise, demands outstrips supply. This has been added to by the removal of GPs responsibility for nights and weekend work. So the slightly ill and the worried well, egged on by a voracious Press who demand an instant solution, go to Accident and Emergency departments in hospitals. There they join the same queue as the significantly ill and the grievously injured. And wait, And wait. And are eventually seen by someone, a junior doctor, who is neither trained nor fully qualified to deal with them. The clue is in the name; Accident and Emergency Department. It is not set up to provide a sort of fall-back general practice. The staff aren't trained for it, and the systems they operate cannot provide it. Junior doctors, who staff it, do not have the right skills or facilities to provide continuity of care.'

'I've experienced that myself, when my mum was admitted.'

'Yes, of course you have. I'd forgotten.'

The shadows began to lengthen as the afternoon wore on, and we turned back towards the car park. I was walking beside him, and we were silent. He had talked himself out about the NHS. But at least he was sensible enough not to offer a simple or one-size-fits-all solution, as the leaders of the NHS are prone to do. His final suggestion had been that there could be an independent non-political review of the options, something like a Royal Commission, to see what we could learn from other health care systems and how the present system might be improved. And we left it at that. But I think I understood some of the problems a little better.

There can be something extraordinarily companionable about silence; most of the time we tend to fill our lives with meaningless chatter, but the closeness of not speaking can be far more meaningful than words. As we came down the last steep path towards the cars, I tripped over my feet and stumbled. He caught me, and for a long moment held me. Now or never, I thought.

'I've got to tell you ….'

But he started to speak at the same time

''This has been…..'

We both stopped, and looked at each other.

'Go on,' I said, 'you first.'

He smiled. 'This has been wonderful. I haven't felt so -' and he searched for a word, '- calm for ages. Thank you. Thank you for being kind, and for being available when I needed you.' He laughed. 'Not many solicitors provide emotional as well as legal advice to their clients.' And he kissed me on the cheek, and then let go of me gently.

And being me, I chickened out. How could I ruin such a day. So we drove home in our different directions, my secret still unshared.

CHAPTER 30

The day of the Court of Appeal hearing was warm and sunny, with that hint of warmth in the air that gives a lift to the spirits. Or it would have done to mine the weight of my cock-up wasn't weighing me down. Appeal Court hearings are held in the same place as the High Court – the Royal Courts of Justice. Before these courts were built half way through Victoria's reign, the hearings were held in Westminster Hall, that wonderful repository of history in the Palace of Westminster, where kings and queens have lain in state, where Sir Thomas More and Charles the First stood trial, and where Nelson Mandela and Aung San Suu Kyi addressed parliament. Secretly, I always rather wished that hearings were still held there rather than in the forbidding Gothic buildings in The Strand. The grandeur of the place, and its history, would have lent more gravitas and significance to the decisions made there. However, the Royal Courts were much more practical, if a lot less imposing, so it was to the Royal Courts that we went, a month after my failure to pluck up courage to tell him my secret on Box Hill. We met, Brooks, Nick Malenkov and I, in the seedy little café over the road from the courts, as we had six months ago, before the High Court proceedings.

'Morning.' Brooks was his usual calm self, but this time he seemed almost cheerful. 'All set? I'm feeling optimistic today. Perhaps, for once, the gods are on our side. They ought to be, given the new evidence.'

I made encouraging noises as well. I wasn't entirely sure whether we were encouraging ourselves or our client. He had been so devastated by the first hearing that he probably didn't believe a word we said. His faith in the fairness of the law had been damaged for ever. Looking at him today, withdrawn and distant, I saw a man on death row, the whole of his professional life once again held in balance.

'I've got the listings of who is going to hear us today,' Brooks said, 'and it's another bit of good news.'

Appeal Court hearings are heard by three Lords or Ladies of Appeal. These are exceptional people. They are nearly at the top of the legal tree. Sure enough, the Supreme Court Justices are the pinnacle of judicial decision-making in England, but the Lords of Appeal are on a par with them intellectually. Because they are hearing matters that are of often of a significance above and beyond the case itself, containing implications for precedence and future interpretation of the law, they nearly always sit as a tribunal of three. I suppose common sense says that three heads are better than one.

'The chairman of our hearing is Lady Gardner-Castle,' Brooks said, 'and the wingers are Davies and Batchelor. I don't know much about either of them, but Lady G-C is an absolute star. She goes straight to the heart of a case, and doesn't suffer fools gladly, if at all. She has a history of understanding the problems faced by people having to make snap judgements in difficult circumstances, and not falling for the abstract idealism of experts. We couldn't have any one better – or wiser for that matter.'

My doctor perked up a bit. 'Does that mean she is on our side?'

'I don't think that any judge of her experience or calibre could ever be said to be on anybody's side.' Brooks answered thoughtfully. 'What I mean is that she is aware of the realities of decision-making in the real world, of how people, especially professionals, often have to opt for what may be the least bad option in a given situation, and that being wise after the event, not taking all the circumstances into consideration, as experts looking at a situation later tend to do, is not just unfair, but unjust as well. And she believes strongly that her role is to deliver justice in the full sense of the word.'

'That's encouraging.' I chipped in, as much to encourage him as to contribute to a description of Her Ladyship. I had watched and listened to her perform in the past, and like Brooks, admired her sense of justice hugely. 'I don't think we could have anybody better.'

Nick smiled at me, an anxious smile, and I was tempted yet again to touch his arm. Luckily, Brooks got to his feet and marched us across the road and up the imposing staircase once more, past the statues at the top, and on into the part of the building reserved for the Court of Appeal. It was calmer here, with less noise and bustle, and fewer lawyers rushing about, as if the significance of the big decisions made here carried a gravitas all of its own. The little waiting room near the entrance to the Court was less utilitarian too, and had a carpet, and chairs that were almost comfortable.

We hung up our coats, and sat down, and arranged our bundles of papers, but had hardly settled before an usher put his head round the door.

'They're ready for you.'

So we trooped into the Court. It was smaller than the High Court, and somehow less intimidating. It was designed to allow senior lawyers to debate points of law, rather than for the more showy confrontations of the lower court. There were only a few spectators, and the whole atmosphere was calmer. That did not detract, however, from the solemnity of the place, and the significance for the protagonists of what was decided here. The raised judicial bench and the row of high-backed chairs, with the royal coat of arms above them dominating the court all added to the sense of occasion. We took our places on the lawyer's benches, facing the Clerks bench, and settled ourselves quietly, rather as naughty children settle themselves when summoned to the headmaster's study. I watched as, once again, Gwen Richardson made her usual rather triumphalist entrance, followed by Doggart, but even she seemed a little cowed by the stillness of the place. I caught Nick's eye, and smiled at him encouragingly. He did not smile back. This must feel to him like the road to the gallows again, I thought.

There was a long quiet pause, and then the door to the side of the raised bench opened, and the two Lords and one Lady of Appeal came in. Because this was a civil, not a criminal, hearing, they wore the long zip-up robes with vertical gold clerical bands. They did not wear wigs, as in all the lower courts, and this added to the impression that the debate here was about issues and points of law, not about personalities and evidence. Somehow this small fact made the Court of Appeal judges more human, more objective. I wondered, for the umpteenth time, how long it would be before all the other courts abandoned their archaic headgear, so loved by the wearers, so lampooned by the real world.

The judges bowed to the Court and took their seats, Lady Gardner Castle, as President of this Court, in the centre. Brooks began the process of preparing to make his opening submission. As this was an appeal, it was up to us, the defendants, to show that there were grounds to overturn the High Court judgement, so we kicked off first. He shuffled his papers, opened his legal notebook and put it on the little lectern in front of him, adjusted his glasses, and was in the process of getting to his feet, when Lady Gardner Castle pre-empted him.

'Mr Brooks, before you open your case, I have a statement that my fellow Lords' she glanced at the two judges on either side of her 'and I wish to make.'

Brooks sat down cautiously. What on earth was this new twist to the saga? Had yet another new piece of evidence appeared? Had Mr Justice Harrap put his miserable narrow oar in? We all sat forwards on the edge of our seats. Even dumpy Mr Doggart at the other end of the bench looked interested. I glanced at my doctor. He was sitting rigid, his hands clenched.

Lady Gardner Castle settled herself, and swept the Court with her gaze. I was struck by how penetrating her pale blue eyes were; they looked at me and through me, before returning to the paper she held in front of herself.

'It is in the interests of justice, and in the public interest, that hearings of this nature are dealt with in an efficient and expeditious manner.' She paused, and glanced round the Court again. 'Put in normal English, what we are saying is that there is no point in dragging out the hearing just to satisfy a time honoured traditional process of claim and rebuttal, when it is entirely clear to the judges from the start what the outcome is going to be. We have had the opportunity of reading the submissions of the defendants, and of the plaintiff, who was successful in the lower court. We have perused the record of the Lower Court carefully and in detail, and we have read the judgement of that Court, and the reasoning for it. We have also had the opportunity to examine carefully the new evidence that has come to light, and to judge the effect it would have had on the lower Court, had it been available to it.' She paused again. 'Put simply, and in modern parlance, we are fully up to speed.'

There was a curious sensation in the court, as though someone had released a blast of fresh air, or a shaft of sunlight had appeared. This was a new and novel way to deal with a case. To say, without equivocation, that the Lady and the Lords of Appeal didn't need to hear us lawyers blathering on, making our case; that they had seen all they need to see, read all they needed to read, and had arrived at a conclusion.

'So, unless anyone wishes to object, or to add anything to the very comprehensive submissions which each side has already made,' and she paused again, and those penetrating eyes looked searchingly at Brooks and Doggart in turn, 'I and

my fellow Lords feel able to deliver our unanimous decision.'
She waited for a brief moment, to give the barristers a chance
to object, but we all knew that they would do so at their peril.
When their eyes dropped, and they said nothing, she went on.

'The decision of this Court of Appeal is as follows. The Court
finds that the new evidence provided by the doctor's letter,
found fortuitously from we know not where, is uncontested and
is conclusive. It demonstrates beyond doubt that the plaintiff,
the doctor, undertook exactly the course of action which the
respondent's expert witness said that he should have done in
the difficult circumstances he found himself in. Taken with
all the other evidence heard previously, and the demonstrable
irrelevance of the opinion of hospital experts on the role and
performance of a general practitioner, we find the case against
the doctor not proved. Furthermore, we find that the respondent,
Mr Harrison, has misrepresented the care and the attention
which this doctor exhibited towards him. This misrepresentation
was either deliberate, in pursuit of financial gain, or because of
a complete misunderstanding of his circumstances at the time.
We are unanimous that Mr Harrison received a high standard
of care from this doctor, and that this conformed to the best
standards of medical care in NHS general practice. Whether the
standard of care Mr Harrison received whilst in hospital was of
the same standard is not for this Court to decide, but it is possible
that his time in hospital may have contributed to his mistrust of
the health system locally, and his desire to start treatment afresh
in a new area.'

I stole a glance at my doctor, sitting alongside me. His face was still rigid and expressionless except for a tear at the corner of his eye. Otherwise, he was still, still as a statue.

Lady Gardner Castle paused, and then went on. ' In the light of these findings, and the new evidence of the referral letter, this Court has no hesitation in overturning the decision of the High Court, and finding the allegation of negligence against this doctor not proven. That concludes this hearing.'

We all sat back, dumbstruck. I had expected a long day of legal debate, and then a pause before a judgement. But this decision had happened so quickly, and was so overwhelming, that I could hardly take it in. I looked at Brooks, and he smiled and gave me a small thumbs-up. Then I turned to looked to my doctor. He was sitting slumped forward, his head in his hands, his shoulders shaking. I reached out to touch him, but changed my mind and withdrew my hand.

Doggart and Richardson at the other end of the lawyer's bench looked at the Judge, and then looked at each other. Doggart struggled to his feet.

'My Lady, the matter of costs....'

I watched, fascinated. He took this huge defeat on the chin. Not a word of protest about the speed and unusual process by which the court had reached its conclusion. It would not be clever – or appropriate – to cry foul.

The gimlet eyes looked hard at him from the Bench. 'This doctor did his very best for a patient in difficult circumstances, and has been on the receiving end of public opprobrium as well as private anxiety for so doing. It would be unjust as well as unfair if, as well as these stresses, he had to pay for proving that he acted properly. Your client, Mr Doggart, is, I believe, contracted with your instructing solicitor, and presumably yourself, on a 'no-win no-fee' basis.'

This was news to me. I wondered how Lady Gardner Castle knew it. She went on: 'It is our opinion that the plaintiff in the original hearing should, as is normal, bear the cost of that hearing, and also the defendant's costs. It follows that he should also bear the costs the doctor has incurred in proving his innocence in this Court. '

And she stood up, bowed briefly to us all, and left the Court, followed by her two fellow Law Lords.

*

As usual, there was a gaggle of press photographers loitering outside the Courts of Justice, looking for a story. Their usual prey was footballers or minor film or television stars, or their wives who had been wronged. All grist to the Grub Street mill. Although we certainly did not fall into that category, they snapped away at us as we walked down the grand staircase and through the great doors and onto The Strand. It was a quiet day for them, with no scandal to feed on, but who knows? The unremarkable man walking down the staircase with his lawyers might turn out to be a closet adulterer or wronged aristocrat, and his photograph, the shock still visible on his face, might keep the picture editor happy. So they snapped away, oblivious to individual privacy.

We walked past the photographers and stopped a few yards

up the street, and stood in a group. My doctor still looked shell-shocked, but the colour was returning to his face slowly, and, with an effort, he turned to Brooks.

'I shall never know how to thank you,' he said, his voice breaking a little, and held out his hand to his barrister. 'You have saved me, in all senses of the word.'

Brooks took the hand, and shook it. 'Rubbish,' he said, ever the professional. 'You saved yourself, or rather, you never had anything to save yourself from. You are a good doctor. All we had to do was to demonstrate that.' And he smiled, touched my doctor gently on the shoulder, and walked away up the street. Job done.

I waited, my back to the high railings, breathless. Was this the moment? If I didn't tell him now, I never would. He turned to me, and for the first time since hearing the decision, he smiled.

'Hello, lovely Antonia. I have to thank you too, more than you can imagine, more than you will ever know. Brooks saved my professional reputation, but you, you have saved my soul.' He kissed me again, gently, on the cheek. And then he, too, turned and walked away.

CHAPTER 31

I was busy for the next few days, but not overly so. I sent a strongly worded solicitor's letter to the local paper that had so publicly demeaned my doctor, pointing out that they owed it to him and also to their professional impartiality as objective reporters to give equal prominence to the Appeal Court findings, and pointing out that failure to do so might lead to 'formal proceedings', that useful veiled threat. I had little hope that this would carry much weight, but you never knew.

I went to see my own solicitor, and talked through options with her. She was calmly sanguine about the implications of my husband's behaviour.

'Let me have an off-the-record chat with his solicitor. You'd be amazed at how effective a little hint about bad publicity can be. Drunken driving is such a stupid slur on a professional reputation when mentioned in a hearing, and such a useful bargaining chip. This is as much about anger management as it is about getting what he wants. We'll respond by being entirely reasonable, and demonstrating that it was he who left you, and it was you who was left, - literally - holding the babies. I've very little doubt that his side will have much trouble in persuading him to back off.'

That made me feel a lot better, but the cloud of guilt about the letter hung unaltered over me, waiting to break. Since neither Lady G-C nor our opponents had asked the leading question concerning its provenance, it didn't seem appropriate for me to bring it up either. As long as nobody asked me directly, I wasn't telling any lies. Brooks had far too much integrity to mention it, and anyway, the likelihood of my doctor seeing him again was slim. This thought carried me through for several days, and I had almost decided to stick to it as a principle, when two things took place that changed my mind.

The first was a coincidence. I was walking down Pall Mall to a meeting with a client a week or so later when I saw two familiar figures come out of the imposing door of the Athenaeum ahead of me. Harrap was familiar, with his narrow sloped shoulders, and small pedantic gait, but the other was less familiar. I had only met Dame Isobel Nicholson's husband once before, at a reception at the Law Society. He had seemed an interesting person, I remembered, in his expensive suit and handmade shoes, which did not go with his position as leader of a Labour council. It wasn't unreasonable that they should know each other, I thought, but it was very surprising that two senior professionals should be conducting an argument in the street. I followed them out of curiosity, down St Martin's Lane. There they stopped, and faced each other, their voices raised.

'You promised me a result, ' I heard Nicholson say quite distinctly. 'You said Keith was guaranteed an outcome and was in the clear.'

Harrap responded with surprising fierceness. 'I did nothing

of the sort. All I said was that I would do my best. I will not be held to account for a distortion of ....' And I could not hear the rest of the sentence. They stared angrily at each other for a moment, then each went his separate way.

I stood shocked on the pavement, while commuters and tourists weaved around me. The implications were plain. There had been some kind of arrangement, a manipulation of legal process, a fix. And Nicholson felt that Harrap had somehow reneged on it.

Perhaps I was naïve, but I had always believed – assumed – that the Courts were above reproach, that no palms were ever oiled, no undue influence was brought to bear. But when I thought about it more clearly, it was obvious that this was not, and never had been, the case. What was plea-bargaining other than a deal, a compromise between the accuser and the accused, coming to an arrangement that permitted one side to win, at the expense of the other side accepting some culpability, but not all.

But this was something quite different. This was someone possibly trying to influence a judge who might have been susceptible to political or social loyalties – or so it seemed. Had Harrison deliberately concealed the letter, the crucial letter, from the prosecution? And had Nicholson known about this? And had – the very thought was unacceptable – Harrap himself known? Vanishingly unlikely. It was more likely that Nicholson had believed Harrison's version of events, and assumed that Harrap would as well. And he had, until the truth came out. So many possibilities; so many 'what ifs?' And no chance of getting an answer to any of them.

And on top of all that, the 'what if' that applied to me. What if I had become aware the letter myself, found it in the pocket it had been anonymously stuffed into, and stopped the whole house of cards being built?

All this was whirring in my mind as I sat at home that evening, when the second thing happened. The phone rang – my mobile, not the land line. It was Nick. Asking me out to lunch.

'Yes, I'd love to see you.' and I paused. It was now or never. But not now; I couldn't do it now, over the phone.

So three days later we met. Not Box Hill this time, but a rather ordinary pub which I had chosen at random on line, just south of Gatwick, half way between us. I had hoped that it would be a pretty pub in a pretty village, but it was neither. It was pub-chain garish, with an unattractive carpet, fake beams and a row of slot machines along one wall.

I arrived first, nervous as hell. I cursed my choice of venue, I cursed my nervousness, I cursed the feelings I had allowed to develop for this man, and above all, I cursed my stupid incompetent forgetful self for being the entire cause of the situation. I was just about to get up and leave, hoping to meet him before he came in, so that we could go somewhere more pleasant, when he sat down beside me. The suddenness of his appearance startled me.

'Hello,' I said.

'It's great to see you, Antonia.' He smiled at me. 'What'll you have to drink?'

I wondered if he was as nervous as I was. 'Just a Perrier,

thank you. Driving, and all that'. I smiled feebly.

He went over to the bar, with its synthetic beer pumps and shelves of mixers, and spoke to the smooth young man with the earing who was serving.

'There you are.' he said, handing me my drink. He reached for the menu. 'What do you fancy eating?'

I saw that he was having a Perrier as well. The ice rattled against my teeth as I took a sip. This wasn't how I imagined it would be at all.

'Antonia?' he said, concerned. 'Are you all right? Has something happened? Tell me.'

'It was my fault.' The words came out in an unplanned rush. 'I had it all along, although I didn't know that I had it. The girlfriend gave the envelope to me – she shoved it into my pocket and ran away, but I didn't realise. And then my mum was suddenly much worse and I had to rush down to her, and the hospital was a shambles, and my husband was foul, and ……. I just forgot about her bumping into me. So I never even looked for it…..' I fought back the desire to cry.

He put his drink down. 'What envelope?'

'The one containing the letter. The letter we needed all along. The one that changed everything.'

His expression changed ever so subtly. I watched his face, swallowing.

'I didn't know what it was, of course. She must have just sort of shoved it into my pocket as she barged by, and then everything kicked off, and I never thought of it again.' I looked down at the table 'I didn't even realise it was the girlfriend at the time, I thought it was someone going to attack me, and I was so frightened…..' My voice tailed off, and I could feel tears running down my face. 'And then my mother died….. And I found it in her old raincoat when I was clearing her place out, and it was the one I'd been wearing then.'

There was a long moment of silence.

I'm sorry,' I whispered. 'It was all my fault. I'm so, so sorry.'

'Hm'. He looked down at his hands, his face expressionless. 'So that's how it happened.' He took a long drink of his Perrier, then looked up and met my eyes. 'Not that it matters now that it's all over and done with.'

I looked at his face. Was it to be for the last time?

Then he looked up again, and the corners of his eyes creased, and I could see the beginnings of a smile. He reached across the table and took my hand.

'' Stop snivelling. This really is a ghastly pub. Let's go and find a nicer one.'

EPILOGUE

The sunset in the west was reaching its dramatic crescendo. I had always been fascinated by the optical illusion created as the atmosphere distorted the size of the sun, and its rate of descent into the sea. As we watched from the terrace of the hotel in Ravello, with the precipitous cliffs of the Amalfi coast below us, it performed its usual trick of becoming larger and larger at the same time as its colour changed from yellow to gold, and then to the rich deep velvety red of the classical sunset. It's diameter seemed to expand as it's lowest tip touched the sea, and streaks of red velvet spread out from it. The few clouds above it picked up and exaggerated the refracted light. I was reminded, as always, of the lines of Browning's evocative description of the phenomenon – ' Sunset ran, one glorious blood-red, reeking into Cadiz Bay', although the Cape St Vincent he described as '…fading away to the north-west', lay eight hundred miles from where we were sitting.

We sat in silence, watching the extraordinary sight that was repeated so regularly, yet never failed to amaze. Nick reached across and topped up my wine glass. I had never been much of a drinker, but if times like this were not for enjoying, nothing was.

I had taken me a long time to lose the slight inhibition I had felt in his presence when we first started to become a couple. It was probably a hang-over from our first relationship as client and professional, an inhibition that had prevented me from being entirely natural in his company. I was aware that it made me talk too much, and probably seem rather bossy. When I finally plucked up courage to tell him this, he had laughed, and said that it had never worried him, as he thought that I was much more intelligent than he was, and it was that which had made me hold him at arm's length. And anyway, he quite liked bossy women.

Little did he know. Never before had I been so completely taken over, absorbed, by another personality, although it took a considerable time for me to realise it. I think he had been nervous about learning to like – love – me as well. He had been rejected, like me, by someone who he thought had loved him, and, like me as well, that had left a cautiousness about commitment . He had had to develop a protective shell, a carapace, in order to continue with his professional life. He must have been as reluctant as I had been to let down our respective guards, and to start giving ourselves to another person again, with all the risks that such giving carried.

We had been talking, as we did quite often since we had both reduced our workload, about what it was that had led the National Health Service, such an idealistic concept, to its present state of dysfunction. I was always drawn back to wondering what the root cause of the failure really was, and, sitting watching the sunset, I had asked him once more to explain why he thought it was unable to function properly.

His brow furrowed as he thought about it.

'Do you remember, a long time ago, talking how the balance of unlimited demand and limited supply would inevitably make it fail?'

'Yes, I remember.'

'Well, as it is certain that no one will have the courage to confront the bottomless pit of unlimited demand, the discussion should really be about which bit will fail first. Or whether all parts will just decline together.'

And then he turned to me and smiled, and the sunset lit up his face, and he laughed.

'But it's far too beautiful an evening to talk about tedious things like that, and you are far too beautiful to be worrying about it.'

The blue eyes crinkled at their edges, and it was with a sense of overwhelming gratitude to whatever god there is up there that I took his arm, and together we walked into dinner.

Finis